ONE TO GROW ON

Books by Nathaniel Benchley

SIDE STREET

THE BENCHLEY ROUNDUP (EDITOR)

ROBERT BENCHLEY, A BIOGRAPHY

ONE TO GROW ON

ONE TO GROW ON

NATHANIEL BENCHLEY

McGRAW-HILL BOOK COMPANY, INC.

NEW YORK · TORONTO · LONDON

For Betty Sinclair

❦ 1 ❦

Spring usually catches the city unawares. One day it is wet and cold, and the buildings and the gutters and the pavements glisten bleakly under a heavy sky just as they have all winter, and then the next day the skies are clear and there is a soft, earthy smell in the air, and it is spring. Few people see a tree or a flower; no birds announce the coming of spring and the perennial pigeons and sparrows seem unaware of it; yet the people in the apartments and tenements and hotels and bars know it is spring by the smell in the air, the faint smell that sifts through all the other city smells. Children begin to shout louder, and stay out-of-doors later, and their noises are the more noticeable because people leave their windows open. Spring is the only season that announces its arrival in such a way that city dwellers are aware of it all on one particular day.

In a small New York brownstone apartment building where there happened to be no children, the coming of spring was felt in different ways by the different tenants. In one of the two ground-floor apartments, Ernest Becker awoke as usual at six, got up quietly so as not to disturb his wife,

1

put on his glasses, and went into the kitchen and started the coffee. Becker was a man in his middle sixties, stooped and slightly disheveled, and at this hour in the morning he looked a little like a mole fighting a high wind. There was no real reason for him to get up at six; the firm for which he worked as an accountant didn't require him to be in until quarter-to-nine, but Becker had almost reached the compulsory retirement age, and he felt that if he arrived at the office before everybody else, they might make an exception and keep him on a little longer. To him, the idea of retirement was the same as death. He shaved, and combed his softly waving hair, then walked across and stood by the open window as he buttoned his shirt. The morning air was cool and clean, and the tops of the buildings gleamed with a bright orange light. Becker breathed deeply and smelled the smell of spring. He breathed again and smiled as he went to the closet to select a necktie. He drank his coffee quickly, and was on his way out the door when Martha, his wife, spoke from under a tangle of bedclothes.

"Don't go out without a coat," she said.

"I don't need one," Becker replied. "It's spring out."

"Not that much spring it isn't," she said. "Wear a coat."

"Look out the window if you don't believe me," Becker said. "It's like June. July, even."

Martha raised her sleep-scarred face from the bed. "Ernest Becker, you don't leave this place without a coat," she said. "Every spring you go out without a coat, and every spring you get pneumonia. 'Becker's got pneumonia,' people say. 'It must be spring already.' You should rent yourself out for a calendar. Next time you get pneumonia, you can be the nurse for yourself. I'm sick of it. Wear a coat!"

Becker sighed and went to the closet. "I was just thinking," he said, as he put on his topcoat. There was no response from his wife, and after a moment he went on, "I was just thinking, I wonder if there isn't something I could build around the place here. Is there anything you need?"

2

"Certainly," said Martha from beneath the covers. "I need three more rooms, a laundry, a new kitchen, a swimming pool—lots of things."

"I was thinking of something maybe like a flower box," Becker said. "For the front window, that we could grow flowers in. And maybe have a trellis going up from it, so we could have one of those vine things. Like a sweet potato, or an avocado, even."

"Uh-huh," said Martha, sleepily.

"It's a thought, anyway." Becker opened the door. "I just got the urge to build something." He went out and closed the door behind him. When he reached the street, he took off his topcoat and carried it over his arm, and as he walked briskly to the bus stop he breathed in deep, invigorating breaths and planned how he would build a trellis that would cover the whole front of the apartment building.

The next tenant to notice the spring that morning was Arthur Montgomery, who lived alone in the apartment directly above the Beckers'. He was a small, round man of about fifty, and he was a copy reader on an evening newspaper. At the age of twenty-two, armed with a degree from Princeton and the conviction that he would be a greater writer than F. Scott Fitzgerald, he joined the paper as a reporter, in order to get the necessary experience. He got the experience, but he never quite finished his first novel, among other reasons because he was one of those people who are lightning rods for minor disasters. When a holdup in a nearby saloon led to a flurry of shooting, nobody was hit except Montgomery, who was hiding under a table and caught a bullet in the calf of his leg. He lost his police card so many times that the Department refused to issue any more to him, and he was taken off reporting and put on rewrite. A collie named Flash ate the first three chapters of his novel, and when he came to write them again he found that he had forgotten one of the characters' names, and had lost interest in the others. The one thing that he gained from his work on the newspaper, and the one thing in which he had few peers, was his knowledge of irrelevant facts. He knew the average rainfall in Ned's Testament, Wyoming, and the design on both sides of a *zloty;* he knew where to bite an octopus in order to paralyze it, and the weights of all the leading opera singers; he knew how to read a Plimsoll mark, and he knew how to tan a cougar skin. He also knew a lot of history, both European and American. He knew every show tune written since 1908.

On this particular morning, Montgomery's alarm clock rang for two full minutes before it penetrated his consciousness. He reached out and groped for it with his eyes closed, and finally found the button and turned it off. Then he lay there, still with his eyes closed, and hung onto the bed while successive waves of pain crashed like surf inside his skull. Slowly, the details of the previous evening began to emerge and sort themselves into a pattern, and with them came twinges of remorse, which added to the over-all physical pain. It had all started with dinner at the saloon—or had he *had* any dinner?—and someone at the bar had bet him he couldn't name the last ten Archbishops of Canterbury ... he took the bet, and lost ... then they had gone someplace where they had been denied admission ... he had threatened to denounce the place in the paper ... then they sang in some other place, and were thrown out.... He wondered how he had got home.

Gently, Montgomery eased himself out of bed, testing his various limbs and muscles for bruises. As he tottered into an upright position, he saw that the top of his dresser was covered with quarters and dimes and match folders, and in the middle of the debris was one crumpled dollar bill. He sighed, and began to gather up his clothes from where they had fallen.

By the time he had dressed and had a cup of coffee, he was feeling a little better. He went down the stairs and out

4

onto the street, and the first deep breath he took told him that it was spring. He tried it again and the fresh air made his head spin, but he squared his shoulders and walked happily down the block, with visions of a tall, frosted mint julep forming in his mind.

On the top floor of the building, Duncan Lapham awoke, yawned, stretched, then reached out and turned on the phonograph beside the bed. A record plopped onto the turntable, and after a few seconds the strains of Debussy's "Clouds" floated softly through the room. Lapham ran his own business—an antique store on Third Avenue—and consequently he was able to arrive at work whenever he wanted, which was usually around ten. As he lay in bed and listened to the music, he looked slowly and critically around the room, making mental notes of items that ought to be changed. It began to occur to him that the whole room bored him, to stupefaction; what he had gone to such pains last year to have in the best possible taste now looked to him like a jumble of highly varnished Grand Rapids furniture. That end table, for instance, was so close to the writing table that they fairly screamed at each other, and the curtains had faded to a point where they no longer matched the footstool cover. The entire room needed to be redone; he should throw everything out the window and start from absolute scratch. It would be nice to be able to do that. When you get bored with something, just fling it away, and start all over again. It would be nice to have a shop in Provincetown, or Martha's Vineyard, so you could get out of the bloody city during the summer and meet some new people. Nice people, for a change. Not all these dull, plodding drones you bumped into every time you turned a corner.

Lapham got out of bed, examined himself briefly in the full-length mirror behind the closet door, and then went into the bathroom and began to draw the water in the tub. As he stared dully out the window, it occurred to him that this mood of dissatisfaction came over him every spring, and the only cure for it was to have a complete change. Either do something, or buy something, or destroy something; anything, so long as it was a change. He was considering the various possibilities when the phonograph music stopped, and he went in and took off the Debussy record, looked at the other side, then walked to the window and flung the record out. It soared and zoomed in a swooping arc, then dropped out of sight behind a brick building. Lapham went back to the machine, and from the bookcase behind it picked out two more Debussy records, "The Engulfed Cathedral" and "Afternoon of a Faun," and sent them out the window after the first. Three Chopin records followed, and he was just selecting a Khachaturian when he heard the water overflowing in the bathroom. He dropped the record and ran and turned off the faucet, then returned, picked the record up, and flung it as hard as he could after the others. It disappeared, and after a moment there was a distant crash of glass, and someone was shouting. Quietly, Lapham went back to the bathroom and began to mop up the water on the floor. He felt a little better, but not much.

One floor down and on the opposite side of the building, Evelyn Estes was awakened by the telephone. She rolled over and tried to pick up the instrument, but her hand was asleep, and she had no sooner got the phone from its cradle than it dropped from her limp fingers and hit her in the mouth. She made a noise between a cry and a curse. From the receiver came the voice of Marna Westerberg, her agent.

"Did I wake you?" Marna asked.

Evelyn sat up quickly and took the phone in her other hand. "No, of course not," she said. "I was just reading." Her mind was receptively awake, but it could not yet make much sense on its own.

"Oh," said Marna. "Well, do you think you could play a grandmother?"

"Of course," Evelyn replied. "What kind of grandmother?"

"You know—an old Cockney broad. Eighty or so. I gather there are some good comedy lines."

Evelyn hesitated. "Well, I suppose with the proper make-up," she said. "What's the program?"

"This isn't TV—it's a play."

"A Broadway play?"

"Not for this season, no. They're going to try it out in the barns this summer, and if it seems worthwhile they'll bring it in next fall. You could do a lot worse."

"Oh, I don't know. . . ." Evelyn hunched the phone between her ear and her shoulder, and reached for a cigarette.

"Look, dearie, the TV season is just about over," Marna said. "From now on, the best you can get is a shot on some summer replacement show, and who looks at them? If this thing goes, then you're set on Broadway, and at the very least you've got four weeks' steady work, not counting rehearsal pay."

Evelyn took a long drag on her cigarette. "O.K., then," she said. "When do they want me to start?"

"You haven't *got* the part. They want you to read for it."

"Oh," Evelyn said, and paused. "When?"

"Two this afternoon. The Shubert Theatre."

Evelyn took another drag. "All right," she said. "But tell them that if something better turns up—"

"Oh, come off it, dearie," said Marna. "Just get on over there, and read the lines like they tell you to."

"All right," Evelyn said. "By the way, what's the name of —" she began, but Marna had hung up. She realized that she didn't know the name of the author, the director, or, for that matter, the play.

She finished her cigarette, then stamped it out in the bedside ash tray, and got up. A Cockney grandmother. Well, it was either a Cockney grandmother or a Jewish aunt or an Irish washwoman—anything, so long as the character was middle-aged, and the voice funny enough. The day when

7

she could play a straight part went out with the introduction of sound into the movies, at a time when she had had one year in Hollywood and was considered a rival of Janet Gaynor's for young romantic parts. Then came sound, and suddenly all she could do was play funny-voiced people on the radio, where the fact that she was young and good looking wouldn't interfere with the fact that her voice, no matter what kind of accent she used, was highly unromantic. It wasn't until her features and her figure had begun to settle with age that she could afford to be seen again. She had, in the meantime, mastered a broad range of dialects, but as far as the public was concerned she was practically unknown.

Evelyn regarded herself in the mirror, and the dismal thought occurred to her that, without any make-up, she didn't look far from eighty right this minute. Briefly, she considered going to the reading as she was, without doing anything more to her face than washing it, but that thought evaporated after a quick second look in the mirror. They'd think I was crazy, she told herself. Nobody in her right mind would look this way if she could help it. I'll go looking as young as I can, and then tell them I can be made up to look eighty if I have to. She lit another cigarette, started the water for her coffee, and then went back to her mirror. Summer theaters might not be so bad after all, she thought. It's nice at night, after the show, especially if you're near the water, and there are lots of things you can do when you're not working. Like boating, or lying on the beach, or maybe even swimming. . . .

Evelyn opened her make-up box and whistled a little tune as she rummaged through the creams and powders in search of her eye shadow.

For Anne Waters, who lived on the ground floor opposite the Beckers' apartment, the day was one of terror and foreboding. For perhaps fifteen seconds after awakening, she thought it was like any other day; and then the worry, the problem, and the certainty of the answer came over her and locked out the possibility of any other thoughts. She knew what had happened, just as well as she knew the reason for its having happened, but until she had the definite, medical proof, she couldn't make any plans one way or the other. All she could do was look back, as she had so many times in the last few weeks, and try to see where—aside from the obvious incident itself—she had been wrong. Where she had made the wrong decision, and if, in the final analysis, she had been wrong to fall in love with him.

She had met him at the office Christmas party a year ago. A year, three months, and eighteen days ago, to be exact. She was new then, and nervous, and she didn't want to go to the party, but her boss, an account executive, had insisted that she come and get her feet wet, as he put it. He had added that she would never shake the dust of Pennsylvania from her feet unless she upped periscope and let out her stays a little, and before she could frame a suitable answer he had said, "Good—I'll run interference for you and you'll carry the ball. I knew I could count on you." So she went to the party. She stood at one side of the room and sipped at a syrupy Manhattan, while young girls and old women shrieked and cavorted and slapped men on the back, and the men laughed loudly and told stories and got red in the face and blurry in the eyes. There were presents, accompanied by rhymed cards that were read out loud and greeted with wild laughter, but since Anne didn't know the people involved she could only judge the rhymes on their own merit, which was faint. She was wondering whether she could slip away unnoticed when suddenly a man appeared beside her, and stared balefully at the rest of the room.

"It's not very Christmassy, is it?" he said.

She looked at him. He was tall and thin and had dark hair and dark, deep-set eyes, and the fingers that curled around his highball glass were long and tapering. He looked more like a musician than an advertising man. He also looked completely sober. She smiled slightly. "No, it isn't," she said.

"It's a curious thing," he said. "The management feels compelled to give a Christmas party to which nobody wants to come, least of all the management, but everybody comes because they know it's expected of them, and they feel they can stand it for a couple of hours if they get drunk enough quickly enough. Tiny Tim, hold onto your hat."

"I didn't come because it was expected of me," she said. "I came because I couldn't think of a quick way not to up periscope and let out my stays. Before I could open my mouth, I was carrying the ball."

He looked up at the ceiling, and laughed. "Oh," he said. "You're Greg Higgins' new girl, I gather."

"That's right," she said. "I suppose I shouldn't have said that, but it just kind of slipped out."

"I admire you for it. It showed perception, individuality, and candor. It was also refreshing proof that somebody around here can speak English. I would get down and salaam to you if I weren't sure that Greg would kick me while I was doing it. He's watching me like a red-eyed ferret as it is."

Anne glanced around the room, and saw that Higgins was looking at her. Their eyes met, and he raised his glass and smiled, and she raised hers and smiled back. "It's all right," she said. "He just wants to see if I'm having a good time."

"If that's all he wants, then I suggest that we make sure you have a good time and take you out of here. Would you have dinner with me?"

She stared at him for a moment. His eyes were clear and calm and had no more expression than if he had offered her a cigarette. "I'd love to," she said.

He gave her his arm, and as they went to the coat room he said, "Incidentally, my name is Roy Curtin. Just in case anybody asks you."

She laughed. "Mine's Anne Waters," she said.

They shook hands formally, and he said, "Also for your

information, that happens to be my right name. At these parties many people go under an alias, just to be on the safe side."

"Have you been to many?"

"This is only my second. Before that I was in the Navy, where things were relatively quiet."

"You've learned a lot of the local customs in a year."

"You have to, in order to survive. It's all right to learn them, but the trouble starts when you begin to believe them. Don't ever believe them, or you're done for."

"Thank you, sir," she said. "I'll try to remember that."

It was snowing when they reached the sidewalk, and hunched-up people hurried past with white sparkling on their hats and shoulders. Driven by a gusty wind, the snow swirled out of the darkness above Madison Avenue, and the noises of the traffic were soft and muted. Curtin turned up his collar and squinted into the night. "Where would you like to go?" he asked.

"I haven't the faintest idea," she said. "I've been here for exactly three weeks."

"Where were you before that?"

"Way deep in Pennsylvania. I lived with my family and worked in the local department store." He looked down at her, and she asked, "Why? Does where we go depend on where I came from?"

"No, but I was just thinking. This is the spot where the man says he knows a wonderful little restaurant with home cooking and checked tablecloths, and they go and have lasagne or tripe or sauerbraten, and the owner is a lovable old soul who calls them 'My children.' If you don't mind, I say the hell with that. I should like to go to Voisin."

"I've never heard of it, but I'll go anywhere you say."

He whistled at a lighted cab, and took her by the arm. "Well, I can promise you one thing," he said. "The owner of Voisin isn't going to call us 'My children.'"

The dining room was a soft gray, with a blue carpet, and

was lighted by crystal chandeliers, and Anne felt as though she had come in old tennis clothes. But Curtin was completely at ease, and after a while she relaxed and listened to him talk. He was eloquent on a number of subjects, including the Navy, music, marine biology, and modern painting, but the most frequently recurring theme in his conversation was his scorn of the advertising business. He was in the art department and something of a specialist, and he held the rest of the trade in supreme contempt. He was in it, he said, only to make enough money to go into the art business on his own, and until the time came when he could do that, he would put up with any amount of foolishness just so long as it assured his security.

"I really don't know why *I'm* in it," Anne said. "I guess it was just to get out of Pennsylvania."

"That seems as good a reason as any."

She stirred her coffee slowly. "It's not that it was bad there," she said. "As a matter of fact, I had a very good job offered me in the bank. I just wanted a change of scenery, that's all." She looked around the dining room, at the blue leather banquettes and the wall mirrors that reflected the sparkle of the chandeliers. "And you can believe me when I tell you there's nothing like *this* where I come from."

"Well, please don't think this is my usual hangout," he said. "We came here because I couldn't stand the idea of going somewhere quaint our first dinner together. Next time, it may very well be the Automat."

She smiled. "I'll be perfectly happy to trust your judgment," she said. "So far, I think you've done beautifully."

They went next to a small, dark place where a young man played the piano, and when, after a while, Anne casually glanced at her watch, she saw that it was one-thirty. "Oh my," she said. "I've got to be going."

"What's the rush?" he asked. "There'll be nobody in before noon tomorrow, I can promise you that."

"No, but I had no idea it was so late."

"For that matter, neither did I. I'm afraid I've been doing a lot of talking."

She smiled as she gathered up her purse and gloves. "Not too much for me," she said. "I've loved every word of it."

"Those could be the most fatal words you ever spoke," he said, and laughed.

He was quiet as they rode through the deep snow to her apartment, and she hoped that his silence was not a preliminary to some elaborate proposal. She didn't want the evening to end with an argument, or hurt feelings, and she was rehearsing in her mind the most tactful way to refuse him, when the cab slowed down and she saw that they were at her address.

"Keep your flag down, driver," he said, leaning forward and grasping the door handle. "I'll be with you in a minute."

He took her elbow and guided her gently up the front steps, and when they reached the door she turned and looked at him. "Thank you for the nicest evening I've had in New York," she said.

"Thank you for coming with me," he replied. He shook her hand quickly, then turned and went down the steps.

In her room, Anne closed and locked the door, and then walked slowly across to the mirror. Her features were the same as they had always been: large, gray-green eyes, which had a somewhat surprised look under arched eyebrows; high cheekbones that tapered down to a small, full mouth; and ash-blonde hair that was braided coronet fashion around her head. She examined herself for a minute or so, then quietly took off her coat, hung it up, and began to get undressed. Not a flicker of emotion, she thought. Not even a hint that he was *thinking* of kissing me. Most men made at least a routine gesture in that direction, but he might as well have been saying good night to the janitor. Well, I guess it takes all kinds. . . . Of course, it might be that he's—oh, no.

13

That's impossible. That would have shown up—and if that were the case, then why the invitation to dinner? No. He was just reserved and proper, that's all.

She shrugged, and slowly began to unbraid her hair. It wasn't until she was completely ready for bed that she realized she had forgotten to pull down the shade.

She went home to Pennsylvania for Christmas, and didn't see him again for almost a week. Then one day he came into her office, looked quickly around, and said, "Can we talk without being overheard?"

"Yes, of course," she replied. "Why?"

"Then here's this," he said, producing a large envelope from behind his back. "I know it's late, but I couldn't get it done in time."

She opened the envelope, and in it was a large Christmas card, which he had painted, showing the scene at the office party, with the more prominent members of the staff in highly unflattering caricature. Over in one corner, the figures of Anne and Curtin were watching with undiluted boredom. It was like a picture of *Walpurgisnacht* by Hogarth, and around the border was a design of holly, bells, and a few of the more important sponsors' products. Anne shrieked, then covered her mouth with her hand. "Oh, it's wonderful!" she whispered.

"I thought you might like a memento," he said. "Sort of like bronzing the baby's first shoes, or something like that."

She looked up at him, and her eyes were sparkling. "It's the best present I ever got," she said.

"Are you clear for dinner, by the way?"

"I most certainly am. I'd like a chance to change, though."

"Whatever you say. But this time it's not going to be Voisin. This time I think we might try a saloon."

"No matter where we go, I still would like to change."

"O.K. I'll be wearing brown, in case you want to harmonize colors."

14

They went to a saloon that served excellent steaks, and then went to two or three different places where there was music. This time, when he took her home, he did kiss her, but it was a quick, almost absent-minded kiss, and before she opened her eyes he had turned and was going down the steps. He stopped at the taxi door and waved, and she waved back and then went quietly into her apartment.

They went out about once a week for the next few months, and during the summer it became twice or three times a week. They were completely at ease together, and there developed an unspoken sense of communication between them, as with people who have been married a long time. Although he never said he loved her—or even liked her, for that matter—it was obvious that he was deeply contented just to be with her, and this contentment filled her with a serene kind of happiness. They laughed a lot, although she was never able later to remember anything that had been particularly funny.

Gradually, the days became cooler, and the subway advertising cards had pictures of autumn foliage, and then snow scenes, and then Santa Claus. Bells chimed from loudspeakers along Fifth Avenue; swarms of angry, weary people crushed their way in and out of stores; the traffic degenerated into a seething, honking mass, and the air quivered and rang with Christmas. The office party was indistinguishable from the one the year before, or the year before that; the only difference was that Anne and Curtin went to it together, knowing that they would leave together as soon as they politely could. They stood to one side, where they had stood the year before, and watched the carryings-on until after the presents had been distributed, then he looked at her, and without a word they left.

Outside he gave the cab driver the address of Voisin. She knew, without being told, that after dinner they would go to hear the young man who played the piano; and she also

15

knew, as well as she knew anything else, that at one-thirty they would get up and leave, and that this time she would go home with him.

It was snowing the next morning, and when she woke up she didn't know for a moment where she was. The dazzling white light of the snow glared through unfamiliar curtains, and she had to look all around the room before she was awake enough to remember. From the kitchen came small clattering noises and the smell of coffee brewing. Then he appeared, wearing a blue dressing gown and carrying a tray on which were two cups of coffee and a glass of orange juice. "Good morning," he said.

She sat up in bed, and pulled the covers around her. "Good morning, my love," she said. "It's snowing."

"It certainly is."

"Remember the first time we saw it snow together?"

"I do." He handed her a cup of coffee. "It looks almost as though I'd planned this, doesn't it?"

"I'd like to think you had." She blew lightly on the coffee, and took a tentative sip. "Sit down." She patted the bed.

He sat gingerly on the edge of the bed, and looked out the window while he drank his coffee. "It's really coming down," he said. "We may be holed up here for weeks."

"I think that's the most wonderful idea I've ever heard."

"The office would love it, wouldn't they?"

"Pooey on the office. We'll just tell them we're sick."

"Oh-ho." He took a pack of cigarettes from his pocket, and offered her one. She shook her head, and he bit it out of the pack and lighted it. "What about the people at your place?" he asked. "Are they going to be scandalized at your being out all night?"

"As far as the people at my place are concerned, I could spend the night in Kiska and it wouldn't make any difference to them."

"Why? Aren't they friendly?"

"They're just nothing. Nobody speaks to anyone else—you

nod sometimes in the halls, but that's all. I think the people across from me are named Becker, but the only way I know that is from the mailbox."

"It must be kind of dismal. Here, at least I know a *couple* of people."

"It might have been dismal, if I hadn't had you."

He finished his coffee, stood up, and glanced at his watch. "I suppose we ought to get going," he said. Then he turned and looked at her, and walked over to the bed and kissed her. "Otherwise, we really might be here for weeks," he said.

The day after New Year's, he came into her office at closing time, and from the look on his face she knew that something had happened. All that he said was "Let's go have a drink," and then he lit a cigarette while she gathered her coat and purse from the locker. They went to a crowded, noisy bar down the block, and sat at a table in the back of the room, and after he had ordered their drinks he looked down at his knuckles and said, "It seems that I'm being transferred to the Coast."

"Oh, *no!*" she said. "Why?"

He shook his head. "It's not clear yet. It's got something to do with somebody else being transferred, and their needing someone to head up the art department, or some such thing."

"But didn't you tell them? Didn't you—" She stopped, looking for the words.

"What is there I could tell them? What could I do?"

"I don't know. I guess there's nothing."

"It may not be so bad. I have a feeling it's only temporary."

"Why? Did they say so?"

"No, but—you know how the business is."

"Yes, I know, but—"

"For all I know, it might be only a year or so."

"A year is an awfully long time. For me."

"I know. I'll miss you, too."

"*Miss* me? Dear God, I'm not going to *miss* you—I'm going to be dead without you!"

"Oh, now, easy does it. I'm not all that important."

"You don't think so? What do you think I've lived for all this past year?"

"Yes, but this was just last year. You did all right before you knew me."

"That was different. I was home then."

"Well, there it is, anyway. The ball has been taken out of our hands, and I'm afraid there's not much we can do about it."

"I could quit the job here, and get one out there."

"That wouldn't be very smart, everything considered."

"Why wouldn't it? Who would know?"

"Those things get around. They'd find out soon enough."

"Well, what of it? Suppose they did—then what?"

"It just wouldn't look right, that's all."

"I don't see why not. If we love each other, there's no—"

"Just believe me, please. It would be very unsubtle, and it would be bad for both of us careerwise. I mean that."

"If you're sure."

"Yes, I'm sure. I promise you."

"All right, then."

"Now. Would you like another drink?"

"Yes, please. A double."

"Where do you want to go for dinner?"

"I don't feel much like eating, thank you."

"How about Voisin? Just for old times' sake?"

"The way I feel now, I don't ever want to see Voisin again. Wild horses couldn't drag me in there."

"It'll wear off. You'll feel better after a while."

"I suppose being electrocuted wears off too—after a while."

"Come on, please. It isn't the end of the world."

"Well, it's a good imitation."

"Please."

"All right. I'm sorry. I'll try to behave."

"That's better. I knew I could count on you."

"I seem to have forgotten to ask—when does all this happen? When do you leave?"

There was a long silence. "They've booked me out of here on the noon plane tomorrow," he said.

Now, on the morning that spring came to the city, Anne got dressed slowly and deliberately, as though trying to keep the day from getting started. When she was dressed, she transferred the contents of one purse into another, item by item, then went into the kitchen and heated up the coffee and poured herself a final cup. She sipped it slowly, then rinsed out the cup, and the telephone rang. She picked it up, and a woman's voice said, "Miss Waters?"

"Yes," said Anne, knowing already what was coming.

"This is Dr. Lipkin's office. The doctor would like to see you sometime today, if it's convenient."

"Is it about the lab report?"

"I believe it is, yes."

"Can you tell me what it was? Was it—"

"I'm sorry, but we can't give out that information on the telephone."

"Is the doctor there now?"

"The doctor is busy right now, but you may see him around noon if you wish."

"All right. I'll be there."

She went to the doctor at noon, and he confirmed what she had known all along. She ate part of a tuna fish salad sandwich for lunch, and then went back to the office and spent the rest of the day staring at the objects around the room, all of which looked different than they had before. They seemed more clearly in focus, and she noticed small details like the spot on her typewriter where the finish was chipped, and a tiny crack in the rim of the ceiling light, and the smear of white brass polish in the screws under the doorknob. At the end of the office day, she went home and wrote Curtin a letter that ran for fourteen pages, and after mailing it she wandered through the city streets, with the one idea of making herself so exhausted that she could go back to her room and go to sleep.

ꙮ 2 ꙮ

IT WAS ALMOST a week later that Curtin's letter arrived. It had been another soft, smoky spring day, and when Anne came home from work it was still daylight. The letter was in her mailbox, a long, fat envelope with the red-white-and-blue airmail border. She tore it open and started to read it in the vestibule, then after a moment she went into her room and closed the door and sat in a chair and read it through quickly. Then she read it more slowly, examining sentences she had missed in her first rush, and then she read it a third time, to make sure she had read correctly. In the end, she knew every word of it by heart. It ran:

Dearest Anne:

This is going to be the hardest letter I've ever had to write, partially because I can't agree with the solution you suggest, and partially because I can come up with only a very second-rate solution of my own. I feel utterly miserable about it, but I guess that's the way the ball bounces. I'll try to tape it out for you as clearly as I can, and give it to you absolutely on the level.

First, as to your coming out here. That would be even

more impossible now than it was before, because if we were to get married here and you were to have the baby, it would all be so utterly obvious that it would be common gossip within a week. If it were only the gossip we had to worry about I wouldn't mind, but the company is—as I probably don't have to tell you—terribly strait laced when it comes to any hanky-panky between the employees, and they won't stand for even the slightest suspicion of any scandal around the shop. One of the officers out here—a guy, I might say, who is far higher up the ladder than I am—was transferred simply because his wife got him involved in a messy divorce case, and the Big Brass concluded that his usefulness to the team was through. You can imagine what would happen to *me*, therefore, if they ever got wind of anything.

And that brings up the next point. This job of mine is beginning to firm up into something really big—it has all the earmarks, in fact, of being the thing that I've been waiting for the last three years to latch onto—and if I foul up on anything at this particular point, the whole thing may very well blow up in my face. In slightly different circumstances, I might have been able to change jobs and get a slot where we're not known, but this thing has just about come to a boil here, and if I threw it away it would mean starting all over again, and with cold water, so to speak.

Come to think of it, I may have had a premonition all along that we shouldn't get too deeply involved, because although God knows our friendship meant more to me than any other ever has, I somehow had the feeling that I ought to keep my roots flexible, just in case something like this turned up. You may very well say that now is a hell of a time to tell you, but if I can't be anything else to you at least I want to be honest.

So now we come to my solution, which as I see it is the only one possible under the circumstances. You may remember Ned Harkins, the guy who joined us one night at the Blue Angel. Ned has a friend who is a doctor and who can make arrangements for this sort of thing, and I shall write to him— Ned, that is—and tell him you want to see him. I have no idea what the cost will be (you can believe it or not, but I've had no first-hand experience in these matters), but Ned will put up whatever is necessary, and I will pay him over a period of time, longer or shorter depending on the tab. I realize that this is unpleasant, and unromantic, and highly disagreeable for you, but I can honestly see no other course of action.

On reading this over, it comes to me that I haven't made my point very well, and that I come out of the whole business looking like a prime son of a bitch, but please believe me when I tell you that if I saw any alternative I would latch onto it in a minute. I just don't, or cannot, and that's all there is to it. I imagine you will probably hate me, and for that I am deeply, sincerely sorry, and if there's anything I can do for you—anything you need to buy, or want to have—please, please feel that you can call on me at any hour of the day or night.

Love,
Roy

PS
I'm writing Ned right now. I don't know his phone number, but you can find him in the book.

xxx
R.

Anne put the letter down, and stared out the window. No, I don't hate you, she thought. I feel terribly sorry for you. I feel a sadness that gets deeper every moment I think of it.

From outside came the shouts and screams of children playing stickball, and she could see them darting about in the street like sparrows, unaware of the passing automobiles. Then a flower cart came into sight, drawn by a sagging old white horse, and the red, yellow, blue, and white flowers seemed to her to be everything beautiful she had ever known. She took her purse and went outside, where the driver of the cart was calling out a wild chant to the windows above, and she bought a pot of yellow tulips and took them back and put them on her window sill. While she was looking at them, Mr. Becker, the little old man who lived across the hall, came down the street, and he looked at the flowers and then at Anne, and smiled and tipped his hat. She was so deep in her thoughts that she didn't realize what he had done until he had gone past and it was too late to reply. She started up, and then sat back in her chair. All at once, a feeling of panic swept over her, and she wanted to run, scream, break things—anything, just to get away. Her heart pounded in her ears and she began to tremble violently, and for a moment she had the feeling that she was going to go insane. She opened her mouth and breathed in deep gasps, and then the pounding of her heart slowed down a little, and the trembling began to pass. She concentrated on the tulips, and breathed deeply, and after a while she felt a relaxation that began to loosen her limbs, and she lay back in the chair, still looking at the tulips. I can't let that happen again, she thought. I can't let myself get in a state like that or I'll go right out the window. She looked at the tulips for a long time, until the daylight began to fade, and then she let her eyes wander around the darkness of her room. Somewhere in here, she thought, I'll have to make room for a crib, or a bassinet, or whatever. Maybe in a corner, where I could put a screen around it when the lights are on. Well, there'll be time enough to think about that. That and all the other problems, like making enough money to live on, and all that. Plenty of time to think about that. The thing is, it isn't the thinking, it's the doing. And there's nobody except me who can do it. Nobody in the world. A quick flash of the panic returned, but she fought it down.

Just for a second, she considered the possibility of giving up her job and going back home, but the thought of her father's reaction made her dismiss the idea immediately. Her mother might understand, or at least offer to help her, but her father might very possibly hurl her out into the snow, like the fathers in the old-fashioned melodramas. Her parents would have to know eventually, but right now she would sooner go with a troupe of Armenian gipsies than go home.

She stood up in the darkness and went to the light switch,

and in the sudden glare the room looked harsh and ugly. And I'm going to have to do something about this, too, she thought. This is no kind of room to keep a child in, no matter how young it is. I'll have to brighten it up somehow, think of something to make it more cheerful. Maybe like prints, or brighter curtains. And better lights, certainly. Well, at least it'll give me something to do. Something to keep my mind occupied at night and over the week ends.

She moved toward the kitchen, and as she passed the dresser she stopped and looked at herself in the mirror. For perhaps a full minute she stared at her reflection, and then she took a deep breath and made up her mind. Tomorrow the braids come off, she told herself. Get those braids off there, and get another hairdo, and maybe even get a new face. Off with the old and on with the new, and hold your hats in the nickel seats. Or, as someone else once said, Tiny Tim, hold onto your hat. Can't remember who it was that said it, but that's not important. It couldn't matter less. Some sad ad man, probably.

The next day she managed to get an appointment at a hairdresser's for late afternoon. After a long discussion, during which the hairdresser suggested an upswept creation, his assistant held out for a bun in the back, and the manicurist maintained that an Italian cut was the simplest, Anne decided on a pageboy. The hairdresser said that more girls with upswept hairdos became engaged than all the others put together, and Anne said thanks a million but she still preferred a pageboy. When he was finished she looked very sleek and attractive, and completely different from before.

She went next to a ten-cent store and bought two new shades for her lamps, and then went back to her apartment. In the vestibule, she saw the older woman from upstairs, the one who looked like an actress, coming down, and Anne smiled at her and said hello. The woman's eyes were puzzled, and Anne added, "I just changed my hairdo," and the woman said "Oh, yes," and went out. Anne let herself into her apartment, and put the new shades on the lamps, then looked around to see what else she might do. The shades didn't really help a great deal, and she sat down and gazed morosely from one item of furniture to the next. Then she saw her tulips, and she rose from her chair and got a glass of water. As she poured it into the caked earth in the pot, she said, "I'm sorry, fellows. I forgot about you. It won't happen again, I promise." She shook out the last drop from the glass, said, "If you need anything else, just holler," and then took the glass back into the kitchen. She stood for a moment, staring into the sink, her eyes focused on the drain hole and the faint green stains that surrounded it. What I need is to talk to someone, she thought. I don't care who, but anyone. I've just got to talk to someone.

As Evelyn Estes left the apartment building, she thought briefly about the girl who had changed her hairdo, and reflected that even if she hadn't changed it, she might not have recognized her. She knew by sight only two of the tenants in the building; one was the round, blurry little man who lived across the hall and who often sang old show tunes late at night, and the other was the younger, slightly more elegant, man who lived on the top floor and played classical records at full volume. Once or twice, when she saw the older man on his way to work in the morning, she had been tempted to ask him how he knew so many theater songs, but he always looked so glassy-eyed and unhappy at that hour, rather like a sad, wet owl, that she never had the nerve to speak to him.

Now, as she hurried toward the theater for the first cast reading of her play, she realized that, for no rational reason, she was nervous. She had got the part of the Cockney grandmother after three readings, in competition with two other actresses, and her complete ease with the dialect was what had counted most heavily in her favor. It occurred to her that if she handled this role well, and the play were a hit, she might very well establish herself as a character actress on Broadway, instead of a bit player in television. Tonight, all that would happen would be that the cast would read the play through once, and there was nothing that could possibly go wrong, but still she was nervous. Just take it easy, she told herself. You don't have much until the third act, anyway, and by that time everybody should be relaxed and at ease. Just don't tighten up, that's all. Take it easy.

The theater was dark, except for a brilliant, white worklight that hung over the stage and threw sharp shadows in all directions. There was a wooden table, at which were three chairs, and a dozen or so more chairs were arranged in a semicircle facing the table. Evelyn was formally greeted by the director, the producer, and the author, who sat in their shirtsleeves at the table, and she was introduced to the other members of the cast, some of whom she had seen and some of whom she knew by reputation only. She took a seat in the semicircle of chairs, opened her bag and brought out her script, and tried to appear casual as she riffled through its already well-thumbed pages. When everybody had arrived and settled down, the producer arose and greeted them in a brief speech, and turned them over to the director. The director, who had a head that came to a bald, glistening point, stood up and glared at them through dark-rimmed glasses.

"This is just going to be a run-through for words," he said, in a surprisingly mild voice. "Don't try to put anything into it, because all we want to do is listen to the words and follow the thought. Such thought as we devoutly hope exists, that is." He looked at the playwright, and they both smiled tight little smiles, then he sat down and opened his script, which was in a red leather binder. "All right," he said. "Let's go. Remember—just the words."

As the reading progressed and the words flowed from one actor and then another, Evelyn watched the director and the playwright, trying to gauge their reactions. The director looked without expression at whichever actor was reading, and occasionally made light pencil marks in the pages of his script; the playwright looked at the ceiling, or down at the stage, or covered his eyes with his hands, but rarely did he look at an actor. Once, after reading one of her lines, Evelyn glanced up and saw that he was staring at her, and she became so flustered that she lost her place.

When they had finished the second act, the director put his pencil in his script and said, "All right, let's take ten." He and the playwright and the producer stood up and went off into a darkened corner of the stage, and one of the actors began to take orders for coffee and sandwiches. Evelyn ordered coffee and a doughnut, although her stomach had already begun to flutter, and she knew she wouldn't be able to eat much until the reading was over. Her most important scenes were in the third act, and in spite of the fact that she had done them so often during the tryouts that she knew them by heart, she could not bring herself to feel relaxed. The coffee was hot, and the edges of the cardboard container were soggy with steam, but she managed to get down a few sips before the director and the others came back from their conference. The three men sat down, and the director opened his script with a snap. "All right," he said. "Let's hear what this one sounds like."

Evelyn got through her scenes without any trouble, but as the reading of the act went on, she noticed a change come over the men at the table. Instead of looking at the actors, the director was staring blindly at the work-light; the producer had his hands locked between his knees and his chin sunk down upon his chest, and the playwright seemed to be trying to crawl out of sight under the table. When the final curtain line had been read, there was a silence of almost thirty seconds, and nobody moved. Then the director said, "Just a minute, everybody, please."

The three men rose and went off into the wings again, and Evelyn nibbled at her doughnut and drank her cold coffee, while the voices in the darkness muttered, and grew in volume, then faded away. The playwright's voice was the shrillest, and it was muted and softened by the other two voices, and finally there was total silence, and the men came back. The producer kept snapping a cigarette lighter on and off, the playwright looked glumly into the dead and colorless footlights, and the director faced the cast and said, "The first two acts sound pretty good. There's nothing there we can't take care of with a little work. The third act, however, is something else again. I'm afraid the third act is going to need some fairly—ah—extensive rewriting, so I'd advise you all not to bother learning your third-act lines just yet. We'll concentrate on the first two, and hope to have them in good shape by the time we get a new third." He looked around at the producer and the author and said, "Anything else?" and they both shook their heads. He turned back to the cast and said, "All right, then, thank you very much. That'll be all for tonight."

The stage manager, who had been lurking in the wings, called out, "One o'clock tomorrow!" and the actors picked up their belongings, put on what clothes they had taken off, and filed quietly out into the night.

Crosstown buses were scarce at that hour, and it was almost midnight when Evelyn got off and walked down the dark, deserted street toward her apartment. The only sensation she felt was one of resignation and fatigue, and as she let herself into the vestibule she noticed without interest that the door to one of the first-floor apartments was open, the one belonging to the girl who had changed her hairdo. The lights were on in the room, and as Evelyn went past the door she glanced in and saw the girl sitting in a red overstuffed chair, looking out at her. She nodded and started up the stairs, and the girl rose and came quickly to the door.

"Would you like a cup of coffee?" the girl asked.

Evelyn stopped. I wonder what this is about, she thought. She paused a moment, then turned back. "Yes, I'd love one," she said. "I was going to make myself a drink, but I guess coffee would be better."

"I have some vermouth," the girl said. "And a little sherry. Would you like that?"

"No, thanks. Coffee will be fine." Evelyn went into the room, and the girl closed the door behind her.

"I'm Anne Waters," the girl said. "Here—sit down over there."

"I'm Evelyn Estes," said Evelyn. "Or I was until about an hour ago." She sat in the chair Anne had indicated, and stretched out her feet. "Right now, I'm not sure who I am."

Anne went into the kitchen, and came back with a cup of coffee. "I just felt the need to talk to somebody," she said, as she gave the coffee to Evelyn. "This place gets kind of lonely, sometimes."

"You don't know the 'arf of it, duckie," Evelyn said, and sipped her coffee. "It can drive you right art of yer bloody mind, and that's a fact."

"You know, I never realized before that you're British," Anne said. "Do you live over here all the time?"

Evelyn smiled. "I'm about as British as Madame Chiang Kai-shek. That accent is from a part in a play that I'm doing."

"Oh."

"Or rather, was doing," Evelyn said, after a moment. "For all I know, I'll be cut out tomorrow. But I'm sorry about the Cockney, though. I didn't mean to sound so ham."

"Oh, that's all right," Anne said. "I thought it sounded kind of nice."

Evelyn looked at her. "How long have you been in New York?" she asked.

"A little over a year. Why?"

"I don't know. I just wouldn't have guessed that long."

"Oh, yes, I've—been around," Anne said. She rose, emptied her ashtray into a wastebasket, and then sat down and looked at Evelyn, who was staring at her. She smiled quickly, and added, "Quite a bit, in fact. Around New York, that is. I've been to places like Voisin, and Costello's, and Nick's, and the Drake Room, and—and the Blue Angel—and—well, *you* know. Places like that. Then, as a matter of fact, last summer we went once to the Glen Island Casino, and all that sort of thing. As a matter of fact, I guess I've covered New York pretty thoroughly. For just a year, that is. A year and four months, more or less." She realized that she was twirling a strand of her new hairdo between her thumb and forefinger, and that Evelyn was looking at her without having listened to what she was saying.

"What's on your mind?" Evelyn asked. "What's bothering you?"

"Just as I said—I wanted to talk to somebody. That's all."

"I'm sorry. It's none of my business."

"Don't apologize. It's perfectly natural to ask, especially when I dragged you in here in the middle of the night, and all. It isn't as though this had been a formal invitation to tea, or anything. I can see why you might wonder." Anne rose again, and went to the window and looked at the tulips. She thought a moment, and then she said, "As a matter of fact, there is something on my mind, but I don't know exactly quite how to put it."

"Uh-huh." Evelyn took a sip of her coffee, then settled back in her chair. "Well, if you want to tell me, go ahead."

"I just don't quite know where to start, that's all."

"Would you like me to guess?"

"No, that's not the point—"

"Because I think I've got a pretty good idea."

"No, the thing is it's just that—I really don't know you, and—well, it sounds so sort of crude when you just make the flat statement, that's all."

"I can tell you now, it's one of two things."

"Well, probably."

"The trouble is that I can't help you on either one of them. Why do you want to tell me?"

"Well, it's just that you're bound to know sooner or later, and—"

"All right, that narrows it down to one thing. And it's not money."

"Oh, no, it's not money. I wouldn't think of asking—"

"Do you want me to tell you what it is?"

"Are you sure you know?"

"Well, put it this way, then. Has the father-to-be walked out and left you?"

There was a long silence. "Well, not exactly," Anne said. "I mean—well, yes, I guess you could say he has, although—"

"For all practical purposes, then, he has."

"Yes, I guess so."

"Well, there it is, then. Now what?"

Anne shrugged. "What is there?"

"Well, duckie, I wish I could help you, but I certainly don't know anybody you can go to, and I think that's a bad idea anyway. If I were you, I'd go home and have the baby, and chalk it all up to experience, but I don't mean to sound pious about it." She stopped, and thought a minute. "It's so long since I've had any worries like that that I've kind of got the outsider's point of view, I guess. I'm all in favor of having babies. Twenty—no, ten—years ago, I might have had somebody all lined up who would take care of you, but not now."

"That's not the point," Anne said. "I want to have the baby. I want to have it here. I want to go ahead and have it just as though I were married."

"Oh?"

"The point is, everybody in the building is going to have to know. I mean eventually it'll be obvious, and I'd just like to tell somebody the whole thing, so they'll know my side of it. But mainly I just want someone to talk to—someone I can tell things to, and talk to, and be with every now and then. That's all. I don't want to force anything on you, or make you listen to me if you don't want to, but I just had to say *this* much to someone or I'd have gone crazy. Does that make sense?"

"Yes, of course."

"And maybe you can tell the others, so they'll know and I won't have to go through it over and over—"

"I'm afraid I don't know any of the others, but I'll see what I can do. This kind of word usually travels pretty fast, you know."

"Yes, I suppose it does."

Evelyn looked around the room, then drew a deep breath and sighed. "All right, then," she said wearily, as she got to her feet. "I'll do what I can."

"Don't go," Anne said. "Can't you stay a little longer?"

"Duckie, I'd love to, but I'm dead on me feet. Let me think about this for a while, and maybe I'll have an idea. I'll talk to you tomorrow."

"All right. And thank you for listening."

Evelyn made a dismissing gesture with her hand, and went to the door. "Good night," she said.

"Good night." Anne held the door open for her, then closed it gently. She turned back into the room, and all at once she was bitterly angry at herself. That was the wrong thing to do, she thought. That was just about as wrong as I could be. Plucking at the woman's sleeves, imploring her to tell the others my story—she'll be completely right if she never speaks to me again. How could I humiliate myself like that? What possibly got into me, to go crawling and sniveling around—all I've done is frighten her off, instead of making a friend of her. I'm a stupid, stupid, stupid . . .

She flung herself face down on the day bed, and bit into the dusty covering. She stayed there for several minutes, then slowly she got up, and began to get undressed.

❧ 3 ❧

ARTHUR MONTGOMERY was through his duties on the copy desk at five o'clock. His usual routine was to take a short walk before going to the saloon across the street for his dinner, but his left ankle, which had been bitten by a Scottie the day before, was giving him some trouble, so this day he went straight to the saloon from the paper. It was his regular hangout except for week ends, when most of his friends had their days off. Montgomery's days off were Sunday and Monday, which made it hard for him to have any normal week ends.

There were a few people in the saloon when he came in, and those who looked up greeted him with casual nods. He went to the bar and stood alongside Sam Ulm, a blond, blue-eyed reporter in his twenties, who looked like a depressed stork. He was tall and thin, and his shirt cuffs were frayed around the edges. His hands were dirty with carbon smudges, and his tie was slightly askew, but he nevertheless gave the impression that he could look neat if he really set his mind to it. He had the latest edition of the paper folded across the bar as though he were trying to clamp a wrestling hold on it. He didn't look up; he just muttered, "The sons of bitches, oh, the sons of bitches," over and over again, and took a deep drink of his highball.

"What's the matter, Sam?" Montgomery asked. "They spell your name wrong?"

"You know what they did, the sons of bitches?" Ulm said. "They cut out the last half of the story, the last whole goddam half."

"Maybe they had to, for space," Montgomery said, and took a sip of the drink that the bartender had slid in front of him.

"Maybe, but they cut out the half that made the story accurate," Ulm said, savagely. "Without the ending, it's inaccurate. It doesn't make sense." Montgomery chuckled, and Ulm went on, "And you know what happened when I told them? You know what that chipmunk-brain said to me on the phone? He said, 'Well, very few people read more than one paper anyway, and if they see it in the *Gazette* they'll believe it's the truth.' He had the gall! He had the absolute goddam gall to say that to me on the phone!" He pointed toward the phone booth in the rear of the saloon, then seized his highball glass and emptied it down his throat. "Oh, the sons of bitches!" he muttered, choking slightly.

"Let me buy you a drink," Montgomery said, and gestured to the bartender. "I'll tell you something," he went on. "If that's the worst thing that happens to you on this paper, you'll be lucky. You'll be so lucky there'll be a special division of the Nieman Fellowship named just for you. Believe me, this is nothing."

"Maybe to you," Ulm said, darkly. "But to me it's a goddam outrage. It's *dishonest!*"

"O.K., it's dishonest," Montgomery said. "But you won't go to jail for it. It's just journalistic dishonesty, for which there is never punishment, only rewards."

The bartender set a new round of drinks in front of them,

and slid a pile of wet change toward Montgomery. Ulm lifted his glass and looked at Montgomery over it. "Cynical, aren't you?" he said. "Cheers."

"Cheers," said Montgomery, and they both drank. "No, I'm not cynical," he said, after a moment. "Just realistic. And resigned, maybe. But I don't think particularly cynical. I don't know. I gave up analyzing myself a long time ago. You just get depressed if you analyze yourself too much."

"They say that the difference between an African native and a white man," Ulm said, "is that if an African native thinks very hard, he drops off to sleep, and if a white man thinks very hard, he kills himself."

"The suicide rate in this country dropped a total of six per hundred thousand between 1933 and 1955," Montgomery said. "Are you trying to tell me people aren't thinking as hard now as they were in 1933?"

"Nineteen thirty-three doesn't count. There was a depression, and people had nothing to look forward to."

"And what do you call the prospects these days—balmy?"

"Now you've got me confused," Ulm said. "I don't remember what side I was arguing on."

There was a brief silence. "Neither do I," Montgomery said.

"We were talking about suicide. But why?" Ulm motioned to the bartender for another round.

"Search me." Montgomery finished his drink, and set the glass down. "But I know how you can fake a suicide. Make a homicide look so much like a suicide that it'll fool even the medical inspectors."

"How?"

"It's what are called hesitation marks. If a guy goes to cut his wrists or throat, he usually tries a couple of times and flinches before he really does it. The flinches leave little scratches that are called hesitation marks."

Ulm looked at him without expression. "So?"

"So all you do is kill a man by poison or something else

a suicide might try, and then make it look as though he tried to cut his wrists. Put in the hesitation marks."

Ulm considered this for a moment. "I think there are still some bugs to be worked out of it," he said.

Montgomery raised his new drink in salute. "Cheers." He drank. "Of course there are bugs in it. Nothing is perfect the first time. But it's something to remember, anyway."

They had two more rounds, and then Ulm folded his paper under his arm and began to pick his change off the bar. "Well, keep a stiff upper," he said.

"Don't go," Montgomery said. "Have one more."

"No, I ought to go."

"Just one. Please. A quick one."

Ulm looked up at the clock over the bar. "Well, it's just about eight," he said. "It'll be almost half past by the time I get home—"

"Just call your wife and tell her you're on your way. Another couple of minutes won't make any difference, anyhow."

Ulm's eyes clouded for a brief instant, as though he were trying to think of something. Then he shrugged. "O.K.," he said.

Montgomery smiled, and signaled the bartender. "That's my boy," he said. "I knew you wouldn't leave me."

They had another round, and then Ulm said, "O.K., now. One last one on me, and then I really do have to go."

Montgomery chuckled. "I have a plan," he said. "I'll tell you in a minute, as soon as I've worked all the bugs out of it."

After the next round, Ulm said, "I hope you've got the bugs out of it, because here I go, ready or not."

"My plan is simple," Montgomery replied. "You say it will take you about a half hour to get home." They both looked at the clock, and Montgomery went on, "That means that as of now, you cannot get home before nine-fifteen. Right?" Ulm nodded solemnly, and Montgomery said, "My plan is that you call your wife, tell her that you are having dinner with me here, and that she should not bother to wait dinner for you. Just tell her not to wait, and that you'll be home right after dinner. That way, it'll be simpler all around."

Ulm looked at the clock again. He closed one eye and then opened it. "Hmmm," he said. "I'll be frank and say I don't think you've worked all the bugs out of it. However, it might not be a bad idea if I telephoned anyway, just to say I'm on my way." He picked some change from the pile on the bar, and headed for the phone booth.

"That's the coward's way," Montgomery said.

After a few minutes Ulm returned to the bar, and he was quiet and thoughtful. He sipped his drink, and said, "Strange. She said she'd already had dinner. Said she was in bed, in fact."

"Perfect," said Montgomery. "My plan worked out better than I could have hoped. Now we can have dinner here, and no pangs of conscience."

"Uh-huh." Ulm stared at the back bar, and stirred his drink with one finger.

"She didn't sound sore, did she?" Montgomery asked. "I mean, you're not in any trouble, or anything?"

"Not exactly sore, no. Just a little cool around the edges. I don't think I'm in any trouble; it's just that—" He put his arms on the bar, and cradled his head in them. "Oh, Jesus," he whispered.

"What's the matter?" Montgomery asked. "You all right?"

There was a long silence. "This is her birthday," Ulm said, in a low voice. "And I haven't even bought her a present."

"Oh," said Montgomery. He looked up at the clock. "There's one store I know of that's open at this hour. Come on."

Ulm raised his head, and finished his drink in one swallow. "The damage has already been done," he said. "Leo, let's have another round here. Doubles, if you will."

"You sure you want it, Sammy?" the bartender asked. "You sure it'll be good for you?"

"What's good or bad for me is all relative now," Ulm said.

"O.K., but maybe this better be the last." The bartender made them two weak drinks, and Montgomery paid for them.

"Look," Montgomery said. "We can go to that Doubleday's that stays open till midnight. You can get her a book, or a record album, or a piece of art—hell, you can say what made you late was that you spent so much time shopping for her. Nobody could get mad at that."

Ulm shook his head slowly. "We were to have an early supper," he said. "Then go to a movie, or go dancing, or something. I got so goddam mad about their cutting my piece I forgot all about everything else." He downed his drink and stared morosely into the bottom of the glass.

"I still say it isn't too late," Montgomery said. "Come on."

Ulm shrugged and followed Montgomery out the door and into a taxi. Montgomery gave the driver the address of the store on Fifth Avenue, and then the two men were silent as the cab began to weave its way through the crosstown traffic. Finally Montgomery, who had been staring out the window at the blur of passing lights, turned and looked at Ulm. "What are you doing this for, Sam?" he asked.

Ulm stared at him. "Huh?" he said.

"Newspaper work, I mean," said Montgomery. "Reporting, and all that kind of lunacy."

Ulm hesitated. "Well, hell," he said. "A man's got to make a living—"

"This is no living for you, Sam. It's no living for anyone. Get out of it. Get out while you still can."

"Well, I don't intend to spend all my life as a reporter, for Chrissakes. But you get good experience writing, and you get—"

"And don't tell me you're going to be a writer!" Montgomery shouted. "Please, for God's sakes, Sam, don't tell me you want to be a writer. Be a stevedore, be a procurer, be an *actor*, but don't ever, ever try to be a writer. Please."

"What's the matter? Don't you think I can write?"

"Of course you can write. That's the trouble. But you aren't Hemingway and you aren't Faulkner and you aren't Tennessee Williams, so you might as well give it up right now, before it breaks you. Goddammit, I ought to know."

"How do you know I'm not Hemingway? I haven't even tried."

"How do I know? Oh, for God's sakes, Sam, just get out of it, that's all I know. Get out of it before you become an old bum like me."

"Give me a few years, then I'll see."

Montgomery was quiet for a minute. "I'm sorry," he said at last. "It's none of my goddam business. Forget I said anything."

The taxi drew up in front of the store, and Montgomery paid the driver and they got out. Inside, they browsed for a while among the banks of brightly colored books, and finally Montgomery picked up a large volume and examined it. "Here's one she might like," he said. "It's called *Cruising off the Coast of Greece*. Does she like to sail?"

"No," said Ulm, looking at another book. "She hates it."

"Some damn fine pictures, nonetheless." Montgomery closed the book and put it back. "Well—" He looked around, and selected a book behind him. "How about *A Handbook of African Fertility Symbols?* There ought to be a few laughs in that."

"Maybe a record would be best," Ulm said. "She likes music."

"I'll tell you what." Montgomery peered off at one corner of the store. "You get her a record album, and I'll get her something I see across the room, there."

"What is it?" Ulm asked nervously. "What do you see?"

"Never mind. You get your records, and I'll get this."

Montgomery left Ulm and went over to where there were several rows of figurines, reproductions of ancient works of art. He selected a tiny bronze cow, examined it carefully, thought a moment, and put it back on the shelf. Next he picked out a hippopotamus, which he put back almost immediately. He finally settled on a bronze Egyptian horse. It was small and dainty, and as far as he could see it could give no possible offense. He handed it to a clerk, and asked to have it gift-wrapped.

When they got outside, Ulm was feeling more cheerful. He had two record albums in a gift-wrapped package under his arm, and from the size of Montgomery's package he knew, although Montgomery would not tell him, that it contained some *objet d'art*. He felt that, everything considered, he had done as well as could be expected.

"I just wish I could get her some flowers," he said. "Records aren't a very personal gift, after all."

"No florists open this time of night," Montgomery said. Down a side street, he saw the lighted awning of a bar, and he turned and steered toward it. "Let's go in here and think for a minute," he said. "Maybe an idea will come to us."

They had two rounds of drinks, but no ideas came to them.

"The ancient Britons used to give weasel pelts as gifts," Montgomery said, after a while. "But they're kind of hard to get at this time of night, too. Besides, I don't think nowadays a woman would consider a weasel pelt a suitable substitute for flowers. It has a different ring, somehow."

"The thing is, there *is* no substitute for flowers," Ulm said. "You either get flowers or you don't, and there's no in-between. Now, goddammit, it's spring, and there ought to be spring flowers around. Not spring anything else, just plain old spring flowers."

"Forsythia!" Montgomery shouted, clapping Ulm on the shoulder. "We've got forsythia till hell won't have it!"

"Who's got forsythia?" Ulm asked, mopping the spilled drink from his chin.

"We! The city! Central Park is lousy with it!"

"How do you know? You haven't been in Central Park in years."

"We ran a picture on page one yesterday, showing great masses of forsythia. Read your own paper, for Chrissakes, and you'll learn a thing or two."

"You know, you're right," Ulm said, and he began to smile. "A big spray of forsythia would be just the thing. She'd love that. That's a wonderful idea."

"Of course it is." Montgomery slid off his bar stool, and picked up his change. "Where do you live?" he asked.

"Ninety-fifth and Lex," Ulm replied, as he finished his drink.

"Perfect. We can get into the Park at Ninetieth Street, and grab a bunch that'll knock her hat off."

"Hot damn." Ulm set his glass down, and headed for the door. "Come on. Let's go."

At Ninetieth Street, they crossed Fifth Avenue and went into Central Park. They walked down the bridle path a short distance, then angled off into the darkness of the bushes surrounding the reservoir. The forsythia wasn't as spectacular as the pictures had made it seem, but Montgomery said that was because it was night, and the blossoms had closed. Working together, they tugged and wrenched and broke about two dozen branches, and when Ulm gathered them up they made a massive bundle. Montgomery carried the records, and together they groped their way down toward the bridle path. Suddenly, there was the low growl of a siren, and a white-topped police car slid into view along the path.

"Oh, my God, it's the cops," Montgomery whispered. "Try to act natural."

"Natural, hell," said Ulm, through the forsythia. "I can't even see."

A light flashed on them, and one of the policemen shouted, "Hey, you!" The car stopped, and they heard the sound of a door opening, and then Ulm threw the forsythia at the light, and raced off into the bushes. The policeman shouted "Stop!" and the light slashed back and forth across the shrubbery. Montgomery turned and ran in the other direction, into the darkness. He heard a shot, but only one, and then he was at the entrance to the Park, and he slowed down and walked as casually as he could. His heart was pounding, and his mouth was dry and tasted acid. He looked frantically up and down Fifth Avenue as he walked, hoping to find a cab. He went two blocks before one appeared, and he got in and gave his address and then leaned back in the seat and closed his eyes. Only then did he realize that he was still carrying Ulm's package of records. Oh, the poor bastard, he thought. I did this to him. It was I who got him into all this. I suppose I should have stayed with him, but there was nothing I could have done. And it was he who started to run, anyway. I was going to stay there, until he ran. Still, I should have stayed with him. I got him into it, and then I chickened out. Montgomery, you are no bloody good for anything. You're no good for yourself, you're no good for your friends, and you're no good for your country. You'd be doing mankind a great favor if you drove straight down to the docks and went on into the water. Down into the black, oily water, and down and down and down until you got in the mud at the bottom of the harbor, and just stay there. Stay there and let the Staten Island ferry go back and forth over you all day and all night; stay there until you look like that thing that washed up at Brighton Beach last summer. . . .

He opened his eyes. The hell with that line of thought, he told himself. The first thing to do is go by the paper, and have them alert their man at Headquarters to watch out for Ulm. His police card will probably get him off, but still, it might be just as well to have someone looking out for him. And it seems like the very least I can do, after having run out on him. The very absolute least, for the love of God.

He leaned forward and gave the driver the address of the paper, and then leaned back again and closed his eyes.

It was after one o'clock when he got home to the apartment, and as he trudged wearily up the stairs he heard women's voices somewhere above. When he reached the third floor, the voices were coming from the apartment across from his, and he was just putting the key into his lock when the other door opened, and the woman who lived there looked out. He had seen her a few times before, but they had never spoken, so he paid no attention until she said, "Excuse me." Then he turned and looked at her. It was the first time he had looked straight into her eyes, and it changed her face completely. Before, it had just been a middle-aged face; now, he saw that it was alive, and expressive, and he also saw some other quality that he couldn't quite define. He had the feeling that she might just possibly be laughing at him.

"Yes?" he said.

"Would you care to join us in a drink?" she asked.

Montgomery hesitated. He wanted a drink very badly, but he also wanted to know what was going to be expected of him. "Well—" he said, and then stopped, waiting.

"It's all perfectly proper," the woman said. "Miss Waters and I are just having a drink here, and we heard you coming up the stairs and thought you might like to join us."

"That's very nice of you," he said. He put Ulm's records inside his apartment, threw his hat and package in after them, and closed the door. "Yes, I'd love to," he said, and went across the hall.

"My name is Evelyn Estes, by the way," she said, holding out her hand. "I've seen you quite often, but I guess we've never really met." He told her his name, and they shook hands, and as he went into her room she indicated a blonde with long hair who was sitting on the couch, and said, "And this is Anne Waters. Arthur Montgomery."

Anne smiled, and Montgomery had the impression that he had met her before, but he couldn't remember where. She struck him as being if not shy, at least slightly restrained, but he thought that if he had known her, she would have shown more recognition than she did. There was a curious softness about her, and yet she seemed older than what she obviously was, in her early twenties. He tried to make his how-do-you-do cordial enough to cover any possible previous meeting, and yet not be too effusive, and then he rubbed his hands together and looked around the room. It was furnished in quiet good taste, but had clearly not been done by a decorator, because the walls were covered with pictures of people in the entertainment business, mostly radio. "This is a nice place you have here," Montgomery said. "I wish mine were as cheerful."

"Thank you," said Evelyn. "What would you like to drink? We have Bourbon."

"That's exactly what I was going to ask for," said Montgomery, who had been drinking Scotch all evening. "Just with a little water, and it'll be fine." While Evelyn was pouring his drink, he looked closely at one of the pictures, which was a still from an old silent movie. "Well, what do you know?" he exclaimed. "Look at old Lloyd Hughes! And Gladys Brockwell! What do you know about that?"

"How did you recognize *them?*" Evelyn asked. "You couldn't have been born when that picture was made."

"Ha!" said Montgomery, and took the drink she held out to him. "Thank you." He peered at the picture again. "Who's the little broad with them?" he asked.

"That's me," said Evelyn.

He turned and stared at her. "Well, I'll be darned," he said. "I'm sorry."

She laughed. "Don't be silly," she said. "Sit down."

Montgomery sank into a chair, and looked at Anne, who was still smiling, but who had said nothing. "Do you live in New York?" he asked, hoping her answer might give him a clue.

Both Evelyn and Anne laughed. "I live downstairs," Anne said. "I've been here for over a year."

Montgomery passed his hand across his eyes. "I'm batting a thousand tonight, all right," he said. "What else is new?"

The two women looked at each other, and they laughed again, this time much harder. Glancing from one to the other, and then at the Bourbon bottle, Montgomery deduced that they had been at it for some little time. When they had stopped laughing, Anne said, "I'm sorry. It just sounded funny, the way you put it."

He took a sip of his drink. "Yes, it must have," he said. "Well, heigh ho." He took another sip, and fought back a shudder.

"There's something I've been meaning to ask you," said Evelyn.

"Yes?" he said, cautiously.

"How do you know all those old show tunes? Every now and then I've heard you—ah—singing them at night, and I just wondered how you got to know so many."

Montgomery leaned back and smiled. "It's just a hobby," he said. "I seem to remember them, that's all. And then, too, I sing them a lot," he added. "As you so well know."

"There's one I wish I could remember," Evelyn said. "It's from the First War, and it goes—" she closed her eyes and thought—"no, I guess I can't remember it."

"Would it be 'If You Don't Like Your Uncle Sammy'?" Montgomery asked. "Otherwise known as 'Don't Bite the Hand That's Feeding You,' I believe. Or then there's 'If He Can Fight Like He Can Love.' Would that be it?"

"That's it. It has the line 'I don't know how he's doing over there, but he's a bear in any Morris chair.'"

"That's right."

"Sing it for us, would you? Do you remember it all?"

"Of course I do." Montgomery sang the song, and then he sang "On the Beach at Bimini Bay," and then he and Evelyn sang a couple of old George M. Cohan songs. Anne didn't know any of the words, or for that matter even the tunes, but she sat back and laughed and applauded, and enjoyed herself thoroughly.

Evelyn and Montgomery were in the second chorus of

"Heaven Will Protect the Working Girl," when there was a flutter of sharp knocks on the door. Evelyn got up and opened it. She was confronted by Duncan Lapham, the young man who lived on the floor above. He was wearing a green kimono, and on his feet were leather sandals.

"I wonder if you could possibly sing a little more softly," he said, through tight lips. "I find it absolutely impossible to get to sleep."

"I'm very sorry," she said. "I didn't realize."

"Ask him in," said Montgomery, from inside. "Maybe he knows some old songs, too."

"Yes—would you like to join us?" Evelyn asked, tentatively.

"No, thank you," Lapham replied. "I should simply like to get some sleep."

He started to leave, but Montgomery rose from his chair and came to the door. "Wait a minute," he said. "Are you the one who lives on the top floor, over that apartment there?" He indicated the door to his room.

"Yes, I am," said Lapham. "Why?"

"Well, while we're on the subject of noise, then, may I ask that you tone down your goddam record player when you have it on in the morning? It's enough to knock a man out of bed."

Lapham bowed slightly. "I shall try to remember," he said.

"Thank you." Montgomery went back to his chair, and Evelyn closed the door softly.

"Well," she said. "I didn't know we were making so much noise."

"I'm glad it happened," said Montgomery. "I've been wanting to tell him that for a long time."

Anne put down her empty glass, and rose. "It's time for me to go to bed, anyway," she said. "It's way after two."

"Don't go," said Montgomery. "We've got plenty more songs we can sing."

"No, I really have to."

"Every time I just get started doing something, people have to leave." He took a swallow of his drink. "That's the story of my life."

"Well, you don't have to leave," said Evelyn. "Just stay where you are."

"Thank you," he said. "I shall."

Evelyn followed Anne to the door, and Anne turned and put out her hand. "I want to thank you, too," she said. "Thank you for everything."

"Oh, don't be silly, duck. It was nothing."

Anne laughed. "Don't I wish it," she said. "At any rate, thank you thank you thank you."

"Poosh." Evelyn blew her a quick kiss. "Good night."

She closed the door, and came back and sat down. There was a short silence. "What seems to be her trouble?" Montgomery asked.

Evelyn rose, and poured a little more whisky in her drink. "Her trouble is very simple," she said. She held the bottle toward Montgomery, and he put out his glass. "Her trouble is that she's going to have a baby." She poured him a splash, then set the bottle down.

Montgomery thought for a moment. "And we gather the father has blown town?"

Evelyn nodded.

He sat back and closed his eyes. "I guess there's not a great deal we can do about it," he said.

"No, but we can at least be nice about it. She needs someone to talk to. Someone who'll just be with her, and be friendly."

Montgomery took a sip of his drink, and looked at the ceiling. "The last person with whom I was friendly," he said, "is now in the hands of the police. I wonder if I'm just the person she ought to turn to at this particular moment."

Evelyn laughed. "I wouldn't know about that," she said. "But she hasn't specifically asked you, anyway. She just told me, and said she wanted the others to understand."

"I understand, all right. I just thought there might be something constructive somebody could do. Somebody preferably not me."

"I don't know what it would be."

"Well, I'll give it some thought." He finished his drink, and stood up. "But not tonight. Tonight I've done all the good deeds I can without being arrested myself." He went to the door, and opened it, then turned to her and bowed. "It's very nice to have met you, and thank you for the drinks, and I hope you won't be sorry you let me in on this."

She smiled. "Thank you," she said. "I'm sure I won't."

⚜ 4 ⚜

THE FIRST THING Montgomery did when he awoke the next morning was call the paper and ask for Sam Ulm. After a moment, Ulm's voice came over the telephone, and it was barely audible.

"Sam!" said Montgomery. "What did they do to you? Did they jug you?"

"Ah—not exactly. I guess you might say I jugged myself, from what they tell me."

"Didn't Joe Wood get to you? I had the desk tell him to look out for you."

"Yeah, I know. He looked out for me. But I seem to have decided I wanted to sleep in the precinct station." A long pause. "They let me."

"Oh."

"Yeah."

"How are things at home?"

"How do you think?"

"Yeah. I can see."

"Well, thanks for calling, anyway, Art."

"Oh—Sam. I've got your records and that other present

here. I'll bring them down to the paper, so you can take them home tonight."

"Don't bother, Art. I don't think they'll make much difference now."

"Well, hell, you might as well use them now you've bought them."

"O.K. Only don't go to any trouble."

"It's no trouble. And listen, Sam. Do you think it would help if I called your wife and told her what happened? I mean, I feel kind of responsible, after all, and I'd be glad to straighten her out in case she's got any wrong ideas, or anything."

"Please don't, Art. I think it's best you don't talk to her. O.K.?"

"O.K., Sam. Well, I'll bring your stuff over in an hour or so. Maybe we can have a couple of belts in the saloon to make you feel better."

"Well, I'm on the wagon, so maybe it would be better if you just brought them here to the paper."

"O.K., Sam. Whatever you say."

"O.K."

Montgomery hung up and got out of bed. He breathed deeply once or twice, and was happy to see that it didn't make his head spin. He felt, in fact, remarkably well. Maybe I've discovered the secret of drinking, he said to himself as he went into the bathroom. Maybe if I can remember just what I had last night, and in just what proportions, then I'll be able to do it again, and not have a hangover. Far from having a hangover, I feel at this moment better than I've felt in years.

He whistled an Irish jig as he opened the medicine chest, and took out a bottle of vitamin pills. He always started the day with a vitamin pill, and although he felt he didn't need one today, he rolled one out of the bottle and onto his palm, then opened his mouth and tossed in the pill. Or, rather, he tossed the pill toward his mouth, but something was badly wrong with his aim, and the pill missed not only his mouth but his entire head; it sailed over his shoulder like a bird, and hit the wall behind him. He heard it rattle into the bathtub, but when he turned around and looked for it, it was gone. He shrugged, and took another pill and placed it in his mouth with care, then swallowed it with a drink of water, and replaced the bottle. On the glass shelf below the bottle was his tooth paste, and he picked up the tube and took it out of the medicine chest, bringing with it the shelf on which it rested. The shelf dropped from his fingers and shattered in the basin; glass exploded all over the bathroom, and Montgomery found himself standing naked on a glittering carpet of broken glass. He leaned over to pick up some of the larger pieces, and something inside his head rolled forward and hit him behind the eyes. For a moment everything went black, then he straightened up; his head began a rhythmic pounding, and he felt sick. Resignedly, he turned and tiptoed through the broken glass into the other room and lay down. I knew it was too good to last, he said to himself. Nobody could feel that well and not have something go wrong. He sighed deeply, closed his eyes, and tried to go back to sleep.

Downstairs, on the sidewalk in front of his apartment, Ernest Becker was fitting in place the window box he had built. It was a bright, sunny day, although there was a sharp edge to the wind. The Sunday traffic was light; most people who could had gone to the country or to the parks, and the street was full of shouting children. The larger children played stickball, or lounged around doorways and lampposts and jeered at passing girls; the younger children played their own variety of ball, and ran and chased each other and dodged around and under and across the parked automobiles; and the very young children squatted down in the gutter and played mysterious games with bits of string and paper. The infants were wheeled in baby carriages by silent parents, the fathers looking dressed-up and martyred by their weekly outing.

The window box that Becker had made was only about two feet long and eight inches deep, but he knew it would be quite heavy when filled with earth, and he was uncertain as to how best to anchor it to the window sill. He had bought some angle irons at the hardware store, and his problem was to determine which way they would be the most effective. Experimentally, he put the box up on the sill, far enough forward so that the window would close behind it. He jiggled it for stability, then called in to his wife, who was cleaning the room inside. "How does it look, Martha?" he asked. "You like it this way?"

Martha looked up from her cleaning, and squinted at the box. "It's too high," she said. "You put plants in it, and nobody can see out the window."

She went back to her housework, and Becker lowered the box until the top was level with the sill. "You mean more like this," he said.

"That's too low," said Martha, without looking up.

"You mean half-way between?" Becker raised the box about four inches, and wobbled it back and forth. "You mean like this?" There was no answer, and he called, "Martha, you mean you want it like this?"

From the kitchen, Martha said, "Wait a minute already, I can't do everything at once!"

Becker held the box where it was until she came back into the room, and then he said, "Martha, like this it'll wobble. It's got no stability."

"Then do it your own way," she said. "It's nothing to me. I got more important things to worry about than flower boxes." She started back to the kitchen, then turned and looked at him sharply. "Where's your coat?" she asked. "What are you doing out there without a coat?"

"Martha, it's spring. I don't need a coat." He lowered the box to the level of the sill, and half-closed his eyes as he looked at it. "It's best like that, I think," he said. He set the box on the ground, and reached in a brown paper bag for the angle irons.

Martha came to the window carrying an old gray button sweater. "Here," she said, and threw it out to him. "So you won't wear a coat, at least do me the favor to wear this. I'm sick of nursing you with pneumonia."

Becker put the sweater on, and sat down on the steps and began to screw the angle irons onto the box.

He had just started to work when Evelyn Estes came out the door. He looked up at her and smiled and tipped his hat, and she smiled and nodded to him, and as she turned down the sidewalk, Anne Waters came to her window. She had a glass in her hand, and she emptied it into the tulips. "Hello," she said to Evelyn.

Evelyn looked up. "Oh, hello!" she said, and came closer to the window. "Everything under control today?" she asked.

"Everything's fine. Thanks to you."

"Oh, knock it off, dearie. I didn't do anything."

"You did. But I won't keep harping on it."

"Don't. There'll be time enough later."

"Would you like a cup of coffee?"

"I'd love one, but I'm on my way to rehearsal. Although why I go isn't precisely clear, considering what's left of my part."

"Well, you still don't know about the third act, do you?"

"No, but I'm afraid to think. I'll probably be cut out completely."

"Don't let them. Tell them you won't stand for it."

"A fine bloody lot of good that would do." Evelyn laughed. "Is there anything I can get you from the marts of trade?" she asked. "Any dill pickles, or ice cream, or lobster?"

Anne smiled. "No, thanks," she said. "I haven't had any of those cravings so far."

"I'm told some people never do, although I must say I'm not one who'd know anything about it."

"Just wait a while. In a few months you'll classify as an expert."

"Yes. And at my age, too." They both laughed, and Evelyn said, "Well, tootle-oo," and turned away, just as Montgomery came out the door with Ulm's package of records under his arm. He walked carefully, and for a moment he didn't seem to see anybody. Then he recognized them, and managed a weak smile.

"Good morning," he said.

"Good *morning?*" said Evelyn. "Did you just get up?"

"Well, I got up once before, but it didn't seem to take, so I went back to bed. Even now, it may be a mistake. I don't know."

Anne laughed. "I guess I was smart to leave when I did," she said. "Did you two stay up all night?"

"Oh, no," said Montgomery. "We just had a little—ah—chat, and then I wallowed off and to bed."

"Yes," said Evelyn. "I filled him in on the developments along the maternal front."

"Oh." Anne looked at him, and Montgomery smiled.

"Frankly, I think it's kind of charming," he said. "It's somewhat out of my field, but I'd be glad to help in any way I can."

"Thank you," said Anne. "You don't know how nice that is to hear."

"Look, ducks, I have to be off," Evelyn said. She turned to Montgomery. "Are you going over toward Broadway?"

"More or less, yes."

"Come on, then, let's share a bus."

"Done and done." He offered her his arm, and they walked off down the block. Anne turned back inside, and Ernest Becker continued quietly to screw the angle irons onto his window box.

Well, just imagine that, Becker said to himself. I certainly would never have guessed it. I've never even seen her with a man, much less. . . . Well, I guess you just never can tell. He continued to drive in the screws, more and more slowly as a thought began to take hold of him, and finally he stopped work altogether and looked at Anne's window, and the pot of yellow tulips on the sill. He looked at it for a long time, then he looked at his own window, and then back at Anne's. He tightened the last screw, set the box down, and went over and stood so that he could look in at Anne. She was sitting in a red overstuffed chair, staring at nothing in particular, and for a moment she didn't see him. When she did, she jumped, and said, "Oh—hello."

"How do you do?" Becker said, raising his hat. "My name is Ernest Becker. I live across the hall from you."

"Yes, I know." She got up from her chair, and came to the window.

"I've noticed the flowers you have here," Becker said, looking at the tulips. "They look very nice."

"Thank you. They just came from—you know. I got them off that wagon."

"Yes. I think everybody should have some flowers, someplace."

She smiled. "It brightens things up, certainly."

Becker cleared his throat. "What I was thinking," he said, "was that I've made a window box for flowers, and since you already have some, it would be better to put the box under your window, so you can put your flowers in it. If you want it, that is." He stopped, flustered.

"Oh, no," said Anne. "I wouldn't think of taking your box. Thank you very much, but, after all, you made it for yourself, and there—"

"Please," he said. "Listen to me. It will look much better if the front of the house has two boxes, one on each side, so I was going to make two boxes anyway. Maybe even a trellis, I thought, too, so we might have things that grow, like ivy, or sweet potatoes, or something. But what I mean is, since I was going to make two boxes, and you've got already the flowers, it's better you should have the first box. It just makes better sense that way." He paused, and then added, "Provided you want the box, of course. I wouldn't want to force you into something you didn't want."

"Oh, no," she said. "I want it—I'd love to have it—but I still think you should have the first—"

He put up his hand. "You want it, so you'll get it. We don't argue any more." He went back and got the box, put the tools into it, and carried it to Anne's window. "You just show me how you'd like to have it, and I'll put it up," he said. "I'll have it on in a couple of minutes. Then when it's on, we can decide what color you want it, and I'll paint it whatever you say."

"This is really very nice of you—" Anne paused and looked at the box. "I don't really know how I want it. You put it on however you think is best. Do it the way yours is going to be, so they'll match."

"Mine is going to be level with the sill," Becker said, putting the box in place. "Like this. Is that all right?"

"That's fine. I still think— I mean, I don't really have enough flowers to fill it, and—"

"No more arguments," Becker said, as he drove in the first screw. "It's too late now—I've already started."

"Well, thank you. It's awfully nice of you."

Becker looked up from his work, and grinned. "It never hurt to make things look a little brighter," he said. "Especially—" He became embarrassed, looking for a way to phrase what he had started to say. "Especially in the spring," he concluded, lamely. A drop of perspiration ran down his forehead and onto his nose, and he wiped it away with the back of his hand, and returned to his work.

When he had finished, he stood back and surveyed the box. It was true and level, and it seemed to be solid enough. He was pleased with what he had done. "Now," he said. "What color would you like to have it?"

"I don't know," said Anne. "Why not white, like the trim?" She looked at the dirty, peeling woodwork, and dug at a flake of old paint with her thumbnail. "Or, rather, white like what the trim was supposed to be."

Becker considered this, then shook his head. "I don't think so," he said. "White will get dirty too soon. I think maybe something like green would be better, so it won't show the dirt and the stains too much."

"I hadn't thought of that. I guess you're right."

"I'll go look see if I have some green paint," he said. "If I don't, I'll get some tomorrow." He gathered up his tools and went inside, humming a tune. Anne took her pot of tulips, and put them experimentally in the window box. She saw that it would take at least three more pots to make the box look even partly full.

In his apartment, Becker put the tools away in a closet, and went into the kitchen. Martha was slicing some liver-wurst and cheese for lunch. "Do we have any green paint?" he asked.

Martha didn't look up. "No, and we don't have any gold paint," she said. "And we don't have wall-to-wall carpets and we don't have ermine doilies. Why should we have green paint?"

"You painted the kitchen chair once," he said, looking at the chair that peeked out from under Martha's ample frame. It was black, and chipped, and the paint underneath the black was a dull red. "I just thought there might be some around." Martha said nothing, and he went on, "I put the box up for the girl next door. She wanted it white at first, but we decided that would get dirty too quick, so she settled on green."

Martha looked up at him. "For the who?" she said.

"The girl next door. You know—the one who lives across the hall. She's got some flowers in a pot, so I thought I might as well give her this box, and make another one for us."

Martha put down her knife. "What's the matter with you, are you out of your head?"

"No, I just thought I'd give her the box. Why not?"

"Listen to Romeo Becker—'I just thought I'd give her the

58

box'— You ought to be ashamed of yourself, a man your age
sniffing around young girls like he was a high-school cheer-
leader, or something. Remember how old you are—remember how stupid old men look chasing young girls—remember
what happened to—"

"I was not chasing after her—" Becker began.

"Your no-good Uncle Louie who got arrested in a movie
theater. Try doing something around your own home for a
change, and don't go out chasing after the first girl you see.
It's a hard enough time I have around here without I should
have to wonder what *you're* doing all the time."

"Listen to me!" Becker said, raising his voice.

"And don't shout at me, Ernest Becker, or I'll belt you with
a mop! You keep a civil tongue in your head."

Becker lowered his voice. "All right," he said. "I'm sorry.
So at least let me tell you why I thought it was a good idea."

"You don't have to tell me."

"I thought it was a good idea because she's *schwanger*.
She's going to have a baby. And it seemed that—"

Martha's eyes opened wide. "She's what?" she shouted.
"And how do *you* know, if I'm not getting too personal?"

"I just heard her talking with some—"

"And what kind of slut is this goes around saying 'I'm
schwanger' to the first person she meets? Announcing it like
she was announcing a train—like she was proud of it or
something! She's a disgrace to the building!"

"Listen to me, please—"

"She ought to be thrown out in the street where she be-
longs! It's people like that give the place a bad name, while
decent people—"

"Martha, I'm trying to tell you—"

"Shut up! I'm telling you! You stay away from that slut, or
I'll cut your heart out with this—" She picked up the kitchen
knife and waved it at him. "Just stay away!"

"Martha, will you please let me explain? In the first place,
she didn't tell me—"

"I don't care who she told. She said it loud enough so you

could hear. She said it loud enough so probably the whole block could hear."

"She didn't! She was just talking—"

"Oh, I know. You don't have to tell me." Martha turned away, and her voice changed. "God in Heaven, it's like all those long, horrible years again, with you running around like a goat, while I'm just sitting—"

"Martha, I never ran around! I've told you hundreds of times, I've told you thousands of times, I'll tell you a million times—I did not run around!"

"You don't have to lie to me," she sniffed. "It's all done now anyway. But at least you can do me the favor and don't play like you're young again. Don't go make a fool of yourself in front of everybody in the block. That doesn't seem it should be too much to ask. Just stay away from her, that's all."

"I told her I'd paint her window box for her. Can I do that?"

Martha's voice hardened. "And she's so stupid she can't put a little paint on a window box? She's a cripple maybe, or something?"

"No, she's not stupid, and she's not a cripple. I just told her I'd do it."

"But when I ask you to stay away from her, that isn't enough?" The tears were about to start.

"All right all right all right. I'll stay away from her. Only it makes me look like an awful *schlump.*"

For the first time in a long while, Martha smiled. "Thank you," she said.

❧ 5 ❧

ONTGOMERY AND EVELYN boarded a crosstown bus,
on which they had more or less their choice of seats. A tat-
tered, furry drunk slept in a corner seat in the rear, and a
woman with two noisy, cowboy-clad children sat near the
center door; otherwise the bus was empty. They sat up forward, as far from the children as possible, and for a little
while neither of them said anything.

Out of the corner of his eye, Montgomery glanced at Evelyn and tried to estimate her age. Roughly about his own, he
guessed, depending on how old she was when she was in
the movies. The one picture he'd seen had showed her to be
very attractive, and a certain amount of her looks still remained. Her face was more matronly now, but her eyes were
large and clear, and the slight make-up she wore made them
look even larger. The only place where her age really showed
was at her throat and on the backs of her hands, and in the
fact that her hair had an indefinable middle-aged untidiness
about it, a dry, wispy quality that all but defied control. All
in all, she was remarkably well preserved, he thought. He

imagined she must have been really beautiful when she was young.

Evelyn, on her part, was looking at him, and matching what little she knew about him with her earlier, fleeting impressions. He still had that early-morning stunned look, like a mouse who has just had a trap slam shut and miss him, but she remembered that last night his face had been alive and full and happy, especially when he was singing the old songs. Thinking of him in terms of the theater, she could see him cast as a long-lost uncle who returns with great tales of his adventures and has to borrow carfare to get to the unemployment office. Possibly a character from an O'Neill play, mixed with one from John M. Synge. There was poetry deep in his watery eyes, and a certain sadness, but he never seemed consciously to be sad. He just seemed slightly buffeted. Evelyn wished she knew what was troubling him, but she hadn't the slightest intention of asking. She was sure he'd never tell her, even if he knew.

"I've been thinking about that Waters girl," Montgomery said at last. "Anne, I seem to remember her name is."

"Yes," said Evelyn. "That's right."

"I can't figure her out."

"What do you mean?"

"Just that. Sometimes she seems so young I don't know how she ever got—ah—I mean—"

"I know exactly what you mean," she said. "I think it's just that she's always been protected."

"Not well enough, apparently."

"No. Even her young man protected her, in a manner of speaking. I think her problem is that she's never had to do anything on her own."

"Well, she's got something now that nobody can do for her."

"That's right. This is all hers, and I think she's frightened by it."

Montgomery was quiet for a moment. "That's easy to see,"

he said. "Sometimes it takes a long time to get used to being alone. And doing things alone."

Evelyn glanced at him. "True," she said.

There was another silence. "I still don't know what there is that we can do," said Montgomery. "Sure, we can be nice to her, but then what?"

"I don't know. I guess just be around when she wants someone to talk to."

"What about her family? Are her parents living?"

"From what I gather, they are. But also from what I gather, they're not going to be a great deal of help. They live somewhere in Pennsylvania. I don't know if they're Amish, or what."

"That might be the root of the whole thing. You get kids who've been strictly brought up, and they go all to hell when they hit the big city."

"This wasn't a case of going all to hell. She was really in love with the boy."

"Uh-huh." Montgomery settled deeper in his seat. "That still doesn't make our job any easier, though."

"No, it doesn't."

He thought for a minute or so. "I suppose I could take her out for dinner every now and then, just to give her a change of scenery," he said. "No, I guess not," he corrected himself quickly. "That wouldn't work."

"What she needs is to know people," Evelyn said.

"What kind of people?"

"Well, the people in the apartment, just for a starter. Sooner or later, they're all going to know about this, and if they're friendly with her from the beginning, then so much the better."

"Who else *is* there in the apartment?" he asked. "I don't know anybody, except for that mouse who lives above me, and *he'd* certainly be no help. He'd just shriek with laughter, and think it was all a big joke."

"There's that old couple, who live across the hall from her.

I think their name is Becker. I've seen it on the mailbox."

"Oh, yes. I guess that would be a good idea. The old lady could kind of mother her when she needed it."

"Yes. They'd probably be the best bet."

"All right. How do we do it?" Suddenly, Montgomery laughed. "I suppose we could always throw a party for her," he said. "A sort of debutante party, so to speak."

"Well—" Evelyn thought this over.

Montgomery began to be enthusiastic. "You know, it really might work," he said. "We obviously wouldn't say what the party was *for*, but if we could just get some excuse to have one, then we could get everybody together and the rest would take care of itself. It might be a wonderful idea."

Evelyn smiled. "It's possible," she said. "We might do it when my play opens, kind of like an opening-night—oh, my God—" she groped around the seat, looking for some wood to knock on—"What am I saying?" She knocked three times on her head, then paused and said, "The play would be no good, anyway. We ought to do something more immediate, like—like what? The Fourth of July's a long way off still."

"There's Decoration Day next month. Possibly not too appropriate, but still—" He closed his eyes, and put back his head. After a few seconds, he opened his eyes and said, "Of course, we could always have a May party. The Maypole is a fertility symbol from way back. Or a spring rites festival. Spring is symbolic of all sorts of things, and we could work her into that with no trouble at all." He thought for a while more, then said, "Hopi Indian girls have one hell of a time at *their* coming-out parties. They have to grind corn for four days in a darkened room at the house of an aunt, and during that time they can't eat meat or salt, and can scratch themselves only with a certain ceremonial stick. Then they change their hairdress and come out in the open, and bang! they're marriageable." He looked at her. "I throw that in simply for what it may be worth. I don't think it will be much help to us."

64

"Have you made a study of all this?" she asked. "You sound as though you'd taken a doctorate in symbolism."

"No, it just comes to me. If you frequent newspapers and saloons long enough, you will eventually learn everything. Without really trying."

"I can see I've missed a great deal. I thought the radio business taught you all there was to know, but I guess it was all in one direction." She looked out the window.

"What direction was that?" he asked.

"Frustration."

"Oh ho!" he said. "You think *you* know frustration!" He shook his head, and smiled. "You don't know anything."

There was a short silence, and then she straightened up and said, "Well. That's getting us nowhere."

"True." He cleared his throat. "I still think a party would be a good idea."

"So do I, if I could only think of a reason to give one."

"Well, what about just making it a spring party? Why does it have to be anything special?"

"I think it'll look funny if it's not something special. I don't think anyone will come— Oh. Here. Here's where I get off." She tugged at the cord above her head, and rose.

He stood up with her. "So do I." As they made their way toward the center door, he said, "I'll give it some thought and see if anything comes to me. What time will you be through your rehearsal?"

"I guess about nine. If we do the full eight hours, that is."

They got off the bus, and he fell in alongside her. "I might as well walk over to the theater with you."

"That's very nice, but you don't have to, you know."

"I know. But I've got no special time to be where I'm going. The walk will do me good."

"Fine, then."

"I'll tell you what. Suppose I kick this idea around the rest of the afternoon, and then pick you up after you're through, and then we can get something to eat and maybe come up with something concrete. How does that sound to you?"

"It sounds fine, if you're sure you have nothing else to do."

"I don't have another thing to do. And it would be as good a way as any for me to keep out of trouble."

She smiled. "Good. If you need an excuse, then let that be it."

He left her at the entrance to the theater, then turned and walked down in the direction of his paper. His ankle, which had hurt him the day before, now seemed to be completely healed, and he walked easily if not quickly. Below Times Square, the streets were practically deserted, and the noise of the traffic fell to a distant whisper. The air was clean, with no fumes to pollute it, and looking down occasional side streets he felt that he could see all the way to the Jersey shore. A few people wandered about the streets, with no regard for the traffic lights, and couples walked hand-in-hand in the blocks of sunlight as though they were in a country meadow. Today would be a good day to take a boat trip, Montgomery thought. Get on a boat and go out into the Sound. Or, better yet, go down the Bay, and get a whiff of real sea air. There's nothing like fresh sea air to clear the head and cleanse the soul. The excursion boats won't have started yet, but maybe there's a press cutter going down to meet some liner. That would be the thing to do. Go down the Bay in the cutter, and be back in plenty of time to pick up Evelyn. A good place to think, too, with all that sea air, and everything. Hot damn.

He looked around, hoping to find a cab, but saw none, so he quickened his steps and hurried the rest of the way to the newspaper office. By the time he arrived, his ankle was aching again.

Sam Ulm was not at his desk, so Montgomery left the packages by Ulm's typewriter, then picked up a phone and asked for the Barge Office. He found that a cutter was going down the Bay at two-thirty, and that there would be room for him to come along. He looked at his watch and saw that he had a half hour or so to kill, and then a sudden thought struck him. He went into the reference library and asked the librarian if he had any clippings on an actress named Evelyn Estes.

"That her real name or her stage name?" the librarian asked, as he put down his newspaper and stood up.

"By God, Fred, I don't know," Montgomery replied. "That's the only name I know her by, that's all."

The librarian went into the files, and came back a couple of minutes later with a Manila envelope on which Evelyn's name was stamped in large block letters. He pulled out a few clippings, and sifted through them. "This is all we've got," he said. "I guess it's the one you mean." He gave the envelope and clippings to Montgomery, and went back to his newspaper.

Montgomery sat down at a desk and spread the clippings out in front of him. There weren't many of them, and most of them were yellow and brittle with age. There were three reviews of silent pictures in which she had appeared, and one Sunday-supplement feature story, which quoted her as saying: "Actually, I don't feel any different now that I'm a star than I did at the very beginning of my career. It's all happened so fast, I still feel like the druggist's daughter in Tulsa." Then there were a few trade-paper items from the 1930's and 1940's, which referred to her as a "radio character actress," and there were a couple of mentions of her in more recent television columns, and that was all. No mention of any marriage, or divorce, or family of any sort, except for the possibly phantom Tulsa druggist. Montgomery looked carefully at the picture of her in the Sunday feature story; it was a coarse-screen engraving in which the dots seemed the size of buckshot, and it showed her in a standard pose on the diving board of her swimming pool. But even allowing for the age and the generally poor quality of the picture, he could see that she had been really quite beautiful. I wonder what happened, he thought. I wonder what blew everything apart. The talking pictures probably had a hand in it, but still, that shouldn't have kept her from getting married. Under normal conditions, a girl with those looks would be married at least once, and probably several times, before she reached middle age.

He looked through all the clippings once again, and then gently put them together, bound them with a piece of string, and replaced them in the envelope. He went over and laid it on the librarian's desk. "Thanks, Fred," he said.

The librarian didn't look up. "Was that the one you wanted?" he asked.

"Yes," Montgomery replied. He looked at his watch. "I'll see you," he said, and turned and left.

He had time for one drink before going down to the Barge Office, so he went across the street to the saloon, and there found Sam Ulm, standing morosely against the bar. Ulm looked at him, and his expression didn't change. "Oh, God," he said.

"I left the things on your desk, Sam," Montgomery said.

"Thanks." Ulm turned back to his drink.

Automatically, the bartender made a Scotch highball for Montgomery and slid it to him. "Thank you, Leo," Montgomery said. He raised his drink to Ulm, said, "Cheers," and took a sip. "How are things?" he asked.

"Great," Ulm replied. "That's why I stayed on the wagon so long. Things are just wonderful."

Montgomery couldn't think of anything to say, so he just said, "Oh."

"I'm told I don't have to come home," Ulm went on. "I'm told it's all right if I stay at a hotel, or if I stay in the Bowery, or if I stay with you. In that order, I'm told it doesn't matter a goddam what I do, so long as I don't come home."

"I think that's being unreasonable," said Montgomery. "I think she's taking it too hard."

Ulm looked at him, and smiled an icy smile. "Have you any suggestions?" he asked.

"Yes, I think I ought to talk to her. I think I ought to explain that it's not all as bad as she seems to think it is."

"For God's sakes don't!" said Ulm. "Things are bad enough as they are."

Montgomery shrugged. "O.K.," he said. "That would be the only contribution I could make." He took another sip of his drink. "I've got other problems on my mind, anyway. Problems that are a little more far-reaching than yours."

"Oh?" Ulm looked at him and raised his eyebrows.

"Yes. Just one of them is how to get the people in an apartment house to feel sympathetic toward a pregnant unmarried girl."

There was a long silence, then Ulm turned to the bartender. "Leo, let's have another round here," he said. He looked at Montgomery. "Are you kidding?" he asked.

Montgomery shook his head, and finished his drink. "Nope," he said.

Ulm considered this for a while. "Are you the father?" he asked.

Montgomery stirred his new drink with his finger, raised the glass to Ulm, and took a sip. "Nope," he said.

Ulm stared at the back bar.

"It's quite a problem, I can tell you." Montgomery looked at his watch, and downed half his drink in one gulp.

"I should imagine." Ulm tasted his drink, and looked down at the ice as though he were talking to it. "Would you care to clear up a few details for me?" he asked.

"Some other time, perhaps, but right now I'm late." Montgomery drained his glass and let the ice rattle against his teeth, then set the glass down. "I've got to be at the Barge Office," he said. "Thanks for the drink." He turned and left the saloon. Ulm stared at the door a long time after it had closed.

Montgomery hurried to the nearest subway station, and got

a downtown train. When he got off at the Battery, the wind felt much sharper than it had before. The day was still sunny and the air was clear, and he could see down to the Narrows and imagine he saw the bright Atlantic beyond. The wind, coming up the Bay, smelled of salt and smoke and oil, and it blew with a force that scattered the smoke from the passing tugs and ferries. The waves slapped against the pilings under the Barge Office, and occasional bits of spray were flung up into his face; they stung with cold. As he stepped into the rocking, pitching cutter, he wondered if this was going to turn out to be such a good idea after all. He hitched up his coat collar and sat down in a sheltered corner of the boat.

In her room at the apartment, Anne waited for Becker to return with the green paint, or with the word that he had none at hand. When fifteen minutes had passed and there was no sign of him, she went into the kitchen, opened a can of tuna fish, and began to make herself a sandwich for lunch. I wonder why he didn't come back, she thought. It doesn't seem like him not at least to let me know. After all, the whole thing was his idea in the first place; you'd think.... Well, maybe it's too early. Maybe he knows a place where he can buy paint on Sunday. Maybe he's gone to borrow some somewhere. There's no point getting all worked up about it now.

She put the sandwich on a plate, took a bottle of Coca Cola from the refrigerator, then went into the other room and sat in the red overstuffed chair. The secretary's lunch, she thought, as she munched her sandwich. All week long I eat drugstore lunches, and then when I get a chance to have something different, I make myself a drugstore lunch. That's being in a rut for you. And I suppose pretty soon I ought to start thinking about what I'm eating. I ought to see the doctor, and get a diet, and pay a little more attention to myself. A little more attention. That's a laugh. I'm the only one who pays attention to myself, anyway.... No, that's not fair. Evelyn has been very nice, and so has that Mr. Montgomery. And Mr. Becker, perhaps, but still, nobody's really interested in me. In passing, perhaps, but certainly no more than that.

She finished her sandwich, and suddenly got up from the chair. In that case, she thought, there's no point sitting around here feeling sorry for myself. If anything's going to be done, I'm the one who's going to do it, and the sooner I stop looking to other people the better off I'll be. She rinsed off the plate and put it in a rack to dry, and then put the empty Coke bottle under the sink and went back into the living room. Where do I start? What's the first thing I ought to do? She looked around the apartment, and it seemed to her that everything ought to be changed. The curtains were dull and colorless, the rug was worn and dirty, the table and lamp together would give any interior decorator a sick headache, and the red overstuffed chair looked like something from a warehouse fire. The day-bed was depressing to look at, and even more so to sit on, and the pillows scattered on top of it against the wall had a slovenly, cluttered effect. There was no single place to start; everything needed to be thrown out and the whole room started again from the bare plaster.

Maybe the best thing to do is get out and go for a walk, she thought. I'll drive myself crazy if I sit around here all day. A walk in the fresh air will at least give me a change of scenery, and maybe I'll get some ideas in the process. She changed her dress, put on some low-heeled shoes, and after arranging her hair in the mirror, she picked up her purse and went out the door. The mere act of deciding to go out had made her feel better.

Outside, she turned past the Beckers' window, and glanced in as she went by, but could see nothing. Oh, well, she thought. It isn't every day you get a window box given to you, so I suppose I shouldn't complain. Even though I am going to have to buy more flowers to fill it, it's still a nice thing to have. Maybe I can even paint it myself, if I have to. I still would like to know what happened to him, though. He didn't seem like the kind who would just disappear like that. He seemed almost pathetically anxious to do something for me. And there's a problem right there—why should he want to do all this? I suppose I'll find out soon enough, though. There's no point rushing into anything. Right now, I've got other things to think about.

She walked through the bright streets over to the East River, and she stood at a parapet and watched the gray, oily river swirl past the channel buoys, making bubbling wakes behind them as though they were racing through the water. Looking at the current, she wondered how far out to sea it went, and how far it would carry something with it, and for the first time, and completely impersonally, the idea of suicide crossed her mind. She thought that there were probably some people in her position who would simply hurl themselves into the river without thinking twice—in fact, in her earlier panic, she might have done the same thing—but the idea seemed so remote and impossible now that she couldn't imagine it.

A tug with three barges slipped past downstream, carried swiftly by the power of the tide, and little white chuffs of smoke popped from the tug's stack and then were snatched away by the wind. Across the river, the white and ochre masts and cabins of docked ships stood out in sharp contrast to the dull gray Brooklyn pier sheds.

I'd like to get on one of those ships and sail away, she thought. I don't care where, just away. Across an ocean and into some foreign port, and then keep on sailing, from port to port, around the world. Feel the clean air and the sunshine in the daytime, and see the stars and then the harbor lights at night. She remembered the only time she had ever been on a boat, one summer when her father had taken the family to the Great Lakes, and they had had a ride on an excursion steamer. More than anything else about the trip, she remembered how the harbor looked when they came in at night, with the red and green lights winking in the blackness of the water, and the lights on the shore seeming to beckon with all the warmth of home, and also with a promise of something she had never known. When they docked, of course, the lights were just like lights anywhere, but from the water they had a mystery and an attraction that she had never forgotten. That was the night her father chased a boy who had whistled at her—she was eleven, and had just changed her hair-do from pigtails down her back to braids around her head—and her father ran for three blocks, waving his cane and shouting, without catching the boy. Her father had an almost pathological fear of her being insulted; until she was seventeen, he had not allowed her to go to the drugstore alone, for fear that she would be whistled at by boys. If she wanted to have a soft drink with a young man, he said, then invite him to the house, but he was not going to have his daughter made the butt of drugstore cowboys' jokes. He was just as fiercely protective in other ways, too, and yet with it all he was understanding—in his own sort of way—and was always ready to give help or advice when it was needed. He believed that the problems of one member of the family were the problems of the family as a whole, and nothing of either great or minor importance was ever decided without a family conference. It was a comfort, there was no getting around it.

Anne almost smiled as she turned away from the parapet and started back for the apartment. I wonder what he would do with this problem of mine now, she thought. I wonder what the family conference would come up with as an answer for that. She held her breath at the thought, then closed her eyes for a moment and tried to think of something else.

When she got home, Duncan Lapham was coming out of the apartment with a slat-back rocking chair in his arms. An old, dilapidated station wagon stood at the curb, and the back of it was cluttered with furniture. Lapham was wearing dark slacks, an old tweed coat with leather patches at the elbows, and brown suede shoes. His collar was open, and he was perspiring slightly. A strand of dark hair fell over his forehead as he put the rocking chair into the station wagon, and he stopped and ran the back of his sleeve across his face. He saw Anne and nodded to her, then reached into the station wagon for a piece of furniture. Anne went over to him.

"I'm sorry about last night," she said. "We really didn't realize we were singing so loud."

Lapham paused, "Oh," he said. "Well, I was feeling rather irritable myself." After another pause, he said, "Although I must say, I don't think I play my records as loud as your friend implied. I think *his* attitude was rather uncalled-for."

"I wouldn't know anything about that. I do agree he was a little too violent, though. Of course, I live another floor down, so I've never even heard your records."

"That's good." Lapham reached into the station wagon again. "At any rate, I can see I'm going to have to be more careful in the future."

Anne watched him as he dragged a red Windsor chair onto the tail gate. "You're not moving, are you?" she asked.

He smiled. "No," he said. "Just rotating my furniture. Come spring, I can't stand the *sight* of the stuff I've had all winter, so I take it to the shop, and bring a new batch to replace it."

"What shop is that?" she asked. "I'd like to know a place like that."

"It's my own. I run an antique shop."

"Oh." Anne laughed. "I could use a change of furniture myself, but I'm sure you couldn't use any of the stuff *I've* got."

"Oh, you never can tell. Things crop up in the strangest places." He pointed to a maple butterfly table. "*That*, for instance, I found in the back of an electrican's shop in Danbury. This peasant was using it as a soldering table, and I

74

almost screamed when I saw it. He thought I was out of my mind."

"It's beautiful," Anne said, peering through the window of the station wagon. "You should see the table I've got. It's about as dainty as a fire engine."

"I still say you never can tell. It might be worth a fortune."

"Believe me, you're welcome to look at it if you want to. Nothing would please me more than to be able to get rid of it."

"All right, I will." He picked up the red Windsor chair. "I'll bring this along, so's not to waste a trip."

They went into the building, and Anne unlocked her door. "I'm warning you," she said. "It's not only the table. The whole room is awful."

She went in ahead of him, and he followed. He set the chair down, and looked around the room, his face expressionless.

"You see?" she said.

He didn't answer, but went over to the oak table, looked underneath it, and knocked once on the top. "My," he said, and looked around the room again. "You *weren't* exaggerating, were you?"

She laughed. "Not for a minute."

He put one hand to his mouth. "Sweet God, that day-bed," he said. "How long have you lived here?"

"Over a year."

"You must be of absolute pioneer stock." He looked, in a stunned way, from one item to another.

"Well, it's only now that I've taken any interest in it, really. Before now, I was—well, it was just a place to sleep, not a home. Now, I want to do something with it."

"Yes," he said, thoughtfully. "I can see."

"Also, I've got to put a—well, I've got to add a few things, but at the same time I want to do something to cheer the whole place up. Like new curtains, just for one thing."

"Yes." He went into the center of the room, and looked back at the door, then at the window. "How much did you figure on spending?" he asked.

"That's the trouble. Not much. There are going to be lots of other expenses coming up, and I'm going to have to make do with as little as I possibly can."

"I like your flower motif," he said, looking at the tulips in the window box. "There's something fetching about that."

"The man next door made the box for me," she said. "I'm going to have to get some more flowers to fill it up."

"What are these other expenses? How stiff are they going to be?"

"Well—" she said, and hesitated.

"I'm terribly sorry, it's absolutely none of my business. Please forgive me."

"No, no. Well—among the other expenses are the fact that I'm going to have a baby."

"Oh, for the love of God." He put his hand to his mouth again. "I can see what you mean."

"So, obviously, I want to do the other things as cheaply as possible."

"Of course." He thought for a moment. "Come on up to my room, and let me show you what I've got there. Maybe we could work out a rental arrangement, or something like that, that would help a bit."

"Oh, I wouldn't want to take anything good—I mean, I wouldn't want to be responsible for an antique, or anything."

"My dear girl, a lot of this stuff is perfectly dreadful. You may very well not want *any* of it." He picked up the red Windsor chair. "At any rate, you can get an idea from the general décor as to what you might want to do. Come on."

"Well, I'd love to see it, anyway. It's very nice of you to ask me."

"Actually, my dear, I'm just a businessman at heart. Some day, when you're very wealthy, I expect you to bring all your business to me. It's as sordid as that."

They went out into the corridor. Martha Becker was standing in her open doorway, and Anne nodded to her and smiled, but Martha just stared at her, so she started up the stairs. Martha made a sharp clucking noise with her tongue, and Lapham stopped and looked at her. "I beg your pardon?" he said.

Martha glared at him. "For shame!" she said.

"Really, madam, I think you're being a little *fin de siècle*," he said, and turned toward the stairs.

"It's disgraceful!" Martha hissed.

Lapham wheeled back and faced her. "Madam, I have no idea what you're talking about," he said, "but if you're referring to my carrying this chair behind the young lady, I would point out to you that the only person ever to be compromised in a Windsor chair was a twenty-eight-inch midget. I have neither the time nor the interest to debate the point with you further. Good day." He followed Anne up the stairs, and Martha slammed her door. "Really!" he said. "What some people won't do to get their kicks!"

Anne climbed the stairs in silence. "I think it explains something, though," she said, finally. "I don't know how she found out, but this explains something."

"She's just a nosy old biddy," Lapham replied. "When things get dull at home, she has to dream up excitement somewhere else. Some of that kind come into my store, and I get so mad at them I could snatch them bald-headed. God, what a trial they are!"

Anne said nothing, but continued quietly to climb the stairs.

6

As the cutter slapped through the choppy harbor water and headed for The Narrows, Montgomery sat back and closed his eyes and relaxed. All at once everything seemed very far away, and his problems and worries and annoyances began to fade like the receding buildings of the city. He breathed deeply the brisk salt air and felt more at peace than he had for a long time. After a while, he opened his eyes and looked at the other men on the cutter with him. There were two press-association reporters and one photographer, and they were sitting with their backs to a bulkhead, smoking cigarettes and talking. One of the reporters was tall and lean, with black hair and a gaunt face. He was named Perkins, and Montgomery had seen him on and off in various Times Square saloons. The other press-association man, whom Montgomery remembered dimly from the days when he, too, had been a reporter, was named O'Leary, and he was short and fat, and his breath wheezed through the cigarette that was always clamped between his teeth. The photographer, whom Montgomery didn't know, sat with his bulky leather case of equipment behind him, and stared out at the water, while a cigarette burned unnoticed between his fingers. Montgomery got up, and went over and joined them.

"What have they got you on this job for?" Perkins asked, after they had exchanged greetings. "I thought you were a desk man now."

"I am," Montgomery replied. "I just felt like some air, so I thought I'd come along for the ride."

"Jesus," said O'Leary. "A crazy man."

"I don't even know what the job is," Montgomery said. "What's the boat we're meeting?"

"The H.M.S. *Cathartic*," O'Leary sighed, through his cigarette.

"It's the *Carpathia*," said Perkins. "Herr Doktor Bundeswasser is aboard, with the latest poop on Russian rockets."

"Oh," said Montgomery, and he sat down next to Perkins. "I guess he should know, all right. His real name is Petrov, you know."

"Like hell it is," said Perkins.

"Sure. He came to Germany after the Russian revolution and changed his name. He'd been a physicist at the University of Pinsk."

"He was born in Munich," said O'Leary. "I looked him up."

"Would you like to bet?" said Montgomery. "Look him up again."

"You've got a bet," said O'Leary. "Fifty bucks."

"You're on," said Montgomery.

"You're a fool," Perkins said to O'Leary. "Anybody who bets against Montgomery is a fool."

"I looked it up, for Chrissakes," O'Leary wheezed plaintively. "I saw it in a book."

"Look back through the old clips," said Montgomery. "You'll find a piece about him in the *Times* of either May or June, 1920."

"Ah, don't give me that. You're just bluffing."

"Look it up. You can send the fifty to me at the paper."

"I did look it up."

"Well, look it up again."

"I tell you, O'Leary, you're a fool," said Perkins. "That fifty is as good as gone right now."

"Ah," O'Leary said uneasily, and looked out at the water. "Hey," he said. "Get a load of the fog."

They all looked, and saw that the Lower Bay, beyond The Narrows, was blanketed in a thick, white layer of fog, and the Fort Hamilton section of Brooklyn was visible only as though seen through a dirty window. The wind had died down and the water was no longer choppy, and while they watched they could see wisps of fog creep toward the cutter, blurring all the details around them. From somewhere down the Bay came the low, throaty bellow of a ship's whistle.

"Well, I'll be damned," said Perkins. "*That* certainly came up fast."

"I wonder where the ship is," said Montgomery. "Do you think they'll wait outside?"

"I don't know," Perkins said. "Unless it gets worse, they'll probably come in all right. They've got radar."

"Radar is responsible for more accidents than it prevents," O'Leary remarked, sourly. "Crazy bastards get too sure of themselves once they get radar, and go barreling around like a bunch of Sunday drivers."

Nobody offered any further comment; they all stood at the rail and stared ahead into the thickening fog, as the cutter nosed on down the Bay toward the sound of the whistle. Finally, they could see nothing around them; they were completely surrounded by a soft, silent world of white, and only directly overhead could they see a faint trace of the sky, a brightening in the fog. There was a loud blast nearby, so close that the air around them rattled, and the cutter turned and blew an answering blast on its fog horn, and then suddenly, right above them, loomed the towering, gray side of a ship, glistening and damp and studded with rivets. It was making almost no headway, and as the cutter nosed alongside, toward an open baggage port in which stood waiting seamen, they could hear the splashing of the waves against the steel sides. Then they were right under the port, and a few blue-clad officials who had been in the forward part of the cutter jumped off and disappeared inside the ship; the photographer grunted as he shouldered his equipment, and then he and Montgomery and Perkins and O'Leary jumped through the port, and Montgomery could smell polished metal and steam and salt and fuel oil and cooking, and an indescribable ship's smell that is smelled nowhere else. They went down a long, paneled passageway, and up a curving flight of red-carpeted stairs, and then the smell of flowers and perfume was mingled with the others. There was another rumbling blast that made their eardrums quiver, and it was followed by a dim rattling noise, like distant thunder.

"Oh-oh," said Perkins. "They just dropped the anchor."

"That's great," O'Leary rasped. "We'll probably be here all night."

Suddenly, Montgomery remembered Evelyn. "Say, you don't think that's possible, do you?" he asked. "I've got to pick someone up at nine."

Perkins laughed. "Who knows?" he said. "I guess you'll have to take it up with the captain."

"Oh, for God's sakes," Montgomery said, half to himself. Then, almost plaintively, he said, "Oh, damn it all. Damn, damn, damn, damn."

All that happened during rehearsal was that the director went through the script, line by line, and told each of the players where they should stand when they read their various lines, and where they should move when a move was called for. It was a dull and a tiring process, and Evelyn spent most of the time sitting in the wings and drinking coffee from a cardboard container. By the time the eight hours were up, only about half of the second act had been blocked out, and everybody's eyes were glassy with fatigue. The stage manager gave them their call for the next day, and as they filed wearily out into the alley behind the theater, the playwright came up to Evelyn and walked beside her. She hadn't seen him during the rehearsal, and his presence at this moment seemed ominous. He cleared his throat, and she knew he was going to give her bad news. "I've been thinking about your part," he said.

"Uh-huh," said Evelyn, and she closed her eyes and waited.

"It occurs to me that we can do a lot more with it than we have," the playwright said. "I'm building it up some more in the third act, but I think that'll mean we'll have to pad it out some in the first two."

Evelyn could think of nothing to say, so she swallowed and said, "I see."

"I liked the way you read it," he went on. "I think if we can get some more of that kind of humor in the early part of the show, we'll help ourselves a lot."

"Fine," said Evelyn, not believing what she was hearing.

They emerged into the dimly lighted street, and the director came out of the alley behind them. The playwright turned and looked at him. "I've been telling Miss Estes the plans for Granny," he said.

"Good," said the director. "Who knows—she may wind up the central character."

The playwright laughed, and the two men started down the block, then the playwright stopped and looked back at Evelyn. "Can we take you anywhere?" he asked.

"Oh—no, thanks," she replied. "I'm—I've got to—somebody's going to pick me up here. I guess." She looked at her watch, and saw that it was five minutes past nine. "Thanks, anyway," she said, and the playwright waved his hand and turned and left. Evelyn stood at the curb and reviewed what had just happened. Word by word, she went over what the playwright had said, what the director had said, and what she had said, and she felt hotly embarrassed at the stupidity of her answers. I ought to be shot, she thought. A man compliments me, and all I can say is "Fine." He'd be justified in throwing me out on my head. She knew that the director had been joking about her winding up the central character, but she could not stop herself from imagining what it would be like, and trying to see the necessary script changes. It would mean a whole new story line, but perhaps if some of the emphasis were changed, it wouldn't mean too much revision. They could make it a play about the grandmother in her relation to the other characters, and that way keep a lot of the scenes more or less as they were. And then with the new third act. . . . Stop it, she told herself. You're acting like a child. Just read the lines they give you and stop trying to rewrite the play for them. Be glad they noticed you at all, and don't get off on Cloud Twelve like this. She wondered whether she should tell Montgomery when he arrived. She wanted very much to tell somebody, but she was afraid of sounding silly and schoolgirlish. Maybe Montgomery would understand, though; he would probably realize why she was excited. She looked at her watch again, then searched the block in both directions. I hope he hasn't gone and gotten drunk, she thought. He certainly seemed to mean it when he said he'd pick me up. . . . Once again, she looked at her watch. Nine-ten. Well, that wasn't too bad. She'd give him a few more minutes, anyway.

By nine-thirty, a cold anger had begun to settle over her. It was an anger of disappointment, and also an anger at herself, for allowing herself to be disappointed. She should have known better than to expect him to come, but beyond that, she should have known better than to want him to come. If she hadn't wanted him to come, then she wouldn't have waited so long, and it wouldn't have made any difference one way or the other. She lit a cigarette and snapped the match into the gutter. All right, she said to herself. I'll finish this one cigarette, and then if he hasn't come, the hell with him.

When the cigarette was smoked down to the last inch, she dropped it on the sidewalk, ground it out with her foot, and walked slowly down the block.

She had supper in the Times Square Automat, and it was about ten-thirty by the time she got home. She knocked on Anne's door, but there was no answer, so she went up the stairs, and as she approached her own door she heard music from the floor above. Then the door to Lapham's apartment opened, the music swelled louder, and Anne's voice said, "I'll see if she's home yet." She ran down the stairs, and stopped when she saw Evelyn. "Oh, there you are!" she said. "I was just coming to see if you were home."

"Well, here I am," Evelyn said. "What's on your mind?"

"Oh, nothing," Anne said. "Duncan and I are just sitting around and chatting, and we thought we'd see if you wanted to join us."

"Duncan?" said Evelyn. "Oh—you mean—"

"Yes," said Anne. "Duncan Lapham. He's really terribly nice, and we've been having a gay old time, just sitting around with our feet up and sipping sherry. You really should see his apartment. It's beautiful. Come on."

Evelyn looked closely at Anne, and saw that her eyes were bright. "All right," she said. "But just for a couple of minutes. I'm feeling kind of old tonight."

They went up the stairs, and into Lapham's room. It was no bigger than any of the other rooms in the building, but it looked nothing whatsoever like any of them. A large print screen closed off the kitchen and bathroom area, and beside it, in one corner, was an eighteenth-century New England block-front cabinet. The curtains were red-and-white print, the red matching the Windsor chair, and there was a red antique glass bottle on a gate-leg table in a far corner. A green student lamp was on that table, and a yellow student lamp stood on a small table beside a Boston rocker. The bed was gleaming, highly polished brass, with a white silk spread, and the lights and colors and tones of the room were reflected in a circular gilt mirror that hung above it. The room was elegant without being ornate, and above all it looked completely comfortable. Lapham was in his shirt-sleeves, wearing a scarf around his neck instead of a tie, and he was sitting on the floor, going through piles of record albums. He got up when Anne and Evelyn came in, and came to Evelyn with his hand outstretched. "Welcome," he said. "Sit wherever you like, and tell me what you want to drink. You must be exhausted."

Evelyn sank into a nearby chair, and leaned back. "Thank you," she said. "I don't really care what I have. I guess a spot of whisky would be nice, if you have it."

"Coming right up," said Lapham. He darted off behind the screen, and Evelyn looked at Anne.

"I have to tell you," Evelyn said, lowering her voice. "They're making my part in the play bigger. They may even make it—" she checked herself—"they may even make it one of the feature parts."

"Oh, that's wonderful!" Anne exclaimed. "Duncan!" she called. "Guess what! They're making Evelyn's part in the play into a main part! She's going to be famous!"

"I didn't say that," Evelyn protested, as Lapham came out from behind the screen with a drink in his hand.

"How perfectly spectacular," he said to Evelyn, as he gave her the drink. "I think we should all drink to you." He raised his sherry glass, took a sip, and then looked at Anne. "Do you realize, little mother," he said, "that aside from two tins of anchovies and a quarter of a Brie cheese, we have had no solid food?"

Anne laughed. "I hadn't noticed it," she said. "I'm not hungry, anyway."

Lapham went across and sat on the bed and picked up the telephone book. "If you want your child to have strong teeth," he said, "if you want him to have fangs like a wolf, then you must eat something other than rolled fillets of anchovies and Brie cheese. You must have some solid food. Don't argue with me. I read it in a book, by mistake."

"What are you doing?" Anne asked.

Lapham ran his finger down a page in the book. "I know a place that makes Chinese food to take out," he said. "I'm going to see if they're still open." He put down the book, then reached out and softened the volume on the phonograph, and picked up the telephone. Somewhere in the building, a telephone bell was ringing.

"I wonder if that's my phone," Evelyn said, and got up and went to the door and opened it. But the ringing had stopped, and she waited a moment, then turned and went back to her chair.

"Who would be calling at this hour of the night, anyway?" Anne asked.

Evelyn shrugged and sat down. "I don't know," she said. "Nobody, I guess."

It was still daylight when the fog lifted enough for the *Carpathia* to hoist anchor and make her way slowly up the Hudson River, but by the time the ship had docked, and Montgomery was able to get ashore, it was almost nine-thirty. He raced to a phone on the pier and called Evelyn's theater, but there was no answer. He tried her apartment, with no results, so he ran down and into the street and jumped into a waiting taxi and gave the driver the address of the theater. He knew that she would probably have left long ago, but he had to make sure. The theater was dark and deserted, and Montgomery paid the driver, then went to a nearby drugstore and called Evelyn's apartment again. When he got no answer, he put the receiver back on its hook, picked out his dime as it jangled into the coin-return slot, and left the drugstore and walked to Times Square. There were sailors in pairs, and soldiers in groups, and some men with girls, and some men with their families, and they were milling around and hurrying in all directions, jostling and bumping and elbowing each other in the glare of the lights. Montgomery walked slowly toward a bar and grill he knew of, scanning the faces that went past him and the faces he saw in the restaurant windows, but he had no real hope of seeing Evelyn. He just felt that he should keep on looking.

The bar was nearly empty, and he ordered a drink and then went to a phone booth and tried Evelyn's number once more. As he came out of the booth, he smelled the hot smell of cooking in the back room, and it came to him that he had had nothing to eat all day, and he was hungry. He drank his drink, then went into the back room and ordered a steak sandwich, which he ate hurriedly and without much enjoyment, ignoring the garnishing of limp lettuce and sour pickle. Then he had another drink, and called Evelyn again, paid his dinner check, and went to the bar, cursing himself under his breath.

It was after midnight when he got back to the apartment, and as he mounted the stairs he heard music and laughter. He knocked on Evelyn's door, but he could see that her apartment was dark, and after listening for a moment he went across and put his key in his own lock. There was a burst of laughter from the floor above, and Montgomery hesitated a second, then opened his door and went inside. To hell with everybody, he said to himself, as he flipped on the light. To hell with them all, whoever they are. He threw his hat across the room, then sat heavily on the edge of the bed and ripped with fumbling fingers at the laces in his shoes.

❧ 7 ❧

Lapham finished the last of his spareribs, and cleaned his fingers by popping them one by one into his mouth. Then he wiped his hands, took the cover off a dish, and said, "A bit more flied lice, anyone?"

"Not for me," said Evelyn. "I couldn't eat another bite."

He held the dish out to Anne. "Flied lice for the little mother?"

Anne smiled. "Yes, please," she said.

He put some fried rice on her plate, and uncovered another dish. "Snow peas?" he asked.

"Just a couple." He gave her the peas, and she said, "I guess I must have been hungrier than I thought. Thank you."

"You ought to eat three meals a day, and have all sorts of revolting things like calcium and vitamins," he said. He rose from where he had been sitting on the floor, and went to the phonograph. He removed the pile of records that had been playing, and set them to one side. "Now what?" he asked, looking at the albums. "Does anyone feel like a romp with Khachaturian?"

"So long as I don't have to move," said Evelyn, "that sounds fine."

"We'll have a bit of 'Coq d'Or' and you needn't budge," he said. "It will stir your digestive juices into a positive frenzy." He put on the record, poured himself some tea, and sat down. "And now," he said, looking at Anne, "we come to the main question. What to do about you."

"What do you mean, what to do about me?" she said. "What is there *to* do about me?"

"Just about everything, as far as I can see."

She looked at him for a couple of seconds. "For instance?" she said.

"For instance, that room of yours. You ought to throw everything out, and start all over again. A child growing up in that room would be a paranoiac before he was three."

Anne laughed. "I'd love to throw everything out. I'd love to strip the room bare and start from the plaster. The only hitch is that it costs money. And money is one of those things I don't seem to have."

"I know," he said. "That's where we come in."

"We? Who is we?"

"We is I, and Evelyn, here, and perhaps one or two others. We can shop around, and find things that would go well in the room—God knows *I* have enough things lying around to do that place over three times a week. We can just sort of make a game of it."

"That's very sweet of you, but I still couldn't afford it. And I couldn't ask you to do that, anyway."

"You're not asking us. We're volunteering."

Anne leaned forward. "Listen to me," she said. "Please listen, because this is very important. I can't ask anyone to do anything for me—I can't ask a favor from anyone. This is something that I got myself into, and it's something I'm going to have to work out for myself. I appreciate what you're saying—I appreciate it more than I can tell you—but you just can't do it."

"I don't see why," said Lapham. "If it's something we want to do, I don't see why you should feel badly about it."

"Do you know the best thing you can do for me?" Anne said. "Do you know what would please me the most?"

"What?"

"Just do what you're doing now. Just be around, and be someone to talk to, and someone to spend an evening with —" She looked at Evelyn, and said, "You remember what I said that first night?" Evelyn nodded, and Anne went on, "All right. That's the thing I need most, and that's the thing I can't do for myself. All the rest of it, I've got to do alone."

Lapham shrugged. "Very well," he said. "If you want your child to grow up in a bleak, cheerless cell, there's nothing *we* can do about it."

"Of course I don't want him to grow up in that room! I'm going to try to fix it as best I can, and I hope to God to be able some day to move out of here, but unless I can do it myself it's not going to be done. That's all I'm saying and that's all I mean. Is that so hard to understand?"

"I just don't understand why we can't help," he said, softly. "If there are enough of us, it certainly wouldn't be much of an expense—"

Anne stood up so suddenly that the fork fell from her plate and clattered to the floor. "It's simply that I don't want to be a charity case!" she said, and her eyes were wide with anger. "It's as simple as that! I feel badly enough anyway, without having *that* added to it!" She started for the door.

"Oh, now, wait a minute," Lapham said, and he rose.

"Thank you for dinner," she said, and she went out the door and closed it sharply behind her. Her footsteps clattered down the stairs. Lapham started after her.

"Never mind," Evelyn said, from her chair. "Let her go."

Lapham had his hand on the doorknob. "I can't let her go," he said. "She completely misunderstood what I was saying. I can't let her go off like that."

90

"Wait a second," said Evelyn. "Nothing you say now would do any good. Wait until tomorrow, and she'll have cooled off."

"But this wasn't any kind of charity I was talking about," he said. "After all, people do give showers for the bride and the expectant mother and all that sort of thing, don't they?"

"Yes, of course they do. It's just that she's not in the mood right now to have a shower given for her."

"Well, I can see why she might not want it in lights in Times Square, but really! If we want to get together and give her a present or two, I don't see that that's cause for her to zoom off in a trail of magenta flame."

"Give her time," Evelyn said. "She'll be all right in a little while."

Slowly, Lapham came back and sat down. "You do think a shower would be a good idea, don't you?" he said. "Or, at any rate, something like it?"

"I think it would be a fine idea," she said. "Only there's so much she has to have, I don't know where we'd begin."

Lapham was quiet for a moment. "Just what is it that babies *do* need?" he asked. "I'm afraid I've never given it much thought."

"Neither have I," she said. "Clothes, though. They need lots of clothes."

"Do they, now? I'd always thought they wore the same thing, more or less. You know—drab little dresses, and all."

"They need lots of changes of clothes, remember."

"Oh, Lord, yes, I suppose they do. I'd rather forgotten that. Diapers, I suppose. But I think it would be rather belaboring the point if we gave the poor girl a diaper shower, don't you?"

"I think they have diaper services now, anyway," Evelyn said.

"Good God—you mean some grimy little man comes and washes them *for* you?"

"No. They take them away, and bring you clean ones."

"What a perfectly unbelievable way to make a living." Lapham shuddered slightly. "But I suppose that for our purposes we might as well make a list. Just put things down as they occur to us." He got up, went to the block-front cabinet, took out a pencil and a crisp piece of paper, and then came back and sat down. "Now," he said. "I'll put down clothes. That's one thing." He wrote the word on the paper, put a figure "2" beneath it, and looked up at Evelyn. "What else?" he asked.

"This is perfectly awful, but I just can't think," she said. "Let me see—food. They need some sort of food—"

"I rather thought nature took care of that," said Lapham. "For the first little while, or something."

"I don't know." Evelyn began to feel lost and depressed, and for some reason faintly embarrassed. "I really don't know anything about it. But food isn't a present, anyway. Let me think—oh. Bed clothes, I guess. Sheets, and pillows, and all."

Lapham wrote "bed clothes," and looked at the paper for a moment, thinking. "And that leads us to beds," he said, at last. "She'll need a crib, or at least some place for the little nipper to sleep." He looked up at Evelyn again. "What do babies do when they don't sleep?" he asked. "They certainly don't walk, or leap about, or anything like that, do they?"

"No," said Evelyn. "They don't walk. They just sort of lie there."

"Just lie there and scream," said Lapham, and he wrote "crib" on the paper. "Sweet God, what an arrangement." He studied the paper some more. "Do you know what I'd like to see in that room?" he said.

"What?" Evelyn sensed that he was changing the subject, and she was relieved.

"I'd like to see a big brass bed. Like that one." He indicated his own bed, across the room. "With something like that as

92

a starter, you can decorate a room and really *make* something out of it."

Evelyn looked at the bed. "It's certainly good looking," she said. "But aren't they kind of expensive?"

"It all depends. You can pay anywhere from fifteen to five hundred dollars for them. Of course, if you get a cheap one, then you have to have it polished and lacquered, and that runs into money. Naturally, I can get all that done at a discount." He took a sip of his tea. "And I know where there is one," he said, slowly. "But the old bitch who runs the place would try to strip me to my socks before he'd part with it."

"In an antique store?" Evelyn asked.

He nodded. "I think I'm going to try, anyway. It would be worth it."

Evelyn smiled. "I remember a bed I had once," she said. "It was nine feet square, and it had a blue satin canopy over it that was held up by bronze spears. I was always afraid they were going to fall on me."

Lapham stared at her. "My," he said quietly. "Somehow, I'd never have thought...." He let the sentence trail off, and then hurriedly took another sip of his tea.

"It was my agent's idea," she said. "He said little touches like the spears were important. They gave me individuality, he said."

"Oh," said Lapham. "I'd rather hoped it was something more glamorous than that."

"It was glamorous, all right...." She looked at Lapham's bed, but her eyes did not focus on it. "It was glamorous as all Billy-be-damned."

There was a short pause, and then Lapham said, "Now— about this bed. If I can get it—if I can pry it away from that old crone for anything near what it's worth—what should we do? Should we give it to her right away, or wait until we've got a few things to go with it?"

"I'd wait," said Evelyn. "I think we should take this slowly. We'd better give her everything at once, so that it'll look like a shower and not like a lot of handouts."

"You're absolutely right. I'd never thought of that." He was quiet briefly, and then he opened his eyes wide. "I've got it!" he said. "I know just what we'll do!"

"What?" It occurred to Evelyn that when Lapham was excited he suddenly looked like a little boy, and she felt a curious tenderness toward him.

"We'll wait until she goes to the hospital, and then we'll go in there and fix that room up so she'll never recognize it! We can do it over from top to bottom!"

She considered this. "It sounds fine, so long as it doesn't cost too much," she said. "That kind of thing can run into money."

"Not if we shop around! We've got all summer to—" He stopped. "When did this whole ghastly thing happen?" he asked. "I mean—how long *do* we have?"

"I don't know," she said. "But we've got the better part of the summer, I'm pretty sure of that."

"All right, then. We can decide on a motif, and then pick up little bits here and little bits there, just as we see them. You can always find bargains, if you've got enough time."

"It certainly would be a surprise," she said, smiling.

"My dear, it would be a *sensation!* And you—can't you pick up little things when you're in a show—I mean, don't they let you keep things when the whole affair finally closes?"

"You can buy your costumes," Evelyn said. "I suppose you could make off with some of the props, if you really wanted them."

"Well, just keep your eyes open, and see if there's anything she'd like to have." He stood up, crumpled the paper, and threw it in the brass-bound wastebasket. "Oh, I think this is a spectacular idea!" he said. "What kind of motif do you think would be best—Victorian, Colonial, Georgian—what?"

94

"You know more about that than I do," she replied. "What's the easiest to get cheaply?"

"Victorian, I suppose. But it tends to be so bloody ugly."

"Won't it depend on whether or not you can get the bed?"

"No. I can make that bed fit with anything." He paced back and forth, biting his lower lip. "I'd love to see the whole thing done in Empire, but I'm afraid that's a little out of the question."

"Let's be realistic," Evelyn said. "If Victorian is the cheapest to get, then Victorian it's got to be."

"You're right." He dropped into a chair, and nibbled at one thumbnail. "With Victorian, you have to have as little light as possible, to hide the details. We'll just block out most of the light, and have heavy drapes, and lampshades, and all that."

"You know," said Evelyn, "it occurs to me that the idea behind all this was to provide a cheerful place for a baby. We can't get too bloody Victorian, or he'll suffocate."

Lapham stopped chewing his nail, and was quiet. "Damn," he said. "Why did you have to think of that?"

When Evelyn awoke the next morning, she lay in bed for a few minutes, thinking of all the things she and Lapham had planned. She was sure that very little of it would materialize, but it was fun to think about, and if any of it did work out, then so much the better. She thought about Lapham, and the strange, lonely life that he led, and she could see in his enthusiasm all his pent-up longing to be part of something, to belong somewhere. If ever there was a way to make their plans work, she thought, then he would surely find it. And the more she could help, the happier she herself would be. It was a cause for both of them—a small cause, certainly, but one that could be as important as they chose to make it.

She got up, and went into the kitchen and started the coffee. She felt younger than she had in a long time.

After breakfast, she got dressed and then read through her script, and wondered what changes would be made in her part. The wild excitement she had felt about it last night had given way to a more realistic approach, but she couldn't help improvising in her mind, and looking for places where the part could be expanded. This really could be the thing that does it, she thought. This could be the payoff for all the years of devotion to some idea that took everything out of you and never gave anything back in return. The idea of being a great actress, to which everything else was secondary, except of course the matter of eating, until it was too late to be much of anything at all. Too late to be a good wife, too late to be a mother, too late to be anything except a bit player. Maybe this would do it, though. Late though it was, this might be the thing that changed the luck.

There was a knock on her door, and she started, then looked at her watch. She should have left for rehearsal five minutes ago. "Yes?" she said, getting up. "Who is it?"

"It is I," said Montgomery, through the door. "Young Lochinvar, come out of the west."

She opened the door, and he stood there, looking like a sad sheep dog. "Good morning," Evelyn said brightly.

"I just want to say I'm terribly sorry about last night," he said. "I tried to get hold of you, but you weren't in. There was—"

"Please don't apologize," she said. "It didn't make any difference."

"It certainly did make a difference, and I just want to explain what happened. You probably won't believe it, but—"

"Honestly, I wish you wouldn't feel so badly about it." She picked up her script from where she had dropped it, and looked for her purse. "I'm sorry to have to rush off like this, but I'm going to be late for rehearsal."

"Will you just let me tell you what happened?"

"Of course." She picked up her purse, and faced him.

"I went down the Bay on a press cutter, and we got caught in the fog and didn't get back until about nine-thirty. I tried to get you, but your phone didn't answer."

"No. I was out." She moved toward the door.

"Believe me, I would never have done it if I'd had any idea that would happen."

"I know you wouldn't," she said, pleasantly. "It's just one of those things. Please don't give it another thought. There's no reason to worry about it. Now, I really *do* have to—"

"Just one more thing. I had a couple of ideas about what we should do."

"Do? About what?"

"You know." He lowered his voice. "About Anne."

"Oh, yes," she said. "I'd forgotten." She put her hand on the doorknob. He backed out, still talking.

"I think the best thing," he said, "is just to get some people to come to my room for drinks, and that way it'll look informal and nobody'll suspect anything. What do you think?"

"Well, honestly, I don't think that's going to be necessary," she said. She came through the door, and closed it behind her. "I think maybe she's going to do all right on her own."

"I mean like the Beckers. Does she know the Beckers?"

"No, I don't think she does." Evelyn walked past him, and started for the stairs. "I'm terribly sorry to have to run like this, but I am late. We can go into it all later."

She went down the stairs, and Montgomery stayed where she had left him. As he listened to her footsteps going out of the building and onto the sidewalk, a hollow feeling came over him. He went back into his room, and sat on the edge of his bed.

Well, I certainly blew that one, he thought. And I guess I had it coming to me. I should have known better. By this time, I ought to know better than to expect anything good to come of anything I do. I have the sure touch of disaster— the green thumb of Attila the Hun. Wherever I walk, no grass will grow again; in my path I leave nothing but confusion and trouble.

He stood up. And stop feeling sorry for yourself, he said. Stop moping about like a wounded elk, and do something. You want to introduce that girl to the Beckers—all right, go ahead and do it. Do it on your own, and don't expect other people to help you. Invite the Beckers up for a drink—tell them it's your birthday and you want to celebrate. Then get the girl, and there you are. Your Boy Scout deed done for the day, and everybody happy. Leave the rest up to them; don't meddle in their affairs beyond the simple matter of introducing them. And the first thing to do is clean up this room. Get at it right now, before you do anything else.

He made his bed, then went around the room, picking up loose clothes. Next, he gathered up the remnants of the last three Sundays' newspapers, and stacked them in a pile in the closet. That done, he opened the top drawer of his dresser, scooped all the debris from the top of the dresser into it, and surveyed the room. It still looked like hell. The curtains were torn and dirty, and at the top of one of them, between it and the window, was wedged an old gray felt hat. He reached up and pulled the hat down, examined it without recognition, and tossed it in the wastebasket.

Flowers are what I need, he thought. Flowers will always make a place look brighter. That and some new lampshades. O.K., then, that's what we'll get. Maybe this'll be a good thing all around. Do a good turn for Anne, and at the same time spruce this room up a little—and Lord knows it could use it. This'll be the first worthwhile thing I've done in a long time.

He looked in his wallet, to make sure he had enough money, and then went out the door whistling the march of the Grenadier Guards.

It was midafternoon before he had the room looking the way he wanted it. He wrote a note to Anne, asking her to drop up for a drink when she got home from work, and went downstairs and put it under her door. Then he straightened his tie, cleared his throat, and knocked on the Beckers' door.

Martha Becker opened the door a crack, and regarded him without expression.

"Mrs. Becker?" he said, pleasantly.

She nodded.

"I'm Arthur Montgomery," he said. "I live in the apartment above you." Again she nodded, and he went on, "I'm sorry to disturb you like this. May I speak to you for a moment?"

She opened the door wider. "What is it?" she said.

"May I come in?" Montgomery wasn't sure quite what approach he should use, but he knew that he wouldn't get anywhere standing in the hall. He needed time to see how she was going to react.

She stood aside, and he walked into the room. It smelled of laundry and of cooking and of old age. She closed the door.

"I'll tell you, Mrs. Becker, this is a rather strange thing I'm suggesting," he said. "You'll probably think I'm crazy, but I believe it's a good idea nonetheless."

"If it needs money, we can't afford it," she said.

"No, no, no. It's nothing like that. It's very simple, but I think it's kind of fundamental." He looked around for a chair. "May I sit down?" he asked.

She nodded, and he sat in a hard, upholstered rocking chair. She sat down facing him and wiped her hands in her apron.

"In essence, what I'm talking about is this," he said. "What I'm talking about is the fact that we all lead fairly lonely lives." He looked at her, but she showed no reaction, so he continued, "I think that this is unnecessary. I think it's not only unnecessary, but it's wrong. Here we are all living in the same apartment building, actually just within a few yards of each other, and we live here year after year and never get to know one another. I think this is a shame, and I think that something should be done about it."

A faint smile crossed her face and she shrugged. "A person gets so busy," she said.

"I know they get busy, and that's just the trouble. They get too busy to pay attention to the fundamental things. Now, here's what I'm getting at." He knew he was going to have to get to the point sooner or later, and he had just about run out of pious generalities. "When I woke up this morning, I realized that it was my birthday. And I lay there, remembering how much my birthday used to mean to me when I was a boy, and it made me sad to think that now I was going to spend my birthday alone, with no friends to cheer me, no greetings, no anything. It was a far cry from the birthdays I could remember, with the cake and the ribbons and the screaming and the toys." He looked at her carefully, to see if he was overdoing it, but he saw only a slight softening of her features. "So I said to myself, 'Why don't I give myself a birthday party? Why don't I meet some of the people around me—like Mr. and Mrs. Becker, for instance—and why don't I ask them up to have a birthday drink with me?' So that's just what I'm doing. I'm asking you and your husband to come up later this afternoon—whenever he gets home from work; there's nothing formal about it—and get acquainted and have a birthday drink with me. It's as simple as that." He stopped. His heart was pounding, and the palms of his hands were wet.

She smiled. "That's very kind of you," she said.

"No, it's not kind of me," he said. "It would be kind of you if you would accept. It is you who would do me the favor."

"It would be very nice," she said.

"Good," said Montgomery. He started to rise.

"How long have you lived here?" she asked.

"Oh—let me think," he said, and settled back in the chair. "Fifteen years, I guess. . . . No, maybe it's not that long. I think it's nearer twelve."

She nodded. "I knew it was a long time," she said. "Next

only to us, I guess you're here the longest. Twenty-eight years we been here—twenty-nine next September."

"My, my," he said. "Just imagine that." Now that he had made his point, he wanted a drink very badly.

"When we came here, this was a good neighborhood," she said. "The people, the houses, everything about it was good. Like in the old country, it was clean—none of the dirt you get around here now."

"I imagine it was," he said agreeably. "Everything is getting pretty run down these days. They don't seem to care the way they used to."

"It's not the buildings so much I mean as the people," she said. "It's the people that are no good nowadays. You take the Gundekers—you remember the Gundekers, used to live across the hall, there?"

"No," he said. "I don't think I do."

"Such lovely people you couldn't imagine. Real good, like in the old country. Five children they had, only three of them died."

Montgomery made a clucking noise with his tongue.

"Never once in all the time they was married did he look at another woman," she went on. "Always it was for her— everything he did was for her. They made the most beautiful couple you ever know."

Montgomery smiled. "They must have," he said.

"And now what do we get?" she asked. "You know what we get across the hall, there?"

Montgomery swallowed. "Ah—I'm not sure," he said. "What do you mean?"

"Never mind, I shouldn't say it in decent company," she said. "It's a disgrace. All the more pity you didn't know the Gundekers, such a lovely couple they were. Everything he did, he did for her. And such beautiful children they had, too. The ones that lived, I mean. You saw the whole family together, and it was so beautiful you could feel it in your stomach." She sighed. "Ah, well, you don't get people like that these days."

"About the person across the hall," Montgomery said, beginning to perspire. "Is there any special problem there?"

Her face hardened, and she looked at him for a moment. "You can keep a secret?" she asked.

"Yes," Montgomery said, and he swallowed again. "Of course."

"This girl that lives across the hall—this baggage—she goes around telling people how she's having a child. It's a disgrace! She should be thrown out in the street where she comes from!"

"Well, maybe she's married," Montgomery said falteringly. "Or divorced, or maybe even—"

"So she's married so why doesn't she wear a ring?" Martha said savagely. "So she's married so why don't we see her husband around somewhere? A year she's been here, maybe even more, and not one man do we see with her! Married! She's married like a cat in the alley! It's a disgrace!"

"I didn't know," said Montgomery. He rose.

"I said we shouldn't talk about it with decent people," she said. "Enough trouble there is in the world already, without we should dirty ourselves talking about baggage like that." She stood up, as Montgomery tottered toward the door. "Perhaps about six o'clock we will come up and see you," she said, and smiled.

"Yes," Montgomery said, and he opened the door. "Yes—that will be fine." He went out, and when the door closed behind him he suddenly found he had to sit down. He sat on the front steps, and stared through a kind of fog at the bright and noisy street. After about five minutes his head cleared, and he took a piece of paper from his pocket. He wrote "Sorry—plans changed" on the paper, then stood up and went inside and put it gently under Anne's door. Then he went upstairs to his room to await the arrival of the Beckers.

❧ 8 ❧

SUMMER IN THE CITY has a dead, a heavy quality that is a mixture of oppressive heat and the smell of hot tar and the feel of wet and sticky clothes. Air-cooled bars and movies give temporary icy relief, but the heat is always waiting; it rises like a cloud from the soft pavements and reflects in orange brilliance from the sides of buildings and roars through the subway tunnels like the blast from a cannon. Gasoline and Diesel fumes hang blue and heavy in the air, and the traffic sullenly growls and groans and bangs. People sleep on floors and fire escapes and roofs, and their faces in the morning are drawn and blank, as though still half asleep. Tempers are short, but fights seldom last long; the heat drains away energy and leaves only listless anger.

When a storm strikes, especially in the muggy silence of a week-end afternoon, the city comes briefly to life. With the first heavy clouds come gusts of cool wind, which pick up papers and dust in the gutters and whirl them about in tiny spirals. Then, as the wind rises and the first rain splatters on the pavements, there comes the banging and clattering and screeching of windows being slammed shut. People scurry for cover and stand in doorways and subway entrances, and the wind and rain slash down, wrenching and banging at loose awnings and making the pavements smoke with spray. Brown water boils through the gutters and the thunder crashes in a strange metallic way, and then suddenly the rain stops, and the awnings drip and the streets steam in the sunlight, and for a little while the air smells good. People come out from their hiding places, and go on as though nothing had happened.

One Saturday, Anne had gone to Third Avenue to look for furniture, and a sudden thunderstorm came up. She ducked into an antique store, the window of which she had been scanning from the outside when the rain began to come down. The store inside was piled high with furniture, costumes, lampshades, bric-a-brac, glassware, and figurines. Overhead hung chandeliers of all descriptions, some glass, some bronze, some wrought iron; and the shelves along the walls glittered with red, blue, green, and amber glasses. She had the sensation of being in a damp, dim grotto, one that was encrusted with mineral deposits and accumulated debris. Something moved in a far corner, and presently a man emerged and came toward her. He was middle aged, and thin, and he had a high forehead and an arched nose and an expression as though he were going to sneeze. He wore a flowered sports shirt, which hung outside his khaki trousers, and blue sneakers.

"Yes, Ma'm?" he said, folding his hands together. He glanced quickly at her maternity dress, although his eyes never seemed to leave her face. "May I help you?"

"No, thank you. I'm just—looking around." Anne laughed nervously. "As a matter of fact, I only came in to get out of the rain."

The man pursed his lips in a smile and bowed slightly. "Of course," he said. "Make yourself at home, do."

There was a crash of thunder, and he turned away. Anne

picked up a small, blue cut-glass bottle and examined it. She hadn't seen a bottle like it in many years. It reminded her of a perfume bottle she had once had—her first perfume bottle, in fact—and she removed the stopper and sniffed tentatively at the top. The smell was faint and unrecognizable, like a sound heard from a long distance, but the shape and the feel of the bottle were familiar, and she held it and rotated it between her fingers, and looked out at the rain. She remembered the first night she had been allowed to go unchaperoned with a boy to a dance—she must have been sixteen, or even seventeen, before her father had consented to her going out without an adult member of the family in attendance. Even then, it had required a family conference before he finally gave in, and at the conference he set up a list of rules for her conduct that would have passed muster in the strictest seminary. Then she and her mother went to the city to buy her a dress, and the only dress in the whole store that appealed to her was a white, strapless affair, with blue ribbons around the top.

"Your father would never permit a dress like that," her mother said, but her voice was soft with admiration as she reached out and felt the material.

"Oh, Mother, why not?" Anne cried. "It isn't indecent— look." She held the dress against her, and made the top come a little higher than it normally would. "There's nothing wrong with it—he *couldn't* object! I mean, *really!*"

"All the young ladies are wearing them, Ma'm," the sales-girl said. "They're considered very proper, if you know what I mean."

Her mother was still hesitant. "I don't know," she said. "I really don't know."

"Mother, if we buy it, then that will settle it!" Anne said. "He *can't* do anything once we've bought it! Please, Mother, just this once, let's do it first and ask him later. *Please!*"

Her mother's eyes flickered, and she smiled. "All right,"

she said. "We'll do it. Just this once, we'll do it first and ask him later." Her face did not show it, but she was laughing.

The night of the dance, Anne dressed early, taking great care to put on just enough make-up and not too much. Then she put on her dress, hitched the top of it up so that it came almost to her throat, and went to her father's study and knocked on the door. When he told her to, she opened the door and went in.

Her father was reading a book by the light of a green student lamp, and after a moment he glanced up at her. She never forgot the look on his face as he took off his glasses. In fact, she never forgot a single detail of that room—the light from the lamp throwing shadows around the heavy, Victorian furniture; the dark red curtains that rose up into the gloom of the ceiling; the worn fringe on the red table runner, and the massive steel engraving of a stag that hung behind the black leather couch.

Her father regarded her in silence for almost a minute. Then, when he spoke, he spoke slowly and with infinite scorn.

"You wouldn't dare," he said.

He looked at her for an instant more, then put on his glasses and turned back to his book.

She wore a hastily refitted confirmation dress to the dance, and when her date, a flat-faced blond boy named Junior Wintermussen, suggested that they sit out a couple of dances in his car, she agreed with such alacrity that he began to wonder if he mightn't have started something that he had no idea how to finish. But nobody was much changed by the interlude, although the confirmation dress was never good for much of anything again, and Junior Wintermussen had some difficulty explaining to his mother how he got lipstick stains in one ear and all over his collar. When he called Anne for a date the following night, she was deep in the mire of remorse and refused to talk to him. He made two more futile calls after that, and then gave up.

Now, with the rain pouring down outside the antique shop, Anne looked at the blue perfume bottle and wondered why she always seemed to get more deeply involved in things than she intended. She never intended to let Junior Wintermussen do any more than kiss her good night, if that; she never intended to fall in love—or whatever it was—with Roy Curtin; she never intended to do a lot of things, until suddenly she found herself doing them, and more than a little terrified. Always in over her depth, and always wanting to call for help but never quite daring to. I think I'll buy this bottle, she said to herself. I think I'll buy it and keep it on the dresser, where it'll be a reminder to me not to go around biting off more than I can chew. Not that it isn't a great deal too late for now; it still might be of some help for the future.

She went to the back of the store, where the man was sitting at a desk, riffling papers under a dim gooseneck lamp.

"How much is this?" she asked, holding out the bottle.

He took it from her, and turned it back and forth under the light. "Eighteen dollars," he said. There was a jangling of bells as the front door opened and closed, and the man rose. "Shall I wrap it for you?" he asked.

"Oh—no," said Anne. "I'm afraid that's—I didn't realize it was so—"

"It's Sandwich," he said, with a tight little smile. "It's worth every bit of twenty-four dollars, but you can have it for sixteen."

"No, that's still—I'm sorry," Anne said, just as Duncan Lapham came up behind her, dripping wet from the rain.

"Ah, yes," the storekeeper said, to Lapham. "Come to haggle some more about the brass bed, I presume?"

"Why, Duncan!" Anne said. "What brings you *here?* Are you getting twin beds?"

He seemed surprised and confused to see her, and for an instant or two he made no sense. "Oh, for Heaven's sakes," he said. "Well—yes and no—what I mean to say is that I *do* want it, yes—but not for—I mean, what a coincidence finding *you* here!"

"Yes, isn't it?" She laughed. "I came in here to get out of the rain. It doesn't look as though you quite made it."

"I was halfway here when the bloody skies opened on me. I'd reached the point of no return, so on I slogged." He looked at the storekeeper. "I *should* like to talk about that bed, though, if you don't mind."

"I'll get out of your way," Anne said, and picked up the bottle from the desk. "I'll put this back where I found it—" She looked from the storekeeper to Lapham and went on, "Can you imagine? I picked this up thinking it was just an old perfume bottle, and it turns out to be Sandwich! Did you ever hear of anything so stupid?"

"Let me see that." Lapham took the bottle, looking straight at the storekeeper as he did. The two men stared evenly at each other. Then Lapham examined the bottle. He looked back at the storekeeper. "Sandwich, did you say?" he asked, quietly.

The man took it from him, and held it back under the light. "Well, what do you know?" he said. "No. That's my mistake." He held the bottle out to Anne. "I'm very sorry," he said. "It's just a very good imitation. I've been reading so much today that my eyes are kind of blurry. No, I think about six dollars would be right for that. . . . We'll make it five, seeing as how you're a friend of Cousin Duncan's, here."

"Oh, that's wonderful," Anne said. "Would you just put some paper around it, please? There's no need to do any fancy wrapping."

"We wrap everything the same way," the man said tightly, as he rolled the bottle in a sheet of tissue paper. "That way, nobody feels they haven't had their money's worth." He put the wrapped bottle in a white box and spun some string around it. "And as for that bed," he said, without looking at Lapham. "I have just found out that that bed is worth not a penny less than three hundred dollars." He said the words almost as though he were singing them.

"I had a feeling that might happen," Lapham replied. "Well—I can wait. The market is bound to change."

"Don't hang by your toes until it does," said the man. He handed the package to Anne and took her five dollars. "Or better yet, why don't you?" he said to Lapham, and smiled broadly.

The rain had stopped when they got outside, and they walked slowly along the damp sidewalk, keeping well away from the dripping awnings. The air smelled clean and a slight breeze stirred the scrawny trees along the avenue.

"My, but I'm glad *you* came along," Anne said. "I wanted that bottle, but I certainly didn't want it sixteen dollars' worth."

"Was that what he asked?" Lapham sounded as though he were thinking about something else.

"First he wanted eighteen, then he came down to sixteen, and I had just given up all hope when you came in." She paused. "I hope I didn't mess up your deal for the bed, though. He sounded kind of cross about that."

"No, no, no. He's just that way naturally."

"What do you want another bed for, anyway? I think the one you've got is just beautiful."

"Oh, it's not for me. It's for a—a customer of mine. Asked if I knew where to find one."

"Oh." They walked on for a while in silence, and then she said, "Duncan."

"What?" He still seemed preoccupied.

"Do you have to go back to your store?"

"Why?"

"I'd like to do something silly. I don't know what—I'd just like to do something gay and giddy and foolish, like— like taking a boat around the island, or going down to Chinatown, or something like that. You know what I mean?"

A faint smile skittered across his face. "I know just what you mean, but I'm afraid I can't join you, much as I'd like to. Saturday's a busy day for me."

"Would it hurt so much to take just one afternoon off? I'm sorry—don't answer that. If you can't, you can't, and that's all there is to it."

"I'd love to, dear girl, but I really can't."

"I know. Tell me—have you heard anything from Evelyn lately?"

"Evelyn? No. Why should I?"

"Just that she said she'd keep us all in touch and tell us how her play was going. I got a post card from her in Falmouth, and that was almost three weeks ago. I just wondered."

"No. I haven't heard a thing."

"Do you know something? I miss her."

He smiled again. "She's a good sport."

"Duncan."

"What?"

"Do you think I'm doing the right thing?"

"Good Lord, what do you mean?"

"I mean the right thing in going on with all this. Having the baby here, and all."

"My dear girl, it's a little late to worry about that now, isn't it?"

"I suppose so. Yes, of course it is."

"Then you must be doing the right thing. Look at it that way."

"I know, but all the lying and pretending I've got to do. I've had to tell the people at the office I'm married, so I had to buy a ring to wear to work—I certainly wouldn't wear it any other time—and, oh, I don't know what all. There are so many things."

"Why do you wear the ring only at the office? Why not wear it all the time?"

"Because it's cheating. It isn't true."

"I wouldn't know anything about these things," he said, as though trying to change the subject, "but I should think that in matters like that, it would all be relative."

She thought about this. "I suppose it is."

"But, as I said, I'm really not the one to be an authority."

"I know. I'm sorry. It's none of your worry."

"I didn't say that. I simply said I don't know."

"But I shouldn't be bothering you about it. I'm sorry."

"There's nothing to be sorry about." He stopped in front of a store and held out his hand. "Here's where I leave you." He took her hand and smiled. "I think the best thing for you is to have your little fling in Chinatown or wherever you want to go, and just stop worrying. Go completely mad for one day and you'll feel a great deal better tomorrow."

"Thank you," she said. "I'll do what I can." She wanted to go in and look at his store, but he was so definite in his good-by that she hesitated to ask him. He turned and went inside, and she continued slowly down the street.

When he got to the back of the store, a young man rose to greet him. "Any luck?" the young man asked.

"Not a damned bit," Lapham replied. "I had to open my big mouth out of turn, and the old bag raised the price to three hundred."

The young man clucked sympathetically. "Oh," he said. "I started to cut that stand down, and then I thought I'd wait and see how high you wanted it to be. I've got it in back."

They went into a small, cluttered workshop, where stood a four-foot-high object that had once been used as a shaving stand. It had three claw feet, which merged into a carved walnut pillar that supported the marble-covered top. It looked like an ornate hatrack with a slab of marble on top of it.

"Well, the first thing you do is take this off," Lapham said, as he lifted the marble and put it to one side. "Cut it with *that* on, and it'll come down and crush your bloody little skull."

"Oh," said the young man. "Yes."

"As for the height," said Lapham. He put his hand about eighteen inches off the floor. "I'd say about like that. Regular coffee-table height. Just cut this center piece out, and squat the top down onto the legs. It makes a very practical coffee table. Or, for that matter, a table for baby bottles," he added, as an afterthought.

"How do you know it will match?" the young man asked. "If you haven't got the bed, how do you know this will match the rest of her stuff?"

"Just leave that to me," Lapham replied. "I shall personally see to it that it matches, bed or no bed, if I have to get every stick of furniture for her myself."

As Anne drifted down Third Avenue, she looked in the shop windows without really seeing any of the details. There was a terrible sameness to all the furniture; it was dusty and drab and Victorian, and it seemed to blend together into one monstrous collection of junk. She had developed a deep loathing for anything Victorian—probably as a result of her father's study, it occurred to her. She had never really thought about it before, but she was always depressed by the sight of heavy drapes, or ponderous furniture, or stained-glass windows, and now that she examined her feeling, she realized that this depression stemmed straight from the house in which she had spent most of her life. She could still see the afternoon sun striking harshly on the arm of a horsehair sofa, while a cloud of motes ran up the beam of light to the lace curtains, and she could smell the smell of cigar smoke and old rugs and furniture polish and cooking vegetables. And then there was the stained-glass window on the stair landing—the red and blue and amber lights in that window had a quality of richness, of almost over-ripeness, that she could practically taste, and it meant to her a feeling of being closed in, away from everything, but not in a pleasant way; rather, in an almost morbid way. Theirs was not a typical Pennsylvania house—nor, for that matter, were they typical Pennsylvania people, since her grandparents had moved there from New England—and the feeling of not quite belonging, of being set slightly and not necessarily advantageously apart from the rest, may have been the cause of some of her dislike of the atmosphere. Perhaps if all her friends had lived in Victorian houses, it might have been different, but she always felt, when she walked up the driveway and saw the *porte-cochère* and the mansard roof and the ornamental scrollwork on the porch, that she was going into a mausoleum rather than into a home.

She remembered one time, when the forsythia was in bloom and the fields were wet and muddy, she came back from school and, because her shoes were caked with red clay, she went in by the kitchen door and took them off and put them in front of the stove. Then, in her stocking feet, she went silently into the front of the house, and the first thing she heard was her mother's voice, coming from the library. It had a half-strangled quality she had never heard in her mother's voice before, the quality of being clogged with tears.

"But, Justin, what is one chair?" her mother was saying. "What possible difference can one chair make?"

"It's out of key, that's the difference," her father replied. "And what's more, it's a monstrosity. Nobody could even sit in a contraption like that."

"Just try it," her mother said. "Just sit in it once, and tell me if it isn't twice as comfortable as the rest of this—this junk around here."

Anne held her breath, and stood still. If she went on, they would see her; if she went back, the creak of the kitchen door might give her away. She stood still and listened, frozen.

"I most certainly will not try it," her father said. "And as for what you call junk, it will one day be worth more than the house itself. I'll have you know that some of this furniture has been in my family for three generations, and it holds up a lot better than this damned modern trash you insist on buying. You can call the store and tell them to send for that chair right now. I won't have it around."

"Do you want to know why I bought it?" The tears were gone, and her mother's voice rose in a kind of wail. "Do you want to know why? I bought it so there'd be something of *me* in this house—I bought it so that *I'd* have contributed something, and there'd be something of *mine* in the middle of all the precious Waters heirlooms! That's why I bought it, and that's why I'm going to keep it! How do you like that?"

There was the sharp sound of a slap, and a gasp, and Anne turned and fled into the kitchen and out the back door. She had run halfway to the garage before she realized she was in her stocking feet, but she kept on going, and stayed in the garage until dark. She was subsequently punished for getting her feet wet, but it was a routine punishment, and neither she nor her parents thought of it as anything more than a gesture.

The chair stayed, but it was kept in her mother's sewing room, upstairs.

Now, as she walked along Third Avenue and looked in the windows of the antique stores, Anne had a sudden idea. I know what I'll do, she thought. I'll make it modern. I'll do the whole room in modern, just as modern as I can get it. And if I can't get it, I'll make it. I'll make a table, and a book case, and maybe even a chair, if I can get someone to show me how. Or get a book on how to do it. They have books on how to do all those things. That's the way to do it. Get a book, and build it all myself. Then take pictures of it, and send them home. "Dear Folks," I'll say on the pictures, "I thought you'd like to see my new line of heirlooms. I made them all myself."

She laughed at the thought, and quickened her step as she looked for a store that might help her.

Two hours later, she sat in her room and stared glassily at the magazine in her hands. Four other magazines lay on the floor beside her, and in her lap was a book called "Building Your Own Home," which told her how to do just that; her last hope lay in the magazine she was trying to read, which featured a Do-It-Yourself section for home owners. She flipped through the pages, past articles titled "Lathe Setup for Running a Long Knurl," "How Can a Single Shaper Cutter Be Made to Run Two Kinds, or Shapes, of Moldings?" "Chucking Arbor Cuts Around Tenons," and "Cantering Device Aligns Work for Milling Keyways," until she came to one that said "Hidden Catch Prevents Child from Opening Drawer." Maybe there's something here after all, she thought. At least it's about children, which is a step in the right direction. She read into the article, and got as far as "The catch consists of a short length of spring steel which is fastened at one end to the outside of the drawer guide and fitted with a dowel at the other end." She stopped, and read the sentence again. There seemed nothing tricky about it, but it made no sense to her. The other end of what? The other end of the dowel—and what *is* a dowel?—or the other end of the drawer guide, or the other end of the length of spring steel? The length of spring steel.... Where do you get a length of spring steel, anyway? And how long is a length?

She laid the magazine down, and looked around the room. I don't *want* a catch to keep a child from opening drawers, she thought. I want my child to open as many drawers as he pleases. I want drawers that *any* child can open.

She looked back at the magazine. Turning the pages, she saw that she could cover her entire house with a plastic made to resemble brick; she could transform a kitchen cabinet into a kennel for a repulsively small dog; she could remove dried calking compound from the tip of a calking gun by heating it with a torch; she could drill holes in concrete faster by alternating a star drill with the carbide-tipped bit whenever the bit contacted a piece of aggregate; and she could draw evenly spaced parallel lines quite quickly by sticking a pointer on the underside of her T-square. She closed the magazine and threw it across the room.

There was a knock on the door. "Come in!" she said.

The door opened, and Duncan Lapham looked in. "Just checking," he said. "I wanted to make sure you weren't lost in the, if you'll forgive the expression, bowels of Chinatown."

"Oh, Duncan, come in," she said. "You're just the person I want to see."

He came in, and closed the door behind him. He looked at the magazines around her. "Building something?" he asked.

"That's what I want to do, but I don't know how to begin. I want to make some things for this room—you know, easy things, like tables and bookcases, and all—but I can't find anything that tells me how to do it. How do you build a table?"

Lapham's expression didn't change. "What kind of table were you thinking of?"

"I don't care. Just something simple. And modern. I think the modern things are kind of good looking, don't you?"

"I think they're perfectly hideous."

"But they're simple. You have to give them that."

"Simple, yes. But if you want a simple table, then all you have to do is get an orange crate and put a slab of linoleum on top of it. That's so simple it'll make you scream."

"Duncan, I'm serious. I've *got* to do something about this room, and I can't afford to buy anything. Whatever I do, I've got to do myself."

He looked around the room. "I really don't know where

to tell you to begin," he said. "Why don't you wait a while, and see if something turns up?"

"What do you mean, turns up?"

"Oh, you know." He made a vague gesture. "Sometimes you see incredible bargains. Things that you can get for practically nothing."

"I keep telling you, I can't afford to buy anything. I want to make it myself, and I want it to be good looking when it's done."

"My dear girl, unless you're a born cabinetmaker, it's bound to look terrible. I don't mean to be insulting, but I really don't think you could do anything that would be worth the time and trouble you put into it. I mean that in all friendliness—don't try."

"I don't see what I've got to lose."

"Just take my advice. Wait a while, and I'm sure that something will turn up."

There were two light raps on the door.

"See who it is," she said.

"If it's that old biddy across the way, I'll spit in her eye," Lapham said, and he opened the door. Montgomery stood there. "Oh," said Lapham. "Come in. I'm just leaving."

"Do you two know each other?" Anne asked. "Officially, I mean?"

The men regarded one another coldly. "I don't think so," said Lapham.

"Mr. Lapham, Mr. Montgomery," said Anne. "Duncan, and—"

"Arthur," said Montgomery.

"How do you do," Lapham said.

Montgomery nodded his head, then looked at Anne. "I didn't mean to interrupt," he said. "I just wondered if—"

"You didn't interrupt a thing," said Anne. "Come on in, and sit down. Duncan, you sit, too. Let's talk about this some more."

"No, I really can't," said Lapham. "I must be going."

"Look—I can come back another time," said Montgomery.

"Oh, don't be silly," Anne said. "Come on. As for you, Duncan, thank you for nothing. I'm going to build something for myself in spite of all you say."

Lapham smiled. "Well, good luck, my dear," he said. He looked at Montgomery. "Pleased to have met you."

"Yes," said Montgomery, and Lapham left. Montgomery closed the door after he had gone. "Is he a friend of yours?" he asked.

"Yes," said Anne. "Or at any rate, I think so. He really can be terribly nice."

"I guess you know more people than I thought," Montgomery said. "I had the impression you didn't know anyone here."

"Oh, I *know* everybody, I guess. I'm not sure exactly how many—" She left the sentence unfinished.

"Yes," he said. "I know. By the way, have you heard anything from Evelyn?"

"Not recently. Have you?"

"No." He shook his head. "I haven't heard anything at all. I didn't really expect to, I guess."

"She said she'd keep us all posted."

"Yes, but I don't think that included me."

"Well, it was supposed to include me, but I haven't had anything except a post card from Falmouth."

He cleared his throat. "By the way, the reason I came in was—"

"Won't you please sit down? I hate to see you standing there like that."

"No, thanks, I want to wash up. The reason I came in was to see if you'd consider having dinner with me. It's Saturday night, and I think everybody ought to have dinner with somebody else on Saturday night. Nobody ought to have dinner alone on Christmas or on Saturday."

She laughed. "I'd love it," she said. "Even if it wasn't Saturday, or Christmas, or even Thanksgiving, I'd still love it."

"Good," he said, and put his hand on the door. "I suppose I ought to warn you that no good ever comes of anything I try to do. The best of my intentions lead only to disaster."

She laughed again. "I think that's perfectly splendid," she said. "What have I got to lose?"

❧ 9 ❧

I WONDER if she knows what she's got to lose, Montgomery thought, as he took a clean shirt from the drawer and began to undo the buttons. I wonder if she knows what's working against her.

For perhaps the twentieth time since he had had the Beckers to his would-be birthday party, he thought back over the conversation, and tried to discover the reason for Mrs. Becker's violent hatred of Anne. He had thought the subject was dropped when he left the Beckers' apartment that afternoon, but they had been in his room no more than ten minutes when Martha Becker had looked at her husband and said, "You remember the Gundekers, used to live next door?"

"Of course," said Becker. "Why not?"

"I was telling Mr. Mountkemmerich about them this afternoon," she said. "Such a lovely couple. Not like what we got across there now."

Becker shrugged. "To me, she looks like a nice girl," he said, and glanced apologetically at Montgomery.

"Nice?" said Martha. "*Nice?* And so what is it you think is nice about her, if it's not too personal?"

Becker shrugged again, and Montgomery said, "As a matter of fact, from what I've seen of—"

"I'll tell you something," Martha cut in. "I'll tell you what I'm going to do. The next time the landlord comes around asking for more money, I'm going to tell him what he's got living next door to us, and I'm going to tell him he's not going to get another nickel until she's thrown out. *Then* we'll see what happens!"

"Now, Martha," Becker began, but she kept on without hearing him.

"And something else I'm going to do, if just once there's anything goes on in that room, I call the police! Decent people don't have to put up with that kind of trash, and just once she gets carrying on, it's the cops are going to be on her, and *then* we'll see!"

"Well, actually, I don't think there's much—" Montgomery began, just as Becker said, "Look, Martha," but she continued as though she were addressing an audience instead of just two men.

"When it gets that decent people got to put up with that kind of thing, then a stop has got to come to it! And if nobody else is going to do it, then I'm going to do it. That's all I got to say." She raised her glass, and looked at Montgomery. "*Alle Glück*," she said, and took a sip. "I'm sorry I should be talking things like this on your birthday."

Montgomery had never been able to figure out the basis of her rage, because it was too violent to be impersonal, and yet she didn't know Anne personally. It was more than just a sense of outraged decency; it was as though some deep, private wound had been inflicted on her, but from what little he knew, this was impossible. And there was nothing in particular he could warn Anne about; she was aware that Mrs. Becker disliked her, and beyond that it would only upset her to go into detail.

He finished buttoning his shirt, selected a tie, and tied it twice before getting the knot he wanted. Well, maybe this will be good for her, he thought. Maybe a night on the town will take her mind off herself for a little while, and let her have some fun.

They went to the saloon across from the newspaper. There were not many people at the bar, and only a couple of them looked up as Montgomery and Anne came in. Montgomery nodded and greeted them casually as he led her into the back room to a table, and he was aware that his appearance with a young and pregnant woman was going to cause considerable speculation among his friends. He didn't care; in fact, he almost relished the thought of the indirect questions that would be put to him later, and the elaborate attempts to make it appear that nobody had noticed or was interested. There was a strict feeling at the saloon that every man's business was his own, and that it was his own business whom he brought there and for whatever reason, but men who stand at bars have nothing to do except think and talk, and if anything unusual swims into their consciousness they will snap at it like big-mouthed bass. As Montgomery and Anne went past the bar, one man was saying, "Who was Nokomis? 'Daughter of the *moon* Nokomis'! I suggest that Nokomis was the biggest literary hoax since—" He paused when he saw Anne, and someone else said, "If there were more people like Longfellow writing today, there'd be less trouble in the world." Then the subject of Longfellow was dropped, and someone said something in a lowered voice.

They sat at a table in the back room, where it was quiet but from where they could still see out to the bar, and when a waiter came up to them Montgomery said to Anne, "What would you like to drink? They have everything here from buttermilk to akvavit."

"I really don't think I want anything," she replied. "I seem kind of to have lost the taste for it."

"That's a depressing thought." Turning to the waiter, Montgomery said, "I'll have a Scotch, please, Otto. And let's have a couple of menus." The waiter disappeared, and Montgomery said to Anne, "This isn't going to be much fun for you, I'm afraid. This isn't the place for someone who's not drinking."

"Don't be silly," she said. "Right now, this looks to me like the most wonderful restaurant in the world."

"Just hold that thought," he said. "You may need it to reassure yourself later on."

"May I ask you something?" she said.

"Of course. What do you want to know?"

"Why do you always apologize for things in advance?"

"Good God, I hadn't thought about it. Do I?"

She nodded. "Two or three times, now, I've heard you kind of down-beat yourself, and for no real reason. I just wondered. Have you had some terrible tragedies happen to you, or something?"

He looked out at the bar and thought, and he was almost smiling. "No, I guess not that bad," he said at last. "Nothing really so terrible."

"I'm sorry if I was impertinent. Maybe I shouldn't have asked, but I just wondered."

"No. I'm glad you did." The waiter brought his drink, and he took the glass and raised it to her. "Cheers," he said, and she smiled and nodded. He took a sip. "I'm glad you did," he repeated. "I imagine it must get kind of tiresome, after a while."

"No, that's not what I meant. It doesn't get tiresome in the least. It's just that it made me wonder, that's all."

"Well, I won't do it any more, I promise."

O'Leary, one of the men who had been on the press cutter, came in from the bar. He had a drink in one hand and a cigarette was clamped between his teeth, and he reached with his free hand into an inside pocket as he came toward the table. He brought out an envelope, and laid it in front of

Montgomery. "Here," he said. "Don't ever say I don't pay my debts."

Montgomery opened the envelope, and saw five ten-dollar bills. "What's this?" he asked.

"You mean you don't remember?" O'Leary wheezed, sending out a shower of sparks from his cigarette. "You mean you've forgot the bet we made?"

"Oh, yes, now I remember. Dr. Bundeswasser." Montgomery laughed. "I guess I did forget it there for a minute. Well, thanks, pal—thanks a lot."

"How do you like that?" O'Leary said, to Anne. "Here I owe him a fifty-dollar bet and he doesn't even remember it! I could have saved myself a half a yard and nobody would have known the difference!" He laughed, and then coughed until his face turned red and mottled.

"Well, thanks very much," Montgomery said. "It was darned decent of you." He laughed again, nervously. "You ought to get something for that cough, there, son."

O'Leary straightened up and shook his head. "Too late," he whispered. "Too late."

"The least I can do is buy you a drink," said Montgomery. "Go tell Leo I said to make you a double. Tell him to put it on my tab."

O'Leary drifted off, still choking slightly, and Montgomery turned to Anne. "I'm sorry about that," he said, in a low voice. "If he'd sat down, we'd never have gotten rid of him. He's a nice enough guy but a little on the coarse side. And he wanted to be introduced to you, which would have given him an excuse to sit down."

"In a way, it's kind of flattering," she said. "When a girl has so obviously been spoken for, to have *anybody* want to meet her. It's the biggest boost my ego has had in a long time."

He laughed. "He's cold comfort to anybody's ego. You can do a lot better than that, I promise you."

124

"Well, the next time someone wants to sit down, you let him. This is the kind of encouragement I need."

"I think I'd better be the judge of who sits down and who doesn't, if it's all the same to you."

"But what can we lose? Nobody's certainly going to *kidnap* me, or anything. What's the worst that can happen?"

"The worst that can happen is that the man approaching us right now should sit down," he said quietly. "Stick with me, and forgive me if I'm rude."

A short man with a large black moustache came up to the table, carrying a Manhattan cocktail. "Ah, there, Arthur," he said, and cleared his throat.

Montgomery pretended not to have seen him, and he looked up as though startled. "Oh—hi," he said, and then turned back to Anne. "Well, what I was trying to say was that—" he began, but the man continued talking.

"I have a story that I think might amuse you," he said, and pulled a chair from an adjoining table. "May I sit down?" he asked, as he sat in the chair.

"Well, just for a second," Montgomery said. "We're expecting another couple."

"This won't take a moment," said the man. "But I know it will amuse you."

"It better had," Montgomery said pleasantly. "I was right in the middle of a sentence."

"Quite so," said the man. "Quite so. I apologize." He raised his glass. "Your health," he said, and took a sip. "And to the lady's," he added, looking at Anne over his glass.

"All right," said Montgomery. "What is this that's going to amuse me?"

"Arthur, do you remember several years ago I was going to buy a farm in Mount Kisco, only I didn't because the water rights hadn't been cleared?"

"No," said Montgomery.

The man took a sip of his Manhattan. "You must," he said.

"I distinctly remember telling you, one night in here with George Kessler, Harry Marlin, and some other chap. I'll think of his name in a minute. A tall bloke, on the blond side."

"Charles A. Lindbergh?" Montgomery asked.

"No, no. It was more like Beach, or Bache, or—Bart. That's it. Stewart Bart. It was the night it was raining so hard the ceiling leaked, and a mouse ran into the ship model to get dry." He looked at a ship model up over the door, and chuckled. "What ever became of him?" he asked.

"Who?" said Montgomery. "The mouse?"

"Of course not. Stewart Bart. I haven't seen him since."

"Neither have I."

"Oh, well. No matter." He took another sip of his Manhattan. "Did I ever tell you about the time when I was in the Guards, and the Colonel's horse went lame?"

"Look, old boy," said Montgomery. "The reason for this visit was to tell me something amusing about the Mount Kisco farm you didn't buy. Remember?"

"Oh, yes. Quite." The man touched his lips to his Manhattan. "I never did buy the bloody thing. Couldn't get the water rights cleared."

"I know," said Montgomery. "Then what?"

There was a short silence. "Not a great deal, come to think of it," the man said. "Just that I dreamed about it the other night. Dreamed the rights were all cleared up and I bought the whole shebang—pond, stream, and all. Most extraordinary dream. All in color. I'm told very few people dream in color." He put his glass to his lips, held it there, then took it away. "Speaking of color, there was one time when I was in the Guards—full-dress parade and all—"

"Look—I'm very sorry," Montgomery cut in, "but the young lady and I have something rather personal to talk about. Would you excuse us?"

"Certainly," said the man. "Go right ahead." He lifted his Manhattan and looked deep into the glass.

"No, I mean just the two of us. Alone at the table. The two of us, alone. Get it?"

"Oh, I see," said the man. "Yes, of course." He stood up. "I hope I wasn't intruding."

"That's perfectly all right," said Montgomery. "I was glad to hear about the farm."

"I thought you would be," said the man, and he turned and wandered back into the bar.

Montgomery took a deep breath. "I hate to be rude like that," he said. "But it's the only way to get rid of him. If you're standing at the bar, you can always move away, but if you're at a table he's got you trapped."

"Is there anyone here you *do* like?" Anne asked.

He laughed. "Yes," he said. "I guess I like most of them. I think I'm probably nervous about the bores because I don't want them to inflict themselves on you. That's always the way when you bring someone here for the first time; the nice guys don't show up, and it's only the head-crushers that you meet."

"Don't start apologizing again," she said. "I'm having a fine time."

"Of course, Saturday nights in the summer are always slow. Most of the people who can get out of town are already gone. Saturday night in the winter or fall is when you ought to be here—then it's really quite nice."

"I said stop apologizing!"

"I'm sorry. I just didn't want you to expect too much." He looked around for a waiter. "Let's order dinner, and I'll have another drink while it's coming—are you *sure* there isn't something you'd like? Not even a half a glass of sherry, or something?"

"No, thank you," she said, laughing. "I really am having a wonderful time."

"Well, I'll bring you here some night next winter, and then you'll really see something."

"Some night next winter, my dear sir, I am not going to be able to go out unless I have a baby sitter. Had you forgotten that?"

"Uh. Yes, I had. Well, maybe you can get your friend Lapham to sit for you. That ought to be right up his alley."

"Don't be mean. He's been very nice to me."

"Well, I'm glad to hear it. By the way, what are you going to do about sitters or whatever when you're at work? Have you got anyone lined up to do that?"

Her eyes clouded, and she shook her head. "No," she said. "I haven't. I haven't the faintest idea what I'm going to do about that."

There was a short and awkward pause. "I'm sorry I brought it up," he said. "The idea tonight was to amuse you, and not worry you. Something is bound to turn up, one way or another."

She smiled. "Oh, certainly," she said. "Something is bound to turn up. Everybody keeps telling me so."

The waiter came with their menus and a fresh drink for Montgomery, and they ordered their dinner. There were only two other couples eating in the back room, but out at the bar the number of customers had increased. They were not particularly noisy, but the decibel count was definitely higher than before, when only the more silent drinkers had been present. Twice, Montgomery was sure he heard Sam Ulm's voice, and he identified the voices of a few other friends, some of whom might be good company for Anne, and some of whom might not. It occurred to him that the main reason he had brought her to the saloon was that it was the only place where he could sign the check, and now O'Leary's fifty dollars made it possible for them to go anywhere they wanted, but he thought it might be a little late to move, considering the fact that they had already ordered their dinner. Just stop worrying, he told himself. She can probably handle herself a great deal better than you think. He took a sip of his drink, and looked at her out of the corner of his eye. She now seemed relaxed and content, and at the same time there was a dignity to her posture that gave her a faintly regal appearance. The thought crossed his mind that if he were twenty years younger, he could very easily fall in love with her. *And you can stop that line of thinking,* he told himself quickly. *You just keep your thoughts where they belong, and don't make any more of a fool of yourself than is absolutely necessary.*

From the bar, Sam Ulm spotted Montgomery, and he left the group he was with and started for the back room. Montgomery leaned his head closer to Anne. "The man coming toward us now," he said, "is named Sam Ulm, believe it or not. He's really a very nice guy, but he's usually in a rage, or depressed about something, so you've got to be prepared. He'll either be full of invective, or have some long tale of woe. After you get to know him, you don't listen too closely, and then he's a lot of fun."

Anne looked, and saw that Ulm was tall, and had a thin, pleasant face, and short-cut blond hair. "He doesn't look so depressed to me," she said. "What's his trouble?"

"I don't know. He takes things awfully seriously. He wants to be a writer, and I think he's kind of accident-prone."

As Ulm neared their table, his face broke into a broad smile. "Hey, Arthur!" he said. "Guess what!"

"What?" said Montgomery.

"I got a new job! I left the goddam paper—excuse me—I left the paper, and took a job on a magazine!"

"Wonderful!" said Montgomery. "When did this happen?"

"Today. I gave them my notice this afternoon, and I start work on the magazine Monday."

"Well, good for you! Let me buy you a drink. Anne, this is Sam Ulm—Anne Waters. Sit down."

"How do you do?" Ulm sat in the chair the other man had left, and looked at Anne. "I'm sorry to get into shop talk," he said. "But I'm still kind of excited about it."

"That's perfectly all right," she said. "Go right ahead."

Montgomery got the waiter, and ordered a drink for Ulm and another for himself. "What's the magazine?" he asked Ulm, when the waiter had left.

"It's a new one," Ulm replied. "Just starting up. I'm going to be feature editor, and do pieces on the side."

"That sounds marvellous."

"You ought to join us, too. I know damn well there's a job for you there."

"I'm afraid not, Sam. I'm where I belong."

Anne turned to Montgomery. "Why don't you try?" she asked. "Wouldn't you like to try something new?"

"When you get to be my age," he said, "you come to the conclusion that there is nothing new. You stick with what you know, and make the best of it."

"Don't be defeatist," she said. "That's just the same as apologizing in advance for something you haven't done."

He smiled and shook his head.

Ulm turned to Anne. "And you, Miss—Mrs.—"

"Anne," she said.

"Anne. Would *you* like a job on the magazine?"

"Oh, I don't do anything like that. I'm just a—a sort of secretary. In the advertising business."

"Well, what could be better? We need secretaries, and researchers, and checkers, and all sorts of people like that. We even need advertising people . . . or, so I'm told."

"You sound more like the personnel director than the feature editor," said Montgomery.

"Got to see that we get the right people," Ulm replied. "The quality of the staff is very important."

The waiter brought their drinks. "Do you want your dinner now, Mr. Montgomery?" he asked. "Or should I keep it on the fire?"

"Bring it now, please, Otto. I'm sure Mr. Ulm will excuse us if we eat."

"Tonight, I'll excuse anything," said Ulm. "Tonight, there's no telling *what* I may excuse." He looked at Anne. "Except your not coming to work for the magazine," he said. "That will neither be tolerated nor excused."

She laughed and felt her face turn hot. "Well, thank you," she said. "But I don't think I should be taking on any new jobs right now."

"We can wait," said Ulm, quietly. He raised his glass to Montgomery. "Here's to you, sir," he said. "And to everything you have given me. The fond parental guidance, the excruciatingly bad advice, the abominable example you have set, and the endless trouble I have got into in following your footsteps. To all this I drink."

"Thank you," said Montgomery, and he raised his glass.

"And I also drink to the rainbow I have reached at the end of this morass," said Ulm. "For without the morass the rainbow would not have seemed so beautiful, and for that, too, I can thank you."

Montgomery laughed. "I gather things are better at home, too," he said.

Ulm finished his drink in one big gulp, and set the glass down and grinned. "That is another story," he said. "A short and an unbelievably funny one. For the moment, I shall simply say that everybody is happy."

"Good," said Montgomery. "I'm glad to hear it."

Out at the bar, the noise level continued to increase. There were more people than there had been before, but they were also talking progressively louder, so that it seemed as though their numbers had quadrupled. At one end of the bar, three men were singing "I Never Knew I Could Love Anybody Honey Like I'm Loving You," in three distinctly separate keys, while next to them four men tried to tell different stories all at the same time. Two men in shirtsleeves huddled silently over their Martinis like eagles guarding their eggs, and they were being jostled by another pair who were demonstrating the no-windup pitch to a third man who didn't really care. The two bartenders, who earlier had been leaning against the back-bar while they polished the glassware, were now hustling back and forth, pouring drinks with practiced haste and sliding glasses along the wet bar surface.

A man detached himself from one of the groups and came into the back room. He was thin and bald, and he had horn-rimmed glasses that kept sliding down his long, pointed nose. He was trembling with rage. "That swine!" he said, in a choked voice. "Oh, that miserable swine!"

"Sit down," said Montgomery. "Miss Waters—Mr. Shaw. What swine, Benny?"

"How do you do," Shaw said, in a normal voice, to Anne. Then he turned to Montgomery, and his voice clouded with anger. "That miserable, no-good, churlish boor," he said. "You know who I mean." He pushed his glasses back up his nose.

"Have a drink," said Montgomery. "You sound as though you're talking about Reprehensible Smith."

"Let me buy this," said Shaw, and to the waiter who had just brought the food he said, "Otto, let's have a round here, on my check." To Montgomery he snarled, "Yes, that's who I mean. Roger F. Reprehensible Smith, the biggest son of a bitch—excuse me—in the United States, Canada, and the Northern Territories. He ought to be hung, drawn, and quartered."

"What's he done now?" Montgomery asked.

Shaw started in on an involved denunciation, and Ulm leaned over to Anne. "I think I ought to explain," he said, in a low voice. "Benny, here, is a Democrat, and Reprehensible is one of those people who thought Taft was a little too far to the left. And I don't mean Bob—I mean William Howard Taft."

"Oh," said Anne. "Is that how he got his name?"

"No," Ulm replied. "He's just generally reprehensible. Picks people's change up off the bar, and things like that."

She laughed. "I shouldn't think he'd be very popular," she said.

"He isn't. But he kind of revels in his unpopularity. I guess he figures it makes him stand out." Ulm watched her as she started to eat her dinner, and after a couple of minutes he said, "Incidentally, I think Arthur has told me about you."

She put down her fork, and looked at him. "Oh?" she said. "What did he say?" She glanced briefly at Montgomery, who was talking with Shaw, then she looked back at Ulm.

"He didn't say anything in particular," Ulm said, quickly. "He just said there was a girl who lived near him, and he thought she ought to meet some people. I gather you're new in town, or something."

"How do you know I'm the one he was talking about?" she asked.

Ulm swallowed. "He just described you, that's all. The hair, and the eyes, and—well, I haven't seen you with him before, so I just kind of assumed you're the one."

She softened, and smiled, then looked back at Montgomery. "That was very nice of him," she said.

A man came past the table and stopped for a moment. He was middle-aged and small, and his collar seemed too big for his neck, but he carried his cigar with an air of assurance that was almost jaunty. Shaw looked up at him. "Don't come near me, you traitor," Shaw snarled.

"Benny, there was nothing I could do," the man said, with a slight trace of a Virginia accent. "I couldn't knee the man in the groin just because he came in between us."

"Nobody should allow Reprehensible Smith to stand next to him at any time or under any circumstances," Shaw said. "And when he elbows his way between two people who are talking, then they both ought to hit him. Sit down and have a drink."

The man sat down, and Montgomery introduced him to Anne as Prescott Rawlings. He bowed to her, and held his cigar far to one side as he said, "I'm very happy to make your acquaintance, Ma'm." Then he looked at Shaw. "Let me buy this round," he said. "It's my turn."

"Like hell it is," said Shaw. "I've already ordered it."

"Then let's play for it," said Rawlings. "That's the only sporting thing to do. Are we all in it?" The men at the table nodded, and reached silently for the match box in the center. Rawlings looked at Anne. "I shall be responsible for the young lady's share," he said.

"She's not drinking," said Montgomery. "There's just the four of us."

"Very well, then," said Rawlings, and he put his hands behind his back. "I challenged, so I come out. Possible twelve. . . ." He looked at the ceiling, squinting through his cigar smoke, and when all the men had their hands behind their backs, he said, "Ready?" and they all put their right fists on the table. "Three," said Rawlings.

In turn, the men guessed the total number of matches held by all. When the last man had guessed, they opened their fists, and counted. The total was five, which had been Ulm's guess, and he put his matches on the table and talked to Anne while the others continued the game. It seemed to Anne that the players were in actual physical pain as they made their guesses; they closed their eyes, gritted their teeth, tossed their heads, and then slammed their fists on the table as though challenging the forces of the psychic world to prove them wrong. Montgomery was the next one to guess correctly, and he dropped out, and there developed a fight to the finish between Shaw and Rawlings, which Shaw finally won. Rawlings broke his matches, put them in the ash tray, and looked around for the waiter.

"Otto," he said. "That was my pleasure. And bring us another round immediately." He selected three new matches, put them behind his back, and said, "I demand revenge. This will be a trilogy, the second game to be for a buck and a drink. All right?"

The men nodded and reached for their matches, and the game resumed.

The noise at the bar gradually began to assume riot proportions. The singing became louder and more disorganized;

the two men who had been demonstrating the no-windup pitch turned from baseball to wrestling, and flattened the third man to whom they were demonstrating the holds; at the far end of the bar, a woman screamed for no reason that anyone was ever able to ascertain, but it was a scream that made the glassware rattle; one man went to the telephone booth, and after three unsuccessful attempts to dial a number he tore the instrument out of the wall; and another man inverted the cheese crock and was doing a passable imitation of a bongo drum until it slipped off the bar and crushed his foot. At the table in the back room, the match game continued, revenge after revenge and trilogy after trilogy. A great deal of money changed hands, and a great deal of liquor was consumed, but it was almost sepulchral in its restraint compared to what was going on at the bar. Once, when the waiter had brought a new round, Montgomery asked him what was going on out there, and the waiter sighed and shrugged.

"It's the full moon," he said. "Every time we get a full moon it's like this."

"True," said Montgomery. "I'd forgotten. I thought it was going to be quiet tonight." He slammed his fist on the table. "Three!" he said.

From apparently nowhere, the man with the black moustache appeared carrying a Manhattan cocktail, and stood behind Rawlings. "Ah, there, gentlemen," he said. "May I join you?"

"No," said Shaw, and the man sipped his Manhattan and moved away.

Then, almost imperceptibly, the noise out at the bar began to die down. There was still singing, and there was still scuffling and shouting, but it had a thinner quality to it, as though the people's hearts weren't really in it any more. Finally, when Montgomery looked up from a hand of matches, he saw that the lights in the bar had been turned out. One man was huddled at the far end of the bar, and one bartender was talking to him, and their forms were lit from below by the glow of the light in the bar sink. They were just blurs of faint light in the darkness, and they were talking in voices too low for him to hear. In a dim corner of the back room the waiter sat, asleep.

"Hey," said Montgomery. "I think they want us to leave."

"One more round," said Rawlings, through the stump of his cigar. "One more trilogy." He put his hands behind his back.

"Look at the drinks we've got here," said Montgomery, indicating the rows of untouched glasses on the table. "We've got to finish these before we can play for any more. We've been playing faster than we've been drinking."

"That's a fine state of affairs," said Rawlings, and he picked up one of the glasses and drank it empty.

"Do you remember 'The Beach at Bimini Bay'?" asked Montgomery. "You remember how it goes?"

"Hell, yes," said Rawlings, and he and Montgomery sang the song. Then they sang "An Orange Grove in California," "I'm Afraid to Come Home in the Dark," "Rio Rita," "I Was Born in Virginia," and a few more. They sang softly, so as not to wake the sleeping waiter, and pretty soon all the glasses on the table were empty.

Montgomery looked at Anne. She was talking with Ulm, and seemed not to be noticing anything that was going on around her. I guess I didn't need to worry about her, he thought. I guess she can take care of herself when she has to. And Ulm, he noticed, was oblivious to everything that was going on around him.

They played one more round of matches, this time just for money, and then they woke the waiter and settled their various bills. There was one taxicab waiting outside, and Rawlings insisted that Montgomery and Anne take it. Montgomery offered to drop any of them off where they lived, but they all declined, so after everybody had said good night Montgomery and Anne got into the cab.

"Home, Arthur?" the driver asked.

"I'll tell you in a minute," Montgomery replied. He turned to Anne. "How do you feel?" he asked.

"I feel absolutely wonderful," she said. "I haven't felt so well in years and years and years."

"Would you like to see something?"

"Anything you say. Whatever you want to do, I'll do it."

Montgomery leaned forward. "Let's go up to Grant's Tomb, Shorty," he said to the driver. To Anne, he said, "It's a little sad, but I also think it's very beautiful."

"What is it?" she asked.

"You'll see. Just wait."

The moon was high and cold in the western sky, and the trees along Riverside Drive made a soft rustling noise as the cab drove beneath them. At Grant's Tomb, they could see out across the Hudson River to the dark Palisades on the Jersey shore, and the river itself was like a mirror of tiny lights in the darkness. Montgomery and Anne got out of the cab, and he took her hand and led her down the bank off the roadway. In the bushes on the side of the bank he leaned down, then took out a cigarette lighter and lit it.

"Look at that," he said.

In the flickering glow from his lighter, she saw a small stone, on which she could barely make out the inscription:

Erected to the Memory of an Amiable Child

St. Claire Pollock
Died 15 July 1797
In the Fifth Year of His Age

"How about that?" Montgomery said, after a moment. "Did you ever see anything like that?"

"No," she said softly. "Never."

They looked at the stone for a minute or so in silence, and then Montgomery snapped off the lighter and straightened up. "That's all," he said, and he took her hand to help her back up the bank. "Just an amiable child, that's all I wanted to show you."

They got in the cab, and the driver started back downtown. For a long time they were quiet, and then Montgomery said, "How can they think of words like that? What kind of people can get that kind of beauty into just one simple word?" She didn't say anything, and he put his head back and closed his eyes. Then his head rolled over onto her shoulder, and his whole frame was shaken by a deep and quivering sadness. He was like a balloon slowly collapsing, and although he made no coherent sound, there was sadness in every part of his body. After a little while, she put one hand up, and ran her fingers along his forehead. Then, pressing harder, she rubbed his temple, and back along the side of his head.

"There, now," she whispered. "There, now." She repeated it, softly and soothingly, until she was sure that he was fast asleep.

❧ 10 ❧

As ERNEST BECKER came out of the apartment and started down the street, he noticed that the box under Anne's window was still unpainted. Every time he thought about it, he felt a shame that made him wince, and his mind tried to shut out the details of what he had done. Or, more accurately, of what he had not done, because after Martha had kept him from painting the box, he had been so embarrassed that he had not wanted to look at Anne and had not even tried to invent an excuse or an explanation. He had simply tried to block her out of his mind. But this had been impossible, partly because the box was always there to remind him, and partly because of the occasional tirades that Martha would get into on the subject of Anne. At such times, he would retreat deep into himself and plan ways in which he might be able to help Anne without Martha's knowing about it, but he knew that nothing would ever come of these plans; they were small attempts to ease his conscience, at times when he couldn't avoid being reminded of her.

It was early morning, and the sun was not yet high enough to heat the pavements. The air was clear, and Becker could almost detect a feeling of impending autumn, but he knew that in another hour there would be no mistaking the fact that it was still summer. He could see in the open windows along the street, and occasionally see dim figures moving about in the darkness inside, like pale animals in a forest. He felt good just to be outside, and he thought back to the times when, as a boy, he had walked through the woods and fields near his home in Wisconsin. He remembered the cold, yellow, November sunsets, seen through the purple lacework of bare trees; he remembered the silent magic of the first snow, and the feathery feeling of the icy flakes on his out-stretched tongue; and he remembered the rushing, bubbling water of the streams in early spring, when the brittle blades of ice still clung to the black rocks, and porous, dirty chunks of snow lay in the hollows. He had always preferred the cooler seasons; to him, summer was a listless, prickly time, when nothing was really worth doing, and he only felt well —really well, that is—when he had something to occupy his mind. His work as an accountant was the basis, the foundation upon which he could build more creative projects, and he felt that he could put up with any amount of physical hardship provided he always kept his mind supple and in use.

He had left the farm in Wisconsin and come to New York when he was fifteen years old, intending to study to become an engineer. He stayed with an uncle in Brooklyn and went to a vocational high school, but his money ran out before he got to college, and he went to work in a grocery store in order to earn his keep. It was there that he met Martha, who had come over with her parents from Breslau a few years before, and who still felt lost and alone in the new country. The flood of immigrants at that time had had a depressing effect on living conditions almost everywhere in the city, and the lonely newcomers gravitated toward each other and clung together like children in a storm.

As he walked toward his bus stop, Becker thought about

140

Martha and her violent bursts of bitterness, and he wondered what had happened over the years to bring this out in her. Certainly things were better now than they had been in the early days of their marriage, and yet she had borne up better under real suffering than she seemed to be doing now. He could remember only once, in their comparative youth, when she had come even close to having hysterics, and that had been when, with the entry of this country in the First World War, he had tried to enlist. Then she had screamed and shouted and cried, and called him a traitor and a brother-killer and a lot of other things, but that had been a lot more understandable than some of her present-day tirades. And as it turned out, she could have saved herself the energy, because he was rejected for recurrent asthma. But even later, when the anti-German feeling was so strong that there were only certain places where she could buy their food, she was not particularly bitter. And when she had a miscarriage, followed by an operation that left her barren, she had been withdrawn and subdued for several months, but she had never complained, nor had she shown much emotion. She simply sat for long hours, staring into space and saying nothing. And then, one day, she got up from her chair and went on about her housework as though nothing had happened. In her spare time, she started work on a knitted scarf for Becker to wear during the winter, and when the scarf was finished she knitted him a sweater, then some socks, and then a pair of mittens. She only stopped knitting when a doctor ventured the opinion that all the wool was acting as an irritant for Becker's asthma.

Thinking back, Becker tried to remember when her emotional outbursts had started, and the first crisis that he could recall—after the wartime one—was when they were in their middle thirties, and she had accused him of having an affair with a woman in his office. The accusation was preposterous; Becker had conditioned himself to accept sex as a sometime thing at the very best, but Martha seized onto the idea and would not let it go. When he tried to prove his fidelity to her the result was a disaster that, as far as she was concerned, confirmed her suspicions. It was several years before he was allowed to come near her again.

Maybe it's change of life, he thought, as he got on the bus and took a seat. Maybe that's what's doing it. Then he thought of her operation, and wondered if that would have any effect on change of life, and then he gave up trying to understand what the trouble was. Whatever it is, she's got it, he thought, and nothing I can do is going to change it. All I can do is just ride along and make the best of it.

When he got to his office, he turned on the lights, hung his jacket in a closet, and rolled up the cuffs of his sleeves. Then he took the pencils from a jar on his desk, sharpened each one to a perfect, needle point, and replaced them in the jar. He adjusted the air-conditioning unit, picked up a paper clip that had fallen to the floor, and then he sat down at his desk. He had been at work for fifteen minutes before the next person arrived.

At a little after eleven, an office boy came up and stood beside Becker's desk. "Mr. McFarlane would like to see you," he said.

Becker looked at him, uncomprehending. "Who?" he said.

"Mr. McFarlane," said the boy. "In Personnel."

"Oh," said Becker. "All right. Thank you." The boy disappeared, and Becker sat for a moment, trying to think. Then, with a numbness in his brain that was like a trance, he rolled down his sleeves, buttoned each cuff carefully, and stood up. He went to the closet and put on his jacket, tightened the knot in his tie, ran his hands back across his hair, and went out of the room, with the definite feeling that he was walking under water.

Harold McFarlane, the personnel director, was a man of about forty-five, round-faced and with rimless glasses. He was deeply tanned, but he still managed to have a well-scrubbed look, and the moons on his fingernails were white and shining. With him, when Becker came into the room, was Chester Talbot, the manager of the department in which Becker worked, and he was tall and thin and had a bald head that was freckled from the sun. Both men rose, and McFarlane came toward Becker with his hand outstretched.

"Well, Mr. Becker!" he said. "It's good to see you!"

Becker muttered something as they shook hands, and he looked at Talbot, who smiled at him.

"Sit down," said McFarlane, drawing a chair near his desk. "Make yourself comfortable." All three men sat, and McFarlane pushed a cigarette box toward Becker. "Smoke?" he asked.

Becker shook his head. "No, thank you," he said. McFarlane took a cigarette, and while he was lighting it, Becker studied the desk. There was a folder on it, but he could not see what it contained; and there was a small square box, made of imitation leather, with a thin gold line around the top. There was a gold letter opener, an ash tray, a telephone, and an intercom, and that was all. The desk was large and highly polished, and it glistened in the cold glare of the overhead fluorescent light.

McFarlane inhaled deeply from the cigarette, then rested it in the ash tray. "Well, now," he said, and opened the folder. "You had a birthday last week, didn't you?"

"Yes, sir," said Becker dully.

"Your sixty-fifth, I believe, if my subtraction is correct," McFarlane went on, smiling. "Is that right?"

Becker nodded and said nothing.

"By God, I hope I look as well as you do when I'm sixty-five," McFarlane said. He turned to Talbot. "How about that, Chet?" he said. "Do you expect to be in as good shape as Mr. Becker, here, when you're sixty-five?"

"You mean *if* I'm sixty-five," Talbot replied, and both men laughed.

"Seriously, though," McFarlane said to Becker, "I suppose you know what I'm leading up to." He took up the letter opener, held it in both hands, and rested his chin in the middle. "The company has a policy of compulsory retirement at sixty-five, and although in many cases the people could go on doing useful work for several more years, we've found that it's best not to make any exceptions. And, in your case, I should think you'd feel you've deserved a little rest. You've been with us—how long is it?" He looked in the folder again. "Thirty-three years?"

"Thirty-four, next February," Becker said. "Next February twelfth."

"That's a very impressive record," said McFarlane. "A very impressive record indeed." He leaned forward and tapped the point of the letter opener gently on the desk. "And I don't want you to think we're not grateful." Then, sitting back again, he ticked the ends of his fingers with the opener and went on, "First off, we have, as you know, a retirement plan, whereby the company matches whatever has been taken from your salary over the years. This, in your case, will come to quite a tidy little sum. Then, secondly, we have a bonus for all those who have been with the company for twenty-five years or more, and, again, I think you'll find that you will not have fared too badly. In fact, you should be able to continue on with no—ah—curtailment of your standard of living. Thirdly, the company will provide you with free advice and counsel if you care to invest any of your money in securities or the like, to the end that it will work for you and provide you with an income, however large or small depending on how much you invest. This, of course, is completely optional." He paused, and looked at the leather box on his desk. "And now," he went on, picking up the box, "there is a little something extra here—something that says what I cannot. I hope that, when you look at this over the years—and I'm sure there will be many, many more of them—that when you look at it, you will remember the people here with as much affection and pleasure as they will be remembering you." He leaned forward, and handed the box to Becker.

144

Becker took the box and held it in his hand for a moment before opening it. Then he lifted the top, and inside, nestling on a square of wrinkled white silk, was a thin, gold pocket watch. It gleamed in the light, and Becker stared at it in silence.

"Turn it over," McFarlane said.

Becker turned the watch over, and on the back, inscribed in fine italic letters, was his name, the name of the company, and the dates he had worked there. He closed the box, and looked at McFarlane. "I'm—I—I mean—" he stammered, and stopped. "Thank you," he said.

McFarlane smiled. "It's *we* who should be thanking *you*," he said. "And that's the only way we can do it." He stood up, and Talbot rose with him.

Mechanically, Becker rose from his chair. He put the box in his pocket. "When does this begin?" he asked. "I mean—when am I through?"

McFarlane spread his hands and smiled. "Right now," he said. "Whenever you want. You're a free man." He laughed, and reached out his hand. "Good luck," he said. "And drop by and see us any time you want to. Keep us posted on what you're doing."

Becker shook his hand, and then Talbot and he shook hands, and Talbot wished him luck and told him to keep in touch. Then he was out in the corridor and walking toward the stairs that led to his office on the floor below.

When he got outside, the noonday sun hit him with a blast that made him perspire behind the knees, and he walked through the hurrying crowds without knowing or caring where he was going. Habit took him to the restaurant where he always had lunch, a dim, quiet place with booths on one side and a counter on the other, and he sat in a booth for a while and looked at the menu that he could have recited from memory, but nothing appealed to him. The waitress bustled up, took out her pad, and smiled at him.

"The salmon in aspic?" she said, writing it down.

Becker shook his head. "No," he said. "Not today." He put the menu down. "As a matter of fact, I don't think I'll have anything today," he said, and got up. "I'm sorry."

"Do you feel all right?" the waitress asked.

"Yes. Yes. I'm just not hungry, that's all." He started for the door.

"Maybe it's the heat," she said. "The heat can do that to you sometimes."

"I guess that's it. That's probably what it is."

"Well, feel better, now. I'll see you tomorrow."

"Yes. Tomorrow. Good-by."

"'Bye now." She wiped the top of the table, and Becker went slowly out into the brightness of the street.

When he got back to the apartment, Martha had just finished lunch. She was putting the remnants of the salami and potato salad back in the refrigerator as he walked into the room, and she turned and looked at him suspiciously. "What's the matter?" she asked. "You sick?"

He shook his head, and sat down. "No," he said. "I'm fine."

"So you're fine, so what are you doing home?" Martha demanded. "You've been fired, maybe, is that the reason?" She came slowly toward him, her eyes wide.

"No, I'm not fired," Becker replied quietly. "I've been retired."

"You've been *what?*"

"They say I'm too old to work. So I'm retired."

"You don't *work* any more?"

Becker shook his head.

"So now what happens?" she said. "So now from where do we get money? Is it that *I* got to go out and make money, too, with all the other things I got to do? I got to go out and make money, while you sit around the house and be retired? Is that what it is?"

Wearily, Becker shook his head. "No," he said. "You don't

have to make money. I'll get enough so we can get along all right. You don't have to worry about that."

Martha was quiet for a moment. "So you're just going to be sitting around the house now, is that it?" she said. "So now I'm going to have to clean up around you and make lunch for you and do all those things for you, as though I don't have enough else to do. Is that what's going to happen?"

He looked at her, and for some reason his voice sounded almost tender. "No," he said. "You won't have to worry about that, either. You won't have to worry about a thing."

Martha turned away, and went back to the kitchen. "So *that* day should come," she said. "The day I don't have to worry is the day they take me away in my coffin. They should have retirement plans for *women*, that's what they should have. *I* should be so lucky *I* should be retired." She laughed shortly, and turned on the water in the sink.

The next day, Becker got up at his usual hour, and went outside and smelled the familiar cool of early morning. But instead of walking to the bus stop, he went in the other direction, toward the East River, and he leaned against the parapet and looked at the water. The tide had a hypnotic effect on him, and he stood for almost an hour with his mind a complete blank. Then the sun became too warm for comfort, and he moved over to a bench in the shade of a building, and sat down. His stomach rumbled, and he realized that he had had no breakfast—and, for that matter, he had not had very much dinner the night before. It occurred to him that it must be almost time for lunch, and he looked at his watch. It was eight minutes past ten. He got up, and walked slowly down the shady side of the street. After a long time, he looked at his watch again, and it was ten-thirty-two. I've got to stop looking at my watch, he told himself. If I keep that up, I'll go crazy within a week.

All at once, he was reminded of the gold watch back at

147

the apartment, still resting in the box in which it had been given to him. I forgot to wind it this morning, he thought. I wonder if it's run down by now. I guess that will depend on who was the last one to wind it, and when. McFarlane probably wound it, when the two of them were waiting for me to come into the office. He probably took it out of the case, and said to Talbot, "I guess the least we can do is wind the old boy's watch for him," and then he probably wound it and set it according to his watch. Well, that wasn't quite twenty-four hours ago, so I guess it hasn't run down quite yet. But I'll have to have a system for winding it; do it every day at the same time, so that it'll get used to a regular cycle. Every living thing needs a routine it can live by, and a watch is as much a living thing as anything else. It has character, and temperament, and individuality; no two watches are exactly the same, just as no two living things are exactly the same, and it will act just like a living thing if you treat it right.

Another thing I ought to do is buy a chain for it, he thought. A chain, or a fob, or something. No, I guess fobs aren't used much any more; a chain would be the best. Well, what am I waiting for? Why don't I do it now?

Suddenly excited by the prospect of something to do, he took out his wallet to see how much money he had. There were eleven dollars in it, so he put it back in his pocket and hurried down the block.

The first jewelry store he came to had no gold watch chain for less than twenty-five dollars. Then he went to a men's clothing store, where there was a matched set of tie pin, collar bar, and watch chain for nine dollars and fifty cents, but the watch chain was thick and supple, like a snake, and had a large key ring the shape of a four-leaf clover attached to one end of it. Next, he went to a pawn shop, and although there was an abundance of watches there were no watch chains, so he walked slowly and without direction up one block and across the next looking in all the store windows he passed. There were butcher shops, and delicatessens, and electrical shops, and bars, and tailor's shops, and funeral parlors, and plumber's shops, and liquor stores, and pet shops, and laundromats, and antique shops, and more bars and grills, and every now and then a jeweler's shop or a pawn-broker. He stopped and looked carefully in all the jewelers' and pawn-brokers' windows, and finally in one, a jewelry store the size of a closet, he saw a key chain that appealed to him. He went inside and asked the price.

The jeweler, who was thin and wizened and the color of a mushroom, looked at Becker for an instant, then said, "Twelve dollars."

"I'm sorry," Becker said, and turned to leave.

"That's gold-filled," the jeweler said, quickly. "Anywhere else, it would cost you fifteen dollars."

"I'm sorry," Becker said, again. "I don't have that much money with me."

"You could put down a deposit, and I'll hold it for you."

"No, thank you. It's more than I want to spend." Becker opened the door.

"Ten dollars," said the jeweler.

Becker stopped, hesitated, then shook his head. "Thanks, anyway," he said.

"Seven-fifty," said the jeweler. "That's rock bottom, and I'm losing money on the deal."

Becker had no experience with this kind of bargaining, and didn't know within five dollars of how much the chain ought to cost, but he knew he would never get a better one for seven dollars and fifty cents. He came back into the store. "All right," he said. "For that, I can buy it."

Out on the street once more, with the tissue-paper package in his pocket, he felt a strange elation, as though he had done a full day's work. Without looking at his watch, he estimated that it must be the middle of the afternoon, and although he had told Martha not to expect him home for lunch, he felt that he ought to get a bite to eat somewhere. Then he thought it might spoil his appetite for supper, and he determined to wait. He was half-way down the block when the sirens started to moan, and he looked at his watch and saw that it was noon.

He stopped, stared at his watch, then shook it and put it to his ear. Even over the noise of the traffic, he could hear the hurried tick-tick-tick. Then, slowly, the thought of the endless afternoon ahead began to creep upon him. Where was he going to go? What was he going to do? The more he thought about it, the more the afternoon seemed like a flat, arid desert, empty except for heat waves and clanging noise that went on and on.

He wandered around until he came to a corner hot-dog stand, and he had a hot dog and a glass of some pallid fruit concoction. Then, a half block away, he saw the marquee of a movie theater, and more to get off the street than for any other reason, he bought a ticket, and went into the cold, musty darkness inside. He sat in a rear seat, and tried for a while to pay attention to what was happening on the screen. Then his eyelids began to grow heavy, and in a little while he was asleep.

The following day, he went over to the river again. This time, he stayed all morning, and around twelve-thirty he drifted back to the apartment, stunned with boredom and becoming nervous in his desire to find something to do. As he came down the block, he saw the unpainted box at Anne's window, and it seemed to leap out at him, growing in size until it was larger than the building itself. He looked at it, and he thought, and he looked at it some more, and he thought some more, and his footsteps slowed until he had come to a complete standstill. He stared at the box for almost a full minute, and then he took a deep breath, squared his shoulders, and walked briskly to a hardware store around the corner. The clerk came up to him and smiled.

"I want a paint brush," Becker said. "And I want a quart of outside paint, a nice dark green."

"Yes, sir," said the clerk. He took the paint from a shelf, and showed Becker an assortment of brushes, from which Becker selected one. "Will that be all, sir?" the clerk asked.

"That will be all for now," Becker replied. "Later, I may want a lot of other things, but for now, that will be all."

"Yes, sir," said the clerk, and he put the paint and the brush into a bag. "Thank you, sir, and come again."

"I will," said Becker, and he went out.

On his way back to the apartment, he thought about the window box, and wondered if there weren't some place where he could get a little earth to put in it. Anne's tulips had long since gone, but she had not replaced them with anything, and the thought came to Becker that if he could fill the box with earth, then seeds could be planted in it, and seasonal flowers could be grown just as in a regular garden. And he could put up the trellis, too, so that she could grow ivy in it all the year round. There must be a lot of things he could do to help make her place more cheerful; things he could build, even, like a cradle . . . but probably nobody used cradles nowadays. Still, it might make a nice present, if she hadn't already got something for the baby to sleep in. He remembered the cradle that his family had had on the farm, and in his mind's eye he reconstructed it, trying to estimate how much material he would need. By the time he got back to the apartment, his step was light and springy, and he was whistling a tune.

Now for the difficult part, he said to himself as he opened his front door. This is going to be unpleasant, but if I'm firm and calm, maybe I can get it over with quickly.

Martha was doing the laundry in the kitchen, and he put down the paint and brush and started to change into his work clothes. She watched him for a moment, and then said, "You can't paint in here; I'm busy in here."

"I'm not going to," he said, stepping into a pair of stained dungarees. "I'm going to paint the window box."

There was a short silence. "What window box?" she asked.

"The one across the way. The one I made for the girl."

"*What?*"

"The wood will rot if it isn't painted soon, so I'm going to paint it."

"Ernest Becker, are you gone crazy?"

"No, of course not."

"After all I said to you, after all I asked you to do, you mean to tell me you're going to go doing favors for that slut?"

"She's not a slut, and I'm going to paint her window box. I may do a lot of other things for her, too." He straightened up, and looked at Martha. "You might as well get used to it right now."

"She's a slut, she's a *Dirne*, she's a tramp!" Martha shouted. "I'll have her arrested—I'll have her thrown in jail!"

"You'll not do any of those things. And you'll make it a lot more pleasant for everybody if you just keep quiet."

"Don't you say that to me!" Martha screamed. "I'll say what I like! I'll call her a slut, I'll call her a—"

"Shut up!" Becker said, and Martha stopped. Her eyes and her mouth stayed wide open, and before she could catch her breath, Becker went on quietly, "The only thing you have against her is she's going to have a baby. You hate anyone who's going to have a baby, and the only reason you liked the Gundekers was that they had three babies die. I don't know why it should happen to you now, you should get so wild like this, but it's not good and it's not right and you got to stop. Believe me, you got to stop soon, or you'll be sick." He put a screwdriver in his pocket, picked up the paint and the brush, and went out of the apartment.

Slowly, Martha sank into a chair. "I'll get her out of here," she whispered. "I'll get her out of here, so help me God!" Then she put her face in her hands, and began to cry.

❧ 11 ❧

MONTGOMERY MUST HAVE PASSED the Tiny Totz store
several hundred times, but it never registered on his consciousness until this particular Monday. He had had lunch
at the saloon, and had decided that the most sensible and
thrifty thing to do would be to spend the afternoon in an air-
cooled movie theater on the East Side. As he crossed Fifth
Avenue, squinting against the glare of the sun, he saw the
pink-and-blue store front, with the name spelled in jumbled
letters on the window. Fascinated, he veered off and headed
for it, and narrowly missed being hit by a taxi that was turning onto the avenue. The driver shouted at him, but Montgomery paid no attention.

The store window was filled with baby clothes of all descriptions, as well as some round, furry toys that had a
curiously polished and impersonal look, and some bits of
apparatus that Montgomery had never seen before and the
function of which he could only barely guess. Here, he
thought, is what I've been looking for. Here is a place where
I can get a practical present for Anne—something she really
needs. I wonder why I never thought of this before. He lit a

cigarette, flipped the match away, and went into the store.

A saleswoman came toward him, smiling. She wore a blue dress with white starched collar and cuffs, and something about her made a whisking noise as she walked. "Good afternoon," she said. "May I help you?"

"Yes," said Montgomery. "I'd like to get something for a—well, I guess you'd say for a baby. For a small child, anyway."

"Yes, of course. How old is he?"

Montgomery hesitated. "I don't know that it's a he," he said. "I mean—it isn't born yet." He looked around for an ashtray, but saw none.

"Oh, yes!" said the saleswoman. "You mean you want a layette!"

Montgomery stared at her. "I beg your pardon?" he said. "What was that?"

"A layette," the woman repeated, her smile fading. "The clothes, toilet articles, bedding. All that."

"Well, I don't want to buy *all* of it," Montgomery replied. "I just wanted to get one thing, or maybe two. Just as a sort of present, in a way. A present for the mother. Well, really for the baby, but to give to the mother."

"Yes, I understand," said the saleswoman. "What was it you had in mind?" She was looking at Montgomery's cigarette, under which he had cupped one hand to keep the ash from falling.

"That's what I don't know," he said. "I thought maybe you might have an idea."

"Well, let me see," the woman said. "Would you like to get her a dozen crib sheets? Sheets always come in very handy."

"No, I don't think so. I think something maybe a little more personal."

"I see. Is this for a member of the family? I mean, is it a grandchild of yours?"

"It certainly is not. It's for a friend."

154

"Ah, then. Well, now." The woman looked around, and picked up a small, furry white sweater, so small that it seemed impossible it was meant for a human being. "These are always nice," she said, holding the little sleeves apart. "And of course when winter comes they're a necessity."

To Montgomery, there was something frightening about the size of the sweater, and he shook his head quickly. A hot ash fell into his hand, and he put it in his pocket. "Don't you have something personal?" he asked. "Like a—like a— I don't know. A sweater seems kind of run-of-the-mill."

"Well, it's hard to say what's personal and what isn't," the woman replied, briskly. "I mean, everything about a baby is personal, in one way or another, and unless—"

"Let's put it this way," Montgomery said. "What are the things a baby needs most? What are the things he can't get along without?"

The woman looked at him coldly. "Everything," she replied. "Clothes, bedding, toilet articles—"

"That's that layette again," Montgomery interrupted. "I don't want to buy a layette—I want to buy one single thing. One present, of a more or less personal nature. Now, what is the one single thing a baby needs most?"

"Diapers," snapped the woman.

"Oh, God," said Montgomery. "Do you have any toys?"

"Yes, of course. We have all sorts of toys." It was now clear that she would give him anything, just to get him out of the store.

"Let me see some toys." He looked back at the sweater, picked it up, and gave it to the woman quickly, as though it had tried to bite him. "I guess I'd better take that along, too," he said. "Just in case."

From the toy department, he selected a large, black-and-white panda. When it and the sweater had been packed in a shiny, beribboned box, he paid the woman thirteen dollars and seventy-three cents, and then hurried out of the store, perspiring freely. Rather than sit through a movie with the panda in his lap, he took it to the saloon and gave it to the bartender to keep for him. He was just leaving when Sam Ulm came in, and they got to playing matches with two other men, and by the time the match game was over it was too late to see the afternoon movie. All in all, the day cost Montgomery thirty-seven dollars and sixty cents, not including carfare.

❧ 12 ❧

I<small>N HER HOTEL ROOM</small> in Boston, Evelyn Estes left her coffee to cool on its wheeled table and rumpled through the morning papers looking for reviews of the play. After the many weeks of playing on tour, with an opening night every new place they went, she knew pretty well what the notices would be like, but the Boston ones would be more important, because Boston was the last stop before New York.

Generally speaking, the notices around the summer circuit had not been bad. The critics had all agreed that the play needed work; a dismal minority had expressed doubt that anything could save it, but the general consensus was that, with some cutting and a lot of rewriting, it would stand a better than even chance on Broadway. Evelyn's personal notices had always been good, although one critic in Chicago had complained that her accent sounded too foreign. Business had been brisk although not capacity, and the audiences seemed, in the main, to enjoy the show. Evelyn could tell that their reaction was never all that it should have been, but the changes in the script had been so major and so constant that the actors had never had a chance to settle down and become secure in their parts. Every day, just before rehearsal, and sometimes after the show at night, the author would appear with a stack of carbon copies, some of them so dim as to be hardly legible; the director would run through the new material with the actors, and they would then be expected to know it in time for the next performance. It was like a monstrous parlor game, in which everybody was supposed to memorize the Gettysburg address and then recite it backwards, leaving out all the words that began with "c."

There had been a few personality problems, too. In Westport, when they were rehearsing a new scene, the leading man turned to the director and said, "How am I supposed to read this line? The one about the cheese."

"Just the way it's written," the director replied. "You ask your wife if there's any cheese in the kitchen."

"Obviously," said the star. "But what's my attitude? *Why* do I ask her?"

In the empty seats, the author rose and walked toward the stage. "What do you mean, *why* do you ask her?" he said. "You want to know if there's any cheese."

"I know," said the star, as though he were talking to a child. "But why? WHY? Do I want to get rid of her? Do I want to get her out of the room? Do I want to make her admit there *IS* no cheese in the house? *Why do I ask her?*"

"You ask her because you want some cheese!" the author shouted. "You ask her because you're hungry!"

The star looked at the other actors, and shrugged. "Because I'm hungry," he said, in a resigned voice. "My God."

"I don't see any problem," the director put in. "Just ask her for cheese, and let it go at that."

"Well, I'll try," said the star. "But I can't promise anything."

"If *you* can think of some better line, why don't you put it in?" said the author. "You have my full permission to insert anything you want in place of the cheese."

"I might just as well," the star sighed. "The actors have written the best part of this bloody play, anyway."

"You can say that again!" the author screamed. "Every

time I turn my back, some goddam actor has changed a line, or put in a joke he heard in a bar, or written something to pad out his part! If I'd left it up to you, you'd have written the whole damned thing to suit yourself!"

"And a good thing, too," muttered the star.

"All right," said the director. "Let's try it, anyway. If it doesn't work, we'll think of something else."

Evelyn, who had worried about the meanings of two or three of her lines, decided not to ask about them. Instead, she read them the way she thought best, and everybody was satisfied. Although her part had not turned into a major one, it was a great deal larger than it had been at the beginning, and it was important enough so that she was mentioned in all the notices.

Now, groping her way through the unfamiliar newspaper, she finally found the drama page. Folding the page back, she started to read. Then her eye caught words like "idiotic," "puerile," "monumental bore," and "trash," and she dropped the paper and picked up another. Her face began to feel hot as she scanned the next review, which included such words as "pretentious," "utterly devoid of value," "stultifying," and "obnoxious." A third was a little kinder, using only words like "flat," "pallid," "dreary," and, as a comparative compliment, "off-beat." She was searching through this review for some mention of her name, when the telephone rang. She picked it up.

"Yes," she said.

"Company meeting onstage at one o'clock," said the assistant stage manager's voice, and there was a click and then silence.

She put the phone back in its cradle and reached out slowly for her coffee cup, still reading the newspaper. Her name was not mentioned, for which she was thankful. Then she put down the paper and started to get dressed.

The stage was lighted by the overhead work-light only, and it made the set look flat and colorless. When the company was assembled, the producer stepped forward. There was absolute silence before he started speaking. His voice was low, and tired, but every word was clear. He said that the notices made it impractical even to play out the remainder of the week in Boston; that so much money had been spent that their only chance of reaching New York would have been to play to capacity audiences here, and that there simply wasn't the money left to take them any farther. If they played out the week, it would be to practically empty houses and at a continuing loss, and the money wasn't there to lose. They had tried to raise more, he said, but the word-of-mouth about the show hadn't been too good, and the money was hard to find. He said that he was sorry, and he thanked them all for the time and the work they had put into the show, and he hoped that he would see them again, under more propitious circumstances. More or less as an after-thought, he said that the stage manager would give them their tickets back to New York, and that their final pay checks would be ready in a couple of hours.

The director said a few words, and then the stage manager said, "All right! Get your tickets here!" and people began quietly to mill around his desk. While she was waiting her turn, Evelyn looked around the dismal stage, and she found herself staring at a small, Victorian footstool. It looked as though it were made of cherry wood, and it had a red-and-gray needlepoint top. It had been one of the props she used in the third act. Until now, she had thought of it only in terms of the play, but it suddenly came to her that it would make a perfect present for Anne's room. When it was her turn at the stage manager's desk, she asked him if she could buy the stool. He looked up from his stack of papers, glanced at the stool and then at her, and winked.

"Take it along, Granny," he said. "You've earned it."

It wasn't until she got outside that the empty feeling began to come over her. The play had been a part of her life for so long that she found it hard to remember anything else, and now, with it ended, she felt slightly hollow. In all the times that she had been out of a job, or had had plans go wrong, this was the first time that she felt she had definitely lost something, something that was a part of her life. Even that day, almost thirty years ago, when her agent told her that the studio had not picked up her option, and added that he wasn't going to try any of the other studios for fear of hurting her prestige; even then, when everything she had built toward had evaporated into hot sunshine, she had not been particularly depressed. She was young, she was good looking, she had talent, and she knew that this was just the beginning. Somewhere, she had told herself, there would be a job where she could use her talents and make a good, solid name for herself.

Now, carrying the footstool as she walked through the crowded, narrow streets to her hotel, she wondered how much longer she could go on making fresh starts. When she first went with the play, she had not expected much of anything to come of it, but after the weeks on tour and the gradual emergence of the play as a dramatic entity, she had come to count more and more heavily on its success. The fact that it had failed did not depress her so much as the realization that she had lost the resilience to shrug off the failure; she was too old to think that there would always be another time. All of a sudden, she wanted very much to be home. She hurried the rest of the way to her hotel, and when she got there she turned her railroad ticket in to the clerk at the transportation desk, and exchanged it for one on an airplane. I want to get home as soon as I can, she thought. I want to get home just as soon as I possibly can.

It was about five o'clock when the wheels of her plane screeched onto the runway at La Guardia Field. In Boston, it had been autumn; the air was sharp and some of the trees were tinged with yellow and red, but the heat of summer still lay like a smoky blanket on New York, and the foliage had a burned-out, lifeless look about it. For Evelyn, who spent most of her time in New York, there was often no such thing as autumn; in the space of a week, the weather would change from hot and still to cold and wintry, and the only traditional signs of fall would be in the subway advertisements, with red and orange and yellow the predominating colors, and falling leaves decorating the advertisers' products.

As she sat in the sleek airport bus and rode toward the city, Evelyn had a feeling of anticipation; she wanted to see Anne, and Lapham, and Montgomery; she wanted to know everything that had been going on since she left; and she wanted very badly to *do* something, something constructive, or creative, or useful. The emptiness that she had felt earlier was a void that had to be filled, and the sooner it was filled the better it would be, both for her and for anybody around her. She thought of Anne's soon-to-be-born baby, and she smiled wryly to herself. *That's* what I ought to do, she thought. I ought to have a baby for myself, and see if *that* didn't give me something to do. Then she stopped smiling. And that's no joke, either, she thought. All it is is about twenty years too late.

It was dusk when she reached the apartment. There was a light in the Beckers' room, and one in Anne's, but Anne's shade was down, and only an occasional shadow flickered across it from the inside. Evelyn wanted to see Anne before she did anything else, but she decided that it would be better to leave the footstool in her own room until she had showed it to Lapham. She carried her suitcase and the footstool upstairs, unlocked her stuffy, airless room, and turned on the light. The room looked the same as it always had, but everything in it seemed dusty and ragged, and the first thing she did was open all the windows she could to let in some air. Next, she washed, and tidied her hair and fixed her make-up, and then she went downstairs.

Anne was holding a collapsed Venetian blind, trying to determine the top from the bottom, when she heard the knock at the door. "Come in," she said. "It's open." Evelyn opened the door, and Anne shrieked and dropped the blind. "Oh!" she said. "It's *you!*" She ran to Evelyn and embraced her, and her stomach bumped gently against Evelyn's. "Forgive me," she said, and laughed. "I forgot I can't get too close."

"You look wonderful," Evelyn said. "Just wonderful. How do you feel?"

"I feel fine. But how about *you?* How's the show? I want to know everything. Sit down and tell me everything that's happened."

"I can tell you the end first," Evelyn said quietly. "We folded in Boston."

"Oh, no." Anne stopped for a moment. "Why?"

Evelyn shrugged and sat down. "Bad notices, no money . . . I guess no play, really," she said. "I wouldn't know."

"Oh, I think that's awful. I'm really very sorry."

Evelyn smiled. "It was fun while it lasted," she said. "Or, rather, I guess it'll seem like fun later on. Right now, I'm still a little punch-drunk."

"Would you like a drink?"

"I'd love one. Whatever you've got."

Anne went into the kitchen. "I've got lots of things," she said. "I've got Bourbon and I've got gin and I've got sherry. I don't drink any of them myself, but I keep them here for the drop-in trade—for my beaux."

"I'd like a Bourbon, please," said Evelyn. "What have I been missing here? What beaux?"

Anne laughed. "Oh, you know," she said. "Duncan, and Arthur Montgomery. They come around all the time, just to see if I need anything." She poured some whisky in a glass and dropped in some ice. "It's a funny thing," she went on. "Just in the time since you've been gone, this place has become more home to me than my real—than my other home. Everybody's been so *nice,* I feel as though we're all one family. And that Mr. Becker—that lovely little Mr. Becker who lives across the way—he painted my flower box, and then he filled it with earth, and now he's growing flowers in it for me. He's got a regular garden going out there."

"Oh?" said Evelyn. "What about his wife?"

Anne gave Evelyn the drink, and sat down. "I don't know," she said. "I know she was the reason he stayed away for so long, but now I don't see her, and he doesn't mention her. Ever since he got retired I haven't seen hide nor hair of her. He's over here almost every day, puttering around with one thing or another, and we talk a lot, and have coffee together like a couple of the girls, but he never once has mentioned his wife."

"Maybe she left him," said Evelyn. "But I don't suppose he could be that lucky."

Anne shook her head. "No. I know he'd have said something about it. He's really quite chatty, once he gets started." She looked down at the blind on the floor. "I'm going to get this thing put up if it kills me," she said, and picked it up. "How do you like it? Don't you think it'll be an improvement?"

"You shouldn't be fooling around with things like that," said Evelyn. "Let me do it for you." She stood up. "How does it go?"

"That's the problem. I don't know. I assume the pulleys go at the top." She opened up the blind, like a magician with an enormous deck of cards. "I got it at a second-hand store, and there were no instructions that came with it. But the pulleys would *have* to go at the top, wouldn't they?"

"I'm sure they would," said Evelyn. "And I think you've got to nail that top strip to your window. Do you have a hammer?"

"Oh, certainly," said Anne. She gave the blind to Evelyn and went back to the kitchen. "I've really become quite efficient since you've been gone. I've done a great deal of carpentering on my own."

"So I see," said Evelyn, looking around the room. In one

164

corner was a white, box-like structure, inside of which were some books and on top of which was a lamp. It looked like an orange crate that had been painted with one coat of white enamel and then stood on one end. Another piece of furniture, more or less resembling a low end table, stood beside the overstuffed chair, and it, too, was painted white. "I think you've done quite well," Evelyn said. "Are you going to have everything white, or is that just the first coat?"

Anne came back from the kitchen with a hammer and some nails. "Oh, I'm going to leave it white," she said. "It gives it that kind of modern look, don't you think?"

Evelyn said nothing, and held out her hand for the hammer. I wonder what Duncan's reaction is to that, she thought. To Anne, she said, "All right, now. I'll get up on the radiator, and then you hand me the blind. Give me just a couple of nails to start with."

"Are you sure you want to do this?" Anne asked. "You could very well break your leg, you know."

"And who are *you* to be talking?" said Evelyn. "Here—give me a hand up."

She pushed a chair in front of the window radiator, kicked off her shoes, and with Anne steadying her, she mounted the radiator and clutched the edges of the window.

"Are you all right?" Anne asked. "Can you hold on?"

"Safe as a church. Only don't go too far away."

"I've got to let go of you for a minute. I've got to pick up the blind."

"All right, but make it quick."

Anne stooped, and gathered the blind together, and handed it up to Evelyn, putting one hand on Evelyn's back as she did. "There," she said. "Now I've got you."

"Good," Evelyn replied. "Now what do I do?" Anne looked up, and saw that Evelyn had the blind in one hand, the hammer in the other, and the nails in her mouth, and was still trying to hold on to the edge of the window. Anne began to laugh.

"Isn't there something you could do with your feet?" she asked. "I think that's the only way you're going to make it."

Evelyn exploded into laughter, blowing the nails out of her mouth like shrapnel. "Stop it!" she said. "Or I'll fall and crush you flat!" She teetered on the radiator, and Anne clutched her around the legs and laughed harder. "Stop it!" Evelyn shrieked, and she dropped the blind with a clattering crash.

"I *can't* stop it!" said Anne, pushing harder as Evelyn began to topple on her.

"Good God almighty, I'm doomed!" said Evelyn, and she laughed so hard that she dropped the hammer. "Doomed! *Watch out below!*"

There was a knock at the door, and Duncan Lapham burst in. "Anne!" he shouted. "In your condition!" He ran and helped ease Evelyn off the radiator and into the chair. "Really!" he said. "You ought to be ashamed of yourself. What *were* you trying to do?"

Gasping for breath, Anne sat down. "Evelyn was just hanging my Venetian blind for me," she said, and then both women were convulsed with laughter.

"Well, I must say," said Lapham. "You looked like a couple of female wrestlers. I didn't know *what* to think." Then, as though for the first time, he noticed Evelyn. "And by the way, welcome home!" he said, and leaned down and kissed her on the forehead. "When did you get back?"

"Just now," Evelyn replied, weakly. "Just a couple of minutes ago."

"Well, you don't do things by halves, I must say," he said. "You're no sooner home than you start climbing around like a mountain goat. No rest for the weary, or whatever the saying is. How's the play?"

"We died in Boston."

"Oh, isn't that a bloody shame. I'm dreadfully sorry."

She shrugged. Then she looked at her watch. "As a matter of fact," she said, "less than twenty hours ago, I was playing a Polish grandmother in front of what turned out to be the most hostile group of critics ever huddled under one roof. We were slaughtered."

"Polish?" said Anne. "I thought you were a Cockney grandmother."

"That was in the beginning," Evelyn said. "That was when the play was about a mad London doctor. Then, briefly, he became a man like Schweitzer and I had to brush up on my German accent, and I finally turned Polish when they made him a doctor in the underground during the war. I can tell you, I've been around."

"It must have made it kind of hard on the star," Anne said. "Having to learn all those accents, and everything."

Evelyn laughed. "No bloody worry about '*im*,'" she said. "His accent stayed the same throughout—low Sardi's, with just a hint of the Studio." She stood up. "Come, now, Evelyn," she said. "We mustn't be bitchy, must we? Duncan, dear boy, do you think *you* can do something about this Venetian blind? I don't think I trust myself on that radiator again."

Lapham regarded the blind without emotion. It was clear that he didn't approve of it, and yet he felt that any change in the room would be for the better. "I can try," he said. "But I think you're going to have to take down that roller shade first. There isn't room to get this up with that still there."

"Oh, of course," said Anne. "How stupid of me." She started to climb on the radiator to remove the shade, but Lapham stopped her.

"Get *down* off there!" he said, sharply. "Do I have to watch over you every *minute?*"

"I'm sorry," she said.

He pulled her aside. "*Really!*" He glared at her, and climbed up onto the radiator.

Anne looked at Evelyn. "We have to humor him at times like this," she said. "Otherwise, he flies into a rage. I sometimes think this pregnancy is harder on him than it is on me."

"And you can say *that* again," said Lapham, as he disengaged the shade. "I've never been through anything like it in my life."

There were footsteps outside, and a knock on the door.

"Come," said Anne. To Evelyn, she said, "You see? I told you there was a lot of drop-in trade here."

The door opened, and Montgomery came in. "I just thought I'd see if—" he started, and then he saw Evelyn. "Well, hello!" he said. "Welcome back!" He went toward her with his hand out, and she took his hand and then, on a sudden impulse, she kissed him on the cheek.

"Thank you!" she said. "It's good to *be* back."

There was a pause. "I'm sorry about the show," Montgomery said. "I saw the Boston papers."

"Would somebody please take this shade?" Lapham called, from his perch in the window. "I'm afraid it'll tangle in my feet if I try to come down with it."

Montgomery went over and took the shade from Lapham. "Is there anything I can do to help?" he asked.

"What we're trying to do is put up a Venetian blind," said Anne. "I had some idea I could do it alone, but I can see I was wrong."

Lapham came down off the radiator. "If both of us got up there," he said to Montgomery, "then one could hold it while the other hammered. That's probably the only way we're going to get it done."

"O.K." Montgomery took off his jacket, and loosened his tie. "Who does what? How are you at hammering?"

"Fair only." Lapham picked up some nails and examined them for straightness.

"Then you're better than I am," said Montgomery. "I'll hold, and you hammer."

"I suppose we might as well choose up sides, too," Anne said to Evelyn. "I'll hold Duncan in place, if you want to hold Arthur."

"Right you are," Evelyn replied. "Compared to what I went through before, this'll be a lark."

"See that you don't make it too much of a lark," said Montgomery, as he picked up the Venetian blind and stepped onto the chair. "When I fall, I fall heavily."

"Don't worry, duck," said Evelyn. "You've got the weight of centuries behind you here."

Precariously, and with a certain amount of tottering and grunting, they managed to get Montgomery and Lapham bunched together on top of the radiator, with the two women pushing at them from behind to hold them in place. Then Montgomery put the blind up, and Lapham began to hammer nails into it. He had to hit backhand and in a limited space, and he bent several nails before the blind was even partly secured. Montgomery, with his face to the wall, began to laugh.

"Go easy on the laughter up there," said Evelyn. "It almost killed Anne and me a while back."

"I was just thinking," Montgomery said. "Who needs to drink, when you can have all this fun cold sober?"

There was a knock on the door. "That will have to be Mr. Becker," said Anne.

"Well, if it's the police, we're lost," Lapham remarked. "They'll never believe our story in a hundred years."

Montgomery started to laugh again, and Anne called, "Come in, Mr. Becker!"

There was a scuffling and bumping on the other side of the door, and then it opened, and Ernest Becker came in, carrying in his arms a three-foot-long cradle. It was made of dark wood, and highly polished. He set it down, then closed the door behind him. For a moment, nobody spoke. "It's something I made for you," Becker said, smiling. "I thought it might come in handy, since I noticed you hadn't already bought something for the child to sleep in."

"You made that for *me?*" Anne said, and she let go of Lapham and went to the cradle.

"Hey!" said Lapham, who was not able to see anything except the Venetian blind. "Come back here!"

"Hold him, Evelyn," Anne said, and Evelyn took one hand

off Montgomery and braced it against Lapham. Anne knelt down and touched the top of the cradle, and it rocked.

"In the old days, everybody had them," Becker said. "Now, you don't see so many of them. I don't know why. Back on the farm, when I was young, we had one like this only a little bigger, and I and all my brothers and sisters slept in it when we were small. Then, later on, it was used for holding wood in the kitchen. There's many things you can use it for."

"But it's so beautiful," Anne said, wonderingly. "It's so really beautiful."

"Of course, it should be made from mahogany," Becker said. "But mahogany is expensive, so I made it from white pine, and then stained it good with mahogany stain. Then on top of that I rubbed wax, to give it a shine. It looks a little like mahogany, but of course it's not such hard wood."

"I don't know what to say," Anne said. "I really don't—" She stopped, and wiped her nose with the back of her hand.

"One thing, it might be good later on to give it another coat of wax," Becker said. "The wax will protect it a little, and being as how it's soft wood, it needs to be protected all it can."

"Yes," she said. "Of course. I'll keep it waxed all the time."

"Just be careful don't wax the baby, too," he said, smiling. "On a baby, I'm told wax is not so good."

Everybody laughed, and then Lapham and Montgomery came down from the radiator and they and Evelyn gathered around and admired the cradle. Finally Anne stood up, and looked at Becker. "Thank you," she said. "Thank you more than I can ever tell you."

"I'm glad you like it," he said.

She looked around the room. "Would you sit down?" she asked. "I think we could all have some refreshment if we want it."

"No, thank you," Becker replied. "I have to get back now. I have to start to make supper."

"Oh," said Anne. "Is your—wife—ill?"

He paused for no more than a second, then said, "No. But since I'm retired, I like to cook. It gives me something to do."

"Oh, of course," said Anne. "I can see." She went with him to the door. "I can never thank you enough for the cradle," she said, as he went out. "Never in a million years."

He smiled. "You should not try," he said. "It was my pleasure. Good night."

"Good night," said Anne, and she closed the door.

He let himself into his apartment, and went through the room where Martha was sitting, staring silently out the window. In the kitchen, he opened a can of lentil soup and put it on the stove to heat, then took some frozen potato pancakes from the refrigerator, put them in the oven, and lighted it. While they were cooking, he fried three pork chops in an iron skillet, turning them often and feeling the sting of the sparks of burning fat. When the meal was done, he made up a tray for Martha, and took it into the other room and put it in front of her. She gave no sign that she saw it, and he said nothing. He just went quietly back to the kitchen, and sat down at the table and ate his supper.

❦ 13 ❦

IN ANNE'S ROOM, Montgomery said, "Who's for having a little dinner? I'm hungry."

Anne shook her head. "Not I, thanks," she said. "I've already made myself a snack, and I've got to watch my weight." She started to pick up the cradle, but Lapham snatched it from her and put it in a corner, by the day bed.

Montgomery looked at Evelyn. "And you?" he asked.

"Come to think of it, I'd love to," she replied. "The last food I had was some coffee and cold toast, this morning." She stopped and thought a moment, then said, "And what a long time ago *that* seems! When I woke up this morning, I was in Boston, and I was in a play, and within another week we were going to open on Broadway." She laughed. "I guess that'll teach me to make plans."

"Well, you can plan on having dinner," said Montgomery. "This time, I promise not to disappear." He looked at Lapham. "How about it?" he asked. "Would you join us?"

"No, thank you," Lapham replied, as he contemplated the cradle. "But I have a couple of things I'd like to talk to you both about, if you have a minute." Then he looked at Evelyn and Montgomery and smiled. "Should we go up to my room?" he asked.

They said good night to Anne, and as they went up the stairs Evelyn said, "I just want to stop off and get something in my room. I'll be right with you."

"Right-o," said Lapham, and he and Montgomery continued to climb the stairs.

Evelyn went into her room and looked at herself in the mirror. I guess there's not much I can do about it now, she thought. But before we go out, I'll put on a whole new face, and see if that won't help. For no good reason, I suddenly feel young; I only wish I could look a little younger.

She patted her hair in place, then picked up the paper-wrapped footstool and took it up to Lapham's room. When she got there, Lapham had uncovered a marble-topped coffee table that was standing in one corner, and was showing it to Montgomery. Lapham looked up as she came in, and said, "Ah, there. How do you like my creation? I cut it down from an old shaving stand."

"I think it's wonderful," she said. "Is it for Anne?"

Lapham nodded. "It'll take the place of one of those dreadful little do-it-yourself things she's got in there now."

"I've got this, here," Evelyn said, unwrapping the footstool. "I don't know how it will go in the room, but it was the most likely thing I could find when we broke up the play."

"Oh, that will do admirably," Lapham said. "That will give just the right touch of color." He paused, and frowned. "I do wish we could keep her from making all these little horrors herself, though," he said. "It just means we're going to have to throw *away* so much when we finally do the room over."

"You don't mean you want to get rid of the cradle?" Montgomery said incredulously.

"Oh, of course not. The cradle will be fine. But these little boxlike structures she insists on making; there's *nothing* that can be done with them. Out the window—that's the only thing."

"Well, I suppose it'll depend on what we've got to replace them," Montgomery said. "I mean, it's all very well to get rid of the junk, but we can't leave the poor girl in a room with a cradle and a coffee table and a footstool. That would be carrying friendship a little too far."

Lapham laughed. "No," he said. "Somehow or other, we'll have to see that she's adequately as well as tastefully furnished. But I do wish I could lay my hands on that brass bed. That would give just the perfect touch to the whole thing."

"Well, I just wish I could contribute *something*," Montgomery replied. "All I've done is buy, God help me, a panda, and a baby sweater, and things like that—" He looked at Evelyn—"and I'd appreciate it if you'd inspect them for me," he said. "For all I know, I could have been sold a midget's outfit. I don't know what baby clothes even *look* like."

"If they're small and furry, then they're probably for a baby," she said. "It's only if they're small and look like evening clothes that you have to be careful."

"Well, these are furry, all right," he said. "They're so furry all hell won't have them."

"Wait a minute," said Lapham. "I just had an idea. You said you'd like to contribute something; how would you like to contribute a spectacular brass bed?"

"I don't know," Montgomery replied. "How much do they cost?"

"This one shouldn't cost over fifty dollars, and I'll be glad to pay you half. The only trouble is that *I* can't get it because the old fool who runs the store hates my guts. If *you* go in and tell him you want an old brass bed, I'm sure you can get it for nothing." He paused, then smiled and went on, "And I tell you what. If he tries to run up the price on you, say you've seen one in *my* store—and mention my name— for fifty dollars, and you're looking for something cheaper. He'll practically give it to you for nothing, I can guarantee."

"O.K.," said Montgomery hesitantly. "Then what do I do?"

"Then bring it back to my place, and we can polish it up and get it ready."

"I may need a little help," Montgomery said. "I don't know quite how I'm going to lug a brass bed around town."

"You can bribe a cabby to help you. I'd loan you my station wagon, only this old bitch would recognize it, and then that would be the end of that. Just whatever you do, don't let him know that I have anything to do with the deal."

"O.K.," said Montgomery. "If you think it will work."

"I know it will work. It can't *help* but work, if you tell him you're thinking of buying one from me."

"O.K.," said Montgomery again. "When should I do this?"

Lapham looked at Evelyn. "As a woman's guess," he said, "how long do you think we have before *le grand jour* arrives?"

"I really don't know," she said. "A month, perhaps. I'm kind of out of things here, you may remember."

"Well, if you can find out when the *accouchement* is expected, then do it just a little bit before that," Lapham said. "That's all I can say. But I suppose the sooner the better. After all, if we know that we can plan on the bed, then the rest of the décor will practically take care of itself."

"There's a question that's been nagging at me," Montgomery said. "And that is, do you think she *wants* us to re-do her apartment for her? I mean, wouldn't it be easier if she got the stuff that she wanted, rather than what we think she might want?"

"We went into that one night up here," Lapham replied. "Evelyn and I suggested that everybody might sort of chip in and help her refurnish her room, and she got quite uppity and independent and said she didn't want any charity, or some such thing. So we decided to do it more or less as a shower, and make the whole thing a surprise."

"Well, O.K.," said Montgomery. "But I just hope she likes it."

"She's bound to like it. I mean, after all, look at what we've already got for her. And I know she'll like the bed; she as much as told me so a while back."

"O.K.," Montgomery said again. "I just wondered." He looked at Evelyn. "Are you ready for dinner?" he asked.

"Oh, Lord, no," she said. "I'm still in me Boston clothes. I'll need at least an hour."

"All right, I'll give you an hour. But in that time I want you to decide where we're going. Tonight, it's ladies' choice."

"Coo, ain't you the gay one?"

"Not gay. Just contrite."

"I'll make it as fast as I can," she said.

Evelyn insisted that she had no idea where she wanted to go for dinner; she said she'd been away so long that she'd forgotten everything. So they went to a French restaurant in the midtown area that Montgomery had heard about, but had never been to. He thought briefly of taking her to the saloon, and then rejected the idea; he didn't want to drink a great deal, and he knew that it was hard to stay in the saloon and not drink. Besides, he felt that, everything considered, he owed her something a little better. The French restaurant turned out to be just right. He ordered snails and she had a *coq au vin,* and between them they had no trouble finishing a whole bottle of Montrachet. When they had ordered their coffee, Evelyn lit a cigarette and inhaled deeply.

"Do you know something?" she said. "It's good to be home."

"It's under kind of unfortunate circumstances, though," Montgomery replied. "A little better luck, here and there, wouldn't have hurt."

"It's too late to worry about that now. It was good experience, and at least I worked all summer. There's that to be thankful for."

"What are you going to do now?"

"I honestly don't know. Back to TV, I guess. Or another

show, if I'm offered it. Or something. Whatever turns up."

Without looking at her, he said, "Did you ever think of getting married?"

"Oh, my, yes. Dozens of times. But back when that was a possibility, I was so set on making a career that I said the other could wait. I saw too many careers *and* marriages go bust trying to combine the two. Oh, I was very clever, I was."

Montgomery examined his coffee spoon. "Do you really like acting?" he asked.

"What a strange question." She stopped, and thought. "It's all I've ever done," she said at last. "I guess I *must* like it. Why?"

"No reason. It just occurred to me to wonder."

"Well, for that matter, do you like newspaper work?"

He smiled. "It's a living," he said. "Everything's a living, only some people do it better than others. Or, as Churton Collins put it, 'The secret of success in life is known only to those who have not succeeded.'"

"*Who* said that?"

"John Churton Collins. An English literary critic. Born in 1848, died in 1908. Not a wildly successful man himself, by most standards."

She looked at him for several moments. "You asked me if I ever thought of getting married," she said. "I think I should ask you if you ever thought of going on a quiz show. I have never in my life met a man with so much miscellaneous information. You could make millions."

"I get mike fright. I can't even be in the same room with a microphone without starting to choke and sweat. I couldn't remember my own name if they asked me on the air."

"Well, it's a great talent gone to waste there. There must be something you could do with it."

"It helps on the copy desk, every now and then."

"Are you sure it's only mike fright you've got? Isn't there maybe some other fright mixed in there, too?"

"I don't know," he said. "Why?"

"Never mind. It was a rude question, anyway. It just crossed my mind."

He laughed. "You and I both seem to have ideas popping into our minds like fireflies, here."

"I know. I guess it's having been away so long. As I said before, it's good to be home again. And there's another thing. It occurs to me that it's a long, long time since I used that word 'home.' But this morning, I wanted to be home—and I mean this home, here—more than I ever wanted anything since I was a little girl."

"In Tulsa?"

"How did you know *that?*"

"Miscellaneous information."

"Well, I must say! What else do you know about me?"

"Not a great deal, really."

"Now I feel at a disadvantage. I know practically nothing about you—except—"

"Except that I drink too much and know a lot of old songs."

"No, I didn't mean that."

"Well, that's about all there is to know."

"Oh, stop it. There's a great deal more than that, and you know it. Right now, just by guessing, I'll bet I could tell you a lot more important things about yourself than that."

"Go ahead."

She looked straight into his eyes. "Well, just for one thing, I can tell you that you're a lot better than you think you are. That's for a starter."

"Try again," he said.

"You're proving my point. And you're denying it just because you want to be flattered."

"Sure. And vanity is the greatest of all flatterers. Does that make me vain, too?"

"Now you're being childish. You're deliberately being silly, just to avoid admitting that I'm right."

"All right, then. I'm a lot better than I think I am. Then what?"

"Then if you keep on like this I'll belt you right in the eye. I'm serious."

"So am I. Would you like a drink?"

"No, thank you."

"Do you mind if I have one?"

"If you feel you need it."

"That's a charming way to put it. All right—I won't have one."

"No—go ahead. It just proves my point still further."

"What? How does my having a drink prove your point that I don't want to admit I'm better than I think I am— Do you know something? I suddenly have the feeling I'm going crazy."

She laughed. "So do I. I guess I got kind of involved."

"Let's back down a bit and start all over again."

"All right. Let's go back to where you asked if I'd like a drink. Yes, please. I'd love a white mint frappé."

He signaled the waiter. "One white mint frappé," he said, "and a—give me a—ah, the hell with it. Make it two white mint frappés." He looked at Evelyn. "I never thought I'd be caught drinking one of *those*."

"You didn't have to, just because I did."

"I know. But I'll tell you a curious thing. I don't *want* anything else. Just what can you make of that?"

"I really don't know. I'd be afraid even to hazard a guess."

When they had finished their mints, she lit another cigarette and said, "I was interested that you asked Duncan Lapham along tonight. I didn't even know you and he were speaking."

"Oh, he's all right. He drops in at Anne's room a lot, and I finally got to know him a little better. As a matter of fact, he's sometimes kind of funny."

"I know that. But I thought you had one of those allergies."

He shrugged. "I'm too old to have allergies." He looked around for a waiter, but none was in sight. After a moment's thought, he said, "But I must say this business about the bed is kind of odd. That's way, *way* out of my league."

"It shouldn't be too hard, if you can get someone to help you."

"No, I guess not."

"I'll be glad to come along, if there's anything I could do."

"You could kind of give it an air of legitimacy, I suppose," he said, and laughed. "But I don't think I could ask you to help carry it. That would be a little too much."

"We'd make a pretty picture, wouldn't we? Tottering down Third Avenue with a brass bed on our backs. . . ." She was overcome by the hilarity of the idea, and buried her face in her hands.

"It could be called 'Come Live with Me and Be My Love,'" he said, and they both laughed so that other people turned and looked.

"Or, 'I Have Been Faithful to Thee, Cynara, in My Fashion,'" she added, in a strangled voice, and Montgomery collapsed and almost fell out of his chair.

They were still laughing when the headwaiter appeared at their table. "Was there anything you wanted, M'sieu?" he asked, with an icy edge to his voice.

Montgomery straightened up and looked at Evelyn. "Another mint?" he asked weakly.

She shook her head, and dabbed at her eyes with her handkerchief.

"I guess not," he said to the headwaiter. "Just the check, please."

The headwaiter produced the check and put it on the table with a backhanded flip of his wrist. Montgomery reached for his wallet, and something cold ran through him when he realized that his inside pocket was empty. He stabbed his hand into the depths of the flat, hollow pocket, then patted himself all over. "My God . . ." he murmured, and took out his handkerchiefs, his keys, and his change. He tried his inside pocket again, and then he slapped himself all over. He looked on the floor, and on the seat, and he stood up and looked where he had been sitting, and then slowly he sat down again, and looked at Evelyn. "My God," he said again. "I had it—I know I had it—I took it out to pay for the cab . . ."

"I know," she said. "I saw you. Maybe you dropped it outside."

"Just a minute," he said to the headwaiter. He got up, and went out of the restaurant, and searched the gutter and the sidewalk in front. He looked under the nearest parked cars, but all he saw were bits of crumpled paper and flattened cigarette butts. A couple came down the street, walking briskly, and for a second he had the insane urge to ask them if they had seen his wallet. Then they were past him, laughing, and he looked around the sidewalk once more, and the steps into the restaurant, and then he went back inside. The check-room girl looked at him as he came in, and he said, "Did anybody by any chance turn in a wallet here?" For a moment she didn't seem to understand him, so he repeated the question, making the shape of the wallet with his hands, and she said, "No, M'sieu. Nobody has brought it here." On his way back to the table he scanned the carpet, but it was dark and he couldn't see much of anything. When he got to the table, the headwaiter was standing slightly to one side, waiting. Evelyn looked somehow smaller than she had before. Montgomery sat down and spread his hands. "Gone," he said.

Evelyn opened her purse. "Look—I've got plenty—"

Montgomery stopped her, and beckoned to the headwaiter. "I seem to have lost my wallet," he said. "Would it be possible for me to sign, and pay you tomorrow?"

"Does M'sieu have an account here?" the headwaiter asked, in a tone that said, "Not on your life, Buster."

"No, but I work on a newspaper. I can give plenty of—"

"Please," Evelyn cut in. "We were paid off today, and I have—"

"Does M'sieu have identification cards?" the headwaiter asked. "A driver's license, perhaps?"

"Of course I do," said Montgomery. "And they're all in my wallet. But if you'd like to call the paper, there'll be somebody there who'll vouch for me—"

The headwaiter shrugged with his eyebrows and his shoulders, and Evelyn pressed a crumpled wad of bills into Montgomery's hand. "Take this!" she snapped. "Stop all this talk and pay the man, and let's get out of here."

"I am afraid we must see some sort of identification, M'sieu," the headwaiter said.

Montgomery turned over the check and looked at it, then took one twenty- and one ten-dollar bill from the bunch, tossed them on the table, and handed the rest back to Evelyn. The headwaiter picked up the check and the money, and disappeared.

"Keep it," Evelyn said, handing the money back to Montgomery. "We'll need it for going home. Give me what's left when we get there."

"No," he said. "There'll be change. Enough to get us to the saloon, and then I can cash a check."

"You don't *have* to cash a check. Look—we certainly can't use all this."

He put the money in her purse. "We're not going to use any of it," he said. "I'm going to cash a check, and then we can go on from there."

She looked at him for a moment, then closed her purse. "All right," she said.

"I don't mean to sound ungrateful, believe me."

"No, I'm sure you didn't."

"Oh, now, wait a minute. Listen to me, please. Of course I'm grateful to you, for God's sakes. I'm obviously grateful to you."

She smiled. "Let's not make a Federal case of it, should we?"

"I'm not making a Federal case. I'm just trying to point out to you that I cannot let you pay for the entire evening, that's all."

"I wasn't offering to pay for the evening. I was simply offering to help."

"I know. And I thank you. And if you'll notice, I have let you help. But I just want to cash a check, that's all."

"Fine. Then let's go where you can cash a check."

"But that's all I was saying, wasn't it?"

"Yes, of course."

"Then what are we arguing about?"

"I haven't the faintest idea."

The waiter came with their change, and Montgomery left a tip on the plate, and pocketed the rest of the money. When they got outside, he looked once more for his wallet, then hailed a cab and helped Evelyn into it.

There were several people in the saloon when they got there. Montgomery nodded to some of them as he led Evelyn past the bar, and they greeted him casually, without seeming to interrupt their talk. Two men were playing matches, and they ignored everyone else, slamming their fists down on the bar and shouting their guesses, while one bartender wiped the bar in front of them and tried to keep them quiet.

"I've often heard about this place," Evelyn said, as they sat at a table in the back room. "A lot of theater people come here."

"A lot of all kinds of people come here," Montgomery replied. "This is the home-away-from-home for people who have nowhere else to go." He signaled a waiter, and asked him for a blank check. "Although I must say," he went on, "they do serve one hell of a fine Thanksgiving dinner. I have had some of the best Thanksgiving dinners I've ever eaten, right at this table. Lentil soup, sauerbraten with potato pancakes—the works." He chuckled. "Of course, they also have turkey, for the traditionalists. One time, a group of us bought a whole turkey here, and took it up to the city room for the guys who had to work that day. Every stick of copy was covered with turkey grease and cranberry sauce."

The waiter brought the blank check, and Evelyn watched Montgomery as he filled it out. He looked more like himself now, she thought. In the French restaurant, there had been the shadow of fear in his voice, although it was evident only to someone who knew him; now, back among his familiar surroundings, he was relaxed and almost confident. He was at home, and on familiar ground, and could do more or less as he pleased. She wondered why he hadn't brought her to the saloon in the first place, instead of going to a restaurant that was totally strange to him. Could it be that he was trying to make an impression? She rejected the thought as absurd, but then she could come up with no reasonable alternative. She smiled to herself, and watched him as he signed the check and handed it to the waiter.

"Now," Montgomery said, before the waiter had left, "what would you like? You don't want to stick with that mint, do you?"

"No, thank you," she replied. "I think I'll just have a cup of coffee."

"All right, Otto," said Montgomery. "Two coffees, please."

"And a Scotch?" the waiter asked.

"No. Just two coffees."

The waiter drifted away, and Evelyn said, "I wish you wouldn't feel you have to have what I have. Why don't you order a Scotch, if you want one?"

"I would, if I wanted one. I just don't happen to want one right now."

"All right, but it makes me feel as though I were a chaperone, or something."

"Well, I can tell you that's the last way it makes me feel.

184

And I can assure you that before the evening is over, I may very possibly drink a glass of whisky. O.K.?"

"O.K." She smiled. "But as far as I'm concerned, I'm not sure how long the evening is going to last. This has been a day that has seemed like two weeks."

"We'll go whenever you say."

"I didn't mean that you had to go. I just meant that I may fold up any minute now."

"I'll fold when you do. I need the sleep myself."

"Now you're making me feel like a chaperone again."

"Damn it all, do I have to draw you a diagram?"

"What do you mean by that?"

"Nothing. Forget it."

The waiter brought their coffee, and gave the money to Montgomery. He took three ten-dollar bills, folded them, and handed them to Evelyn. "Here," he said. "With my deepest thanks."

"Thank *you*," she said, as she put the money in her purse. "Feel free any time."

"I hope not too often. I can't afford to go around losing my wallet every day in the week."

"Did you lose much?"

"Enough, yes."

"You don't suppose it will be returned, do you?"

"I'm certainly not going to bank on it. But I was prepared to spend the money, anyway, so all I've really lost are the papers."

"In a way, I feel kind of responsible."

"*You* do? How could you be responsible?"

"I don't know. But I feel we ought to go Dutch on the evening, or something."

"Now, let's not get into that again."

"No, but still . . ."

"I said let's not get into that again. Please."

She started to speak, and then something happened, and

her eyes filled with tears and she was crying. "Oh, I'm sorry," she said, groping for her handkerchief. "I'm sorry . . ."

"What's the *matter?*" Montgomery asked, in horror. "What happened?"

"Nothing . . . I'm sorry . . ."

"Did I say something?"

"No . . . I'm just tired, I guess. . . . I'm sorry . . ."

"But what can I—"

"Nothing. . . . Just take me home. . . . Please. . . . Take me home. . . ."

They stood up, and she took a deep breath and clutched her handkerchief to her mouth as he led her out past the bar and into a taxi.

❧ 14 ❧

It was nearly two weeks later that Montgomery forced himself to go and get the bed. It had been a cool, crisp week end, unusually cool for September, and on Monday, with most everyone else at work, he had the day to himself. Evelyn was rehearsing for a television show; Anne, despite Lapham's nervous disapproval, was continuing to go to her office; and of all the people in the apartment only the Beckers were available for companionship. Montgomery found that he rather liked Ernest Becker, although they did not have a great deal in common, but he was frankly afraid of Martha Becker, and he stayed as far away from her as he could. Not that this was particularly difficult; she never seemed to go out of her apartment, and Montgomery had no cause to go into it, so he simply avoided anything that might bring them into contact.

On this particular Monday, he slept late more or less out of habit, and when he woke up he lay still for a while, testing his various reflexes to determine how he was going to feel when he got up. Everything seemed to be in order, and his next test was to see how much of the previous evening he could remember. To his surprise, he remembered it all with complete clarity. He and Anne and Evelyn had gone up to Lapham's room for Chinese food, and then after a while Anne and Evelyn had gone to bed, and he and Lapham had stayed up and talked about the theater. Why the theater, he wondered? . . . There must have been something that got them onto that. . . . Oh, yes. First it was Evelyn's play, and then Lapham said that he had once been in the theater, in a musical that died in Philadelphia. That had led to their singing a few show tunes, but Lapham was too young to remember the really good ones, so they just talked about the theater in general, and Lapham knew a great deal about it. Then they had talked about . . . my God! Montgomery came fully awake as he realized that their next subject of conversation had been Lapham's military service. It had been a long story, starting hesitantly and then, with the assurance of a sympathetic ear, pouring out in jumbled, hurried detail.

It started many years back, when Lapham, at the age of eighteen, had become engaged to a girl he had met in art class. He had studied art nights, hoping to be a stage designer. The engagement didn't last long, because the first time he took the girl to his home, his mother had been so hostile that the evening had been a disaster. Later, when he returned after taking the shaken girl to her house, his mother had told him that the girl was no good, and that his father —who had died before Lapham ever knew him, and who was used as a symbol of perfection in everything—would never have allowed her in the house. A furious scene had followed, and the upshot of it was that Lapham had run away from home and attempted to join the Marines. Rejected, he had enlisted in the Army, and had served as a medic during part of the Korean war. It was during the Korean service that he began to be aware that some deep-hidden feeling, or instinct, within him was taking tangible form, and although he managed to fight it off at first, it became progressively stronger, until by the time he was discharged he was drinking heavily in his attempt to combat it. But the drinking only made it worse, and in the end he had had to have psychiatric help in order to face up to what was by then a condition he could not alter.

All in all, Montgomery reflected, it had been quite an evening. Thinking back on it, he was mildly surprised that there had been so much talk with practically no liquor having been consumed; the kind of fundamental truths he and Lapham had exchanged were the kind that usually came out of the second bottle of whisky. Perhaps the explanation lay in Lapham's closing words, when he held the door open for Montgomery to leave, and said, "I hope you'll forgive my boring you like this, but I find that every now and then I have to kind of clear the air and get everything off my chest, so to speak. I'll try not to do it to you again."

Now, as he slowly shaved and dressed himself, Montgomery thought about the evening, and the more he thought about it the more remarkable it seemed to him, from several points of view. First, it was remarkable that Lapham had talked to him as freely as he had; second, it was remarkable that he had listened as patiently and understandingly as he had; and third, it was remarkable that he had been able to get through the evening on only one drink. I wonder what's come over me, he thought.

Then he thought of the bed, and he decided that if he was ever going to buy it, today was the day. The prospect made him uneasy, but there seemed to be no way for him to get out of it, so he determined to go to the saloon for lunch, and see if he could recruit some help from there. He knew that if he tried to do it alone, the result could only be a shambles.

When he got outside, Ernest Becker was nailing a small trellis along the side of Anne's window. Montgomery glanced quickly at the Beckers' window to see if Martha was watching, and then he greeted Becker with a cheery "Good morning."

Becker looked up from his work. "Ah, good morning," he

said. He indicated the trellis with his hammer. "This will be something she can grow things on. Not so much this time of year, of course, but later on, perhaps, in the spring."

"Yes," said Montgomery. "That looks fine." He cleared his throat. "I must say, you've certainly done a lot for her, what with the window box, and the cradle, and all."

Becker smiled. "It's my pleasure," he said. "It's nice to have something to do."

"I guess you're right." Montgomery glanced again at the Beckers' window. "How are things?" he asked.

Becker looked at him a second before answering. "What do you mean?" he said.

"Nothing in particular," Montgomery said, embarrassed. "It was just a rhetorical question—you know, like—like how's tricks, or something like that. Just one of those idiot remarks." He laughed nervously.

"Oh," said Becker, and he smiled. "Good," he said. "Things are good. Is that the answer?"

"Sure. Or things are looking up, or things are first-rate, or things are fine, or things are humming—any one of them will do."

"Things are humming," said Becker. "I think I like that one best." He turned back to the trellis, and drove a nail into the wood with one sharp blow of the hammer. "Things are humming," he repeated, and laughed.

"Well—keep a stiff upper lip," Montgomery said, as he raised his hand in salute and moved off. "See you in church, and don't take any wooden nickels."

"No wooden nickels," Becker said, and he drove another nail into the trellis.

The saloon was crowded with lunch customers when Montgomery got there. They stood two-deep at the bar, jostling each other as they reached for their drinks, and talking and shouting and laughing like a crowd at a football game. The lunchtime customers were a different group from those who came at night; at night there were the newspapermen and the theater people, but at lunch there were businessmen and advertising men and models and women executives— most of whom were commuters and knew of the saloon only as a shabbily fashionable place to have lunch. It always nettled Montgomery that the regulars should have to compete with these people for tables, but there was not much that could be done about it, and Adolf, the headwaiter, always saw to it that no regular customer had to wait too long. Montgomery moved through the crowd at the bar, looking for a familiar face, and about half-way down the line he spotted Sam Ulm, who was looking unusually neat and well-dressed. He went up behind him and touched his elbow. "Sorry," he said. "We don't allow magazine people in here."

"Arthur!" Ulm exclaimed, as he turned and saw Montgomery. "Come in and have a drink. Are you eating?"

"Eventually," Montgomery replied.

"Eat with me. I've got a table. What'll you have to drink?"

"I don't know. Scotch, I guess." He pulled a bill from his pocket, and put it on the bar. "Boy, you certainly have become a magazine type, haven't you?" he said. "'I've got a table,' indeed! And I suppose you slipped Adolf a couple of bucks to hold it for you, just so you could impress someone."

"I did nothing of the kind. He saw me when I came in, and said he'd hold a table for me any time I wanted it."

"Uh-huh."

"And don't jeer at magazine people, boy. You don't know what you're missing."

"Uh-huh."

"You can say 'uh-huh' all you like, I'm still going to get you to come to work for us."

"Uh-huh."

"And that Anne Waters—I'm going to get her to come to work for us, too. Either that, or I'm going to break my neck trying."

"Now, there you might have a little more luck." Montgomery took the drink that the bartender handed him over Ulm's shoulder, and as he sipped it an idea occurred to him. "What are you doing after lunch?" he asked.

"I don't know. Why?"

"There's a little something I could use your help on. Your mention of Anne made me think of it."

"Why? Is it for her?"

"In a way, yes. What difference does it make if it's for her or not?"

"Nothing. I just wondered. You were the one who brought it up."

Montgomery regarded him thoughtfully for a moment. "How are things at home?" he asked.

"I told you, didn't I? That night you were here with Anne."

"You just said everbody was happy, or something like that."

"Oh, that's right. I didn't want to go into details right then. No—the reason everybody is happy is that Sue walked out on me."

"What the hell do you mean?"

"Just that. She packed up and left."

"My God—do you mean I'm responsible? Was it that night that did it?"

"Arthur, it was no particular night that did it. It was an accumulation of a lot of things."

"You sound kind of bland about it, if you don't mind my saying so."

"Well, I'm afraid, if I were to be honest with you, that it's a load off my mind."

"Oh?"

"It wasn't any good, even at its best. She wasn't cut out to be a writer's wife, and I wasn't cut out to be—ah, the hell with it. There's no point boring you with the details."

"Well, I'm not going to try to pump you, but I'd hate to think that I'd been responsible."

"Arthur, believe me—you weren't responsible. And believe me also, the whole thing is much better this way."

"O.K. If you say so."

"I say so. And God knows, I should know."

"I suppose so."

"Now. Tell me what this is we're going to do for Anne."

The headwaiter came through the crowd to Ulm. "Your table is ready any time you want it, Mr. Ulm," he said.

"Thank you, Adolf," Ulm replied. He turned to Montgomery. "Should we go in?" he asked.

Montgomery nodded, and as they went toward the back room he smiled and said, "You'll never get *me* to believe you didn't slip him a couple of bucks."

"Well, that's the magazine business for you," Ulm said, and they both laughed.

By the time they finished lunch, the crowd had dwindled and the saloon was almost quiet. The only noise, in fact, came from a table in one corner of the back room, where eight women in rimless glasses and flowered hats were winding up a lunch that was apparently in honor of one of their number, a thin spinster from the research library at the newspaper. She was wearing a small corsage of pink orchids. There was a great deal of laughter and some shrieking, and then they all took out their compacts and rearranged their faces, after which they stood up, tugged quickly at the rear of their girdles, and filed out, like children at a school picnic. One of them was laughing uncontrollably, and she stopped at the bar for a glass of water, then caught up with the rest and bundled out into the street, still laughing. Two men, who were playing matches at the bar, hunched over a little as the women went past, but otherwise ignored them.

Ulm put down his coffee cup and reached for a cigarette. "All right," he said. "So we get the bed from this character. Then what do we do with it?"

"Then we take it home," Montgomery replied.

"To Anne's?"

"No, to Lapham's. This is supposed to be a surprise."

"How do we get it there?"

There was a short pause. "Well, there are a couple of ways," Montgomery said, hesitantly. "We could take it in a taxi, or—"

"*In* a taxi? You'll never get a brass bed *in* a taxi."

"I know. But maybe the guy would let us strap it on top."

"And what's the other way?"

"Well, we could always walk with it."

"How far is it?"

"I don't know. I've got the address in my pocket somewhere. I don't think it's far."

Ulm dragged deeply on his cigarette, then talked through the smoke as it came out. "Common sense tells me to stay out of this," he said. "But for some hideous reason, I can't say no to you. I know I'm going to regret it as long as I live."

"Which may not be long," Montgomery said. "Come on, let's go to the bar, and I'll buy you a drink for courage."

They paid their lunch checks, then went out to the bar and ordered two highballs. One of the match players was Prescott Rawlings, the small man with the Virginia accent. He looked at them and said, "Gentlemen, you are just in time for a short game of skill and chance. A drink and a buck is the current stake, but we can revise it on request. Be so good as to join us, won't you?"

"No, thanks," Montgomery replied. "We have work to do."

"Nonsense. If you're having a drink, you might as well play for it."

"I guess he has a point there," Montgomery said to Ulm. "Who knows? We might even win."

Ulm shrugged, and took three matches from a box, and Montgomery also selected three, and they put their hands behind their backs and secretly sorted the matches.

"Gentlemen, this is Roger Streeter," Rawlings said, nodding at his companion. All four men had their hands behind their backs, so they simply nodded their greetings. Streeter, who was short and bald, was smoking a cigarette, and the smoke filtered into his eyes so that he could hardly see.

They played one round, which Rawlings lost. He demanded revenge, so they played one more, which Montgomery lost. Then Rawlings suggested that they make it a trilogy, so they played another, and Montgomery lost again. When the third round of drinks had been served, Montgomery said, "This is all very well, but Sam and I have an errand to do. I'm going to pay my bill and get out of here, charming though your company may be."

"Don't go," said Rawlings. "Let's play just one more trilogy."

"No," said Montgomery. "Flatly, no."

"I dare you. As a gentleman, I dare you."

"I can't. I told you, Sam and I have an errand to do."

"You're a coward, sir. A rank, miserable, sniveling coward."

"Hey," Ulm said to Montgomery. "I have an idea."

"What?"

"Why don't we take these two gentlemen with us? I have a feeling we're going to need some help."

Montgomery looked at Rawlings for a moment. "Would you like to help a lady in distress?" he asked.

"Sir, you have come to the right man," Rawlings replied. "Who is the lady, and what do I have to do?"

"The lady is the one you met here with me the other night, and all you have to do is help us buy a brass bed for her."

"A charming idea," said Rawlings. "I think that is a perfectly charming idea. Where can we find one?"

"I have the address," Montgomery replied. He looked at Streeter. "Would you care to join us?" he asked.

Streeter shook his head. "Too many cooks spoil the broth," he said.

"Coward," said Rawlings.

"It's all very well for you to talk," Streeter replied. "Press agents can take the whole day off if they want to. It just so happens that I have to work." He finished his drink, said good-by all around, and left, bumping into the door with a furry thud.

"What does he do?" Ulm asked.

Rawlings looked at the door, where Streeter had gone out. "It's supposed to be a secret," he said. "But I hear he's a spy."

"For us, or for them?" said Ulm.

Rawlings shrugged. "I don't think in his case it makes much difference," he said.

There was a customer in the antique store when they got there, so they stood to one side and waited. Montgomery was faintly apprehensive, but the mere presence of the other two was of some comfort to him. "Remember," he said to them in a low voice, "you let me do the talking. You're just here to help me."

"Check," said Ulm.

"Hey," Rawlings said, looking into a cluttered corner of the store. "What do you know about that?" He went across, and came back holding an eighteen-inch marble nude with a gold clock in her stomach. "I haven't seen one of these since I was a boy," he said. "I wonder how much he wants for it."

"I don't know," Montgomery replied. "But if you drop it, it's yours."

"I think I'll ask him," said Rawlings. "I'd kind of like to have one around, just for old times' sake."

Ulm laughed. "How're you going to carry the bed and the clock too?" he said.

"Hell, that's easy," Rawlings replied. "We let the lady ride. Put her on the bed, and carry her that way. Any Southern gentleman could tell you that."

For some reason, this struck them both as uproariously funny, and Rawlings laughed so hard he almost dropped the clock. Nervously, Montgomery tried to quiet them. "Hey, take it easy, fellows," he said. "Let's not get the guy sore at us right away."

"What's he got to be sore about?" Rawlings asked. "He's about to make a stupendous sale. They're damn few people would want to buy a thing like this, I can tell you."

"Nevertheless," said Montgomery. He was about to say something more, when the storekeeper came up to them.

"May I help you gentlemen?" he asked tentatively.

"Oh—yes," said Montgomery. "We'd like to buy a brass bed."

At the same time, Rawlings held up the nude and said, "How much is this lady, here?"

The storekeeper surveyed the three men quickly, trying to estimate the situation at one glance. He cleared his throat, and put the tips of his fingers together. "Perhaps if we take things one at a time," he said. And then, pointing limply to the nude, "That clock is sixty-five dollars."

"Whoo-ee!" Rawlings exclaimed, and he wheeled back and replaced the nude where he had found it. The storekeeper turned to Montgomery.

"And now," he said. "You were interested in buying a brass bed?"

"Yes," Montgomery replied. "We—I wondered if you had one." His throat felt dry, and his face was suddenly hot.

"Well, that all depends," said the storekeeper. "How many people would you want it to—ah—accommodate?"

"Oh, this isn't for me—I mean, for us—" Montgomery stammered. "What I mean is that it's just a single bed that we're—that I'm looking for. A bed for one. Brass. You know." He tried to indicate a brass bed with his hands, and failed utterly.

"Yes, I think I have one," said the storekeeper. "Would you like to look at it?"

"Yes, please," Montgomery said. "How much is it?"

"A hundred dollars."

They had started toward the rear of the store, and Montgomery stopped. "Oh, no," he said. "That's much too much."

"This bed is in excellent condition." The man's voice was icy.

"That may be, but I can't pay anything like that."

"I'm very sorry."

There was a pause, and Ulm said to Montgomery, "What did he tell you it was supposed to cost?"

"Nobody told me anything," Montgomery said quickly. "I guess we'll have to go back to the other place."

"What other place?" said Ulm, mystified. "The saloon?"

"No," Montgomery said, and he turned to the storekeeper. "There's a place I know where I can get one for fifty dollars," he said, and the storekeeper raised his eyebrows and shrugged.

"What are you talking about?" Ulm said. "I thought this was the place we were supposed to come."

"I think the whole thing is a trap," said Rawlings to Ulm. "Can you imagine anyone wanting sixty-five dollars just for a lady with a little old clock in her belly?"

In desperation, Montgomery said to Ulm, "There is another place I didn't tell you about, where I saw a bed for fifty dollars. I thought I might be able to get one cheaper, that's all." He moved toward the door, trying to shepherd the other two ahead of him. "I guess we'll just go back to Lapham's, and buy the one he has."

"I don't get it," Ulm said, shaking his head. Propelled by Montgomery, he started out, but the storekeeper stopped them.

"I beg your pardon," he said. "But where did you say you saw the bed?"

"It's a place up the avenue," Montgomery replied, smiling to himself.

"No, but you mentioned the name."

"Actually, I don't know the name of the shop, but I think

it's run by a man named Lapham. Duncan Lapham." Montgomery turned to Ulm. "Come on," he said. "Let's go."

"Boy, this is all over my head," said Ulm. "I thought that Lapham was—"

"Just a minute," the storekeeper broke in. "I think that if you want to take this bed without a mattress, I could come down a little in the price for you."

"Oh?" said Montgomery. "How much?"

"Well, it's a very good mattress. In fact, I know I can get fifty dollars for it. So suppose we say you can have the bed without the mattress for an even fifty. And I wouldn't do this for many people, believe me."

"At Lapham's, I can get a bed *with* a mattress for fifty," Montgomery said. He was immediately sorry he'd said it, because the storekeeper turned away in exasperation. Now I've blown the whole deal, Montgomery thought. What am I going to do next?

From near the door, Rawlings said, "Hey, gentlemen, look at this, will you?" He held up a stuffed woodpecker in a glass bell. The bird was perched on a branch surrounded by pink and blue paper flowers, and one of its eyes was missing. "Do you think Leo would like this to put up over the bar?" he said. "We could all chip in and give it to him as a present." He and Ulm laughed, and then the bell tinkled and another customer entered the store, almost knocking the bird from Rawlings' hands.

"I'll tell you what," the storekeeper said suddenly to Montgomery. "I'll give you the bed, without the mattress, for forty dollars, and that's the last word I'll have to say on the subject. Take it or leave it."

"Done and done," said Montgomery. To the others, he said, "Come on, men, we've just bought a bed. Let's go back and pick it up."

"Don't bother to wrap it," said Rawlings. "I'll sleep in it on the way home."

The minute they got on the street with the bed, they knew that taking a taxi was out of the question. Montgomery had the head piece and one side bar, Rawlings had the foot piece and the other side bar, and Ulm had the spring, and among them they took up as much space as a squad of riflemen.

"All right, then," said Ulm. "So we walk it. How far do we have to go?"

"Not far," Montgomery replied, as he started down the street. "Only about fifteen blocks."

"Jee-*zus!*" said Rawlings, hurrying to catch up with the others. "That's more than I walk in a *month!*"

"Well, you can do your month's quota today," said Ulm. "Then you can ride everywhere you go for the next four weeks."

"There is one thing that leaves me absolutely cold," Rawlings said, panting. "And that's gallows humor."

In New York, a man can stand on a street corner and shout himself hoarse, and people will walk past him with only an occasional backward glance; the minute a policeman comes up to him and tells him to move along, people will stop and form a silent circle to watch. Nobody is interested in another person's trouble until that person is so deeply into it that he cannot ask for help. Thus it was that the sight of three men dragging the pieces of a brass bed along the sidewalk brought no more than passing attention and a few jeers from children playing in the streets, and the entire trip would have gone virtually unnoticed if they had not been spotted on a side street by a police patrol car, and stopped for questioning. The police make it a practice to investigate anything unusual —a man carrying a television set down the street, for instance, is almost sure to be questioned by any policeman who sees him, simply because most people don't carry television sets down the street—and to the police in this particular prowl car, three men with a brass bed was definitely something unusual. The driver pulled over to the sidewalk, and stopped the car just abreast of Montgomery.

"Hold it a minute, there, Bud," he said.

"I knew it!" Ulm said to Rawlings. "I knew it! I knew it! I knew it!"

"This is just a bed, officer," Montgomery said. "We bought it for a friend."

"Oh? Where'd you buy it?"

Two boys, who had been playing punch ball in the street, stopped their game and came over to listen.

"We bought it in a store on Third Avenue," Montgomery said. "I don't know the name, but I can give you the address."

"You got a bill of sale?"

"No."

"Who's the friend you bought it for?"

"I don't see that that makes any difference—"

The driver opened his door and got out of the car, and with the same motion his partner got out the other side. "All right, now," the driver said. "Let's not get wise, or we'll end up with a busted lip." His partner circled in front of the car, and stood by Ulm and Rawlings. "Let's go back to this store," the driver said. "We'll see if you bought a bed or if you didn't."

"All of us?" Rawlings said incredulously.

"All of you," said the driver. "You're all in this together."

"Look, officer," Montgomery said, trying to keep his voice calm. "There's no point our dragging the bed all the way back to the store. If one of you wants to stay here with these two gentlemen and the bed, I'll go back with the other, and the man at the store will identify me. Wouldn't that be all right?" He was suddenly aware that they were surrounded by a circle of people, some quiet and some whispering, but all waiting for something to happen.

The driver looked at him for a moment. "O.K.," he said. "You come with me." He turned to his partner. "You keep these two here, George," he said. "You'd better frisk them," he added, and his partner nodded. The driver ran his hands over Montgomery's pockets, then ushered him into the car. "O.K.," he said. "Now let's see where this place is." As they drove off, Montgomery saw that the other policeman had made Ulm and Rawlings face a building with their hands high against the wall, and he was going through their pockets from the rear.

When they got to the store, the policeman followed behind Montgomery as he went in. In the back of the shop, the storekeeper looked up from his desk, and he blinked when he saw Montgomery and the policeman. Then he rose. "Now, wait a minute," he began, but the policeman cut him off.

"This man says he bought a bed from you," the policeman said. "Do you recognize him?"

"Why, yes," said the storekeeper. "And I don't see that he has any cause for complaint. I gave him an exceptionally reasonable price, and—"

"He's not doing any complaining," the policeman said. "I just want to know if he got it from you legally."

"Oh," said the storekeeper. He relaxed, and his mouth puckered in a tight smile. "Why, yes. Of course."

"You should of give him a bill of sale," the policeman said. "I see these guys dragging a bed down the street, and for all I know they lifted it somewhere. You ought to give a bill of sale when you sell something like that."

"Yes, of course I should have," the storekeeper said smiling. "I guess it just slipped my mind. I'm sorry."

"All right," the policeman said, in a disappointed tone. "I just wanted to make sure." He gestured to Montgomery, and they went out and into the prowl car. The bell tinkled as the shop door closed behind them.

By the time they got back to Ulm and Rawlings, a crowd of fifty or sixty people had gathered. The pieces of the bed were stacked against a building, with Ulm and Rawlings sitting on the ground in front of them, while the policeman kept the crowd back and periodically told people to move on. Montgomery got out of the prowl car, and the driver called to his partner. "O.K., George," the driver said. "They got it legitimate." To Montgomery, he said, "I didn't want to make you any trouble, Mac. We just got to check these things, you understand."

"Oh, sure," said Montgomery. "I understand."

The siren growled as the police drove off, and the crowd began to break up. Montgomery looked at Ulm and Rawlings. Nobody said anything, and they picked up the pieces of the bed and started down the street. They had gone about five blocks in silence, when Ulm said, "Maybe one of these days I'll learn."

"Learn what?" Montgomery replied. "We didn't get arrested, did we?"

"I don't know what happened to you," said Rawlings, "but I sure as hell felt as though *I'd* been arrested."

"This was nothing," said Montgomery. "You should have been along the last time Sam and I went out together."

"No, thanks," said Rawlings.

Ulm began to laugh. "I guess we got off easy, at that," he said. "Maybe your luck's changed, Arthur. Maybe from now on you're going to spread good luck wherever you go."

"All I ask is that we get this bed back home," Montgomery said. "That'll be good enough luck for me."

Their arms were tired and their backs ached when they got to the apartment, and Rawlings leaned his pieces of the bed against the wall, then sat on the front steps. "Wow," he said.

"Just a little bit more," said Montgomery, as he opened the door. "We've got to get it up to Lapham's room."

"And I suppose he lives on the top floor, too," said Rawlings, as he got wearily to his feet.

"Don't worry about that," Montgomery said. "It's not a very tall building."

They had dragged the pieces of the bed to the second-floor landing and were starting up to the third, when Evelyn opened her door and looked out. Montgomery saw her, and smiled. "See?" he said. "We made it."

"Yes," she said, and her voice sounded unnatural. "Can I speak to you for a minute?"

"Just as soon as I get this up there," he replied. "Is Duncan in?"

"No," she said quietly.

"Well, we'll just leave it by his door." Montgomery struggled the last of the way up the stairs, and set his load down with a clattering crash. Panting, he looked at the other two and said, "I think I owe you gentlemen a drink."

"Not for me, thanks," said Ulm, as he leaned the spring against the wall. "I've got to get back to work."

Rawlings, who was glistening with perspiration, wiped his face with a handkerchief. "Me too," he said, and he started slowly back down the stairs.

"Well, I'll buy you all one later, then," Montgomery said. "I really appreciate this—I couldn't have done it without you."

"And you almost didn't do it with us," Ulm said. He nodded to Evelyn, who was still standing in her door, then waved his hand to Montgomery. "See you later," he said, and followed Rawlings down the stairs.

Montgomery went to Evelyn and saw that she was badly upset. "What's the trouble?" he asked.

"Come in." She motioned him into her room and closed the door behind him. "Anne's disappeared," she said.

"*What?*"

"When I got back from rehearsal, she was in her room in a terrible state—crying, and carrying on, saying she was going to go back home, or kill herself, or whatever. From what I gather, she's been evicted from the building—or at least told they won't renew her lease—and she's acting as though it's the end of the world."

"Where'd she go?"

"I don't know. I came up here to get a seconal for her, and when I got back down she was gone."

"Did she take anything with her?"

"She didn't have time. I was only up here a couple of minutes."

Montgomery saw that Evelyn was trembling, and her voice was strained. "You have no idea where she could have gone?" he asked.

She shook her head. "There were only two things she mentioned—either home, or—or the other."

"Let's take a look in her room," said Montgomery. "If she's gone home, she'll have taken at least something. Maybe we can figure out."

They went downstairs and looked through Anne's room, but nothing seemed to have been touched. Her clothes were all in order, and there were no empty hangers, and on the shelf in the bathroom were a green, scraggly toothbrush, a gnarled and nearly empty tube of tooth paste, and an assorted array of lipstick, eye shadow, powder, and bobby pins.

"That settles it," said Evelyn. "She wouldn't have gone home without the make-up."

Montgomery looked around the room. Everything in it was familiar to him, but it had suddenly taken on a dead, empty look, as though he had never seen it before. The Venetian blind was slightly askew, and near the door the rug was worn all the way through to the floor boards. The edges of the hole were stringy and ragged. "Then where else *could* she have gone?" he asked.

"I never should have left her," Evelyn said. "I should have *known* better than to leave her when she was in a state like that. . . ."

"How long ago was this?"

"I don't know—a half hour, maybe. An hour—I don't know."

"And she didn't say anything else?" Montgomery asked, wishing that the East River hadn't just occurred to him.

"No. Just—what I told you."

"Well, I guess I'll go out and take a look around," he said, trying to sound as casual as he could. "You stay here with the

seconal in case she comes back, and I'll walk around a few
blocks and see if I run into her. She may have taken a walk
to settle herself down."

"I only left her for a minute," Evelyn said. "Or only two
minutes at the most. I guess I should have known. . . ."

"I'll go out and take a look," he said, and he went to the
door. "I'll let you know if I find out anything."

He went out, and his first impulse was to walk over to the
river. The afternoon shadows were dark and long, and the
sky to the east was a smoky blue. The air was turning cold,
and the river would probably be windy. There's no point
going there first, he thought. That really wouldn't do much
good, anyway. He circled to the west, and had gone about
five blocks when an idea came to him. He checked his pockets
for change, then stepped into a cigar store and dialed the
number of the newspaper.

✌15✌

I T WAS ALMOST DARK when he came out of the phone booth.
There had been no reports about Anne with either the police
or the city hospitals, and it was clearly too soon to expect that
anything might be on the press-association wires. The man
on the city desk had said he'd keep an eye out for anything,
and beyond that there wasn't very much that could be done.
Montgomery thought briefly of checking the bus stations and
airports, but it seemed such an outside chance that he gave
up the idea almost at once. He walked aimlessly north for a
few blocks, and then found himself circling back toward the
river. All right, then, he said to himself. You might as well go
there and get it over with. You won't be satisfied until you've
looked, for whatever little good it may do.

There weren't many places where a person could actually
get to the river's edge. Montgomery chose the nearest one,
which was a little park with a parapet overlooking the water.
He looked out across the darkening river, and at the lights
of Brooklyn beyond, and then he looked along the parapet,
to see if anything had been left there. He could see nothing.
He stared at the water for a while, wondering what he would

do if he were in Anne's place. He also wondered what had brought about the cancellation of her lease, and then suddenly he remembered Martha Becker's words: "I'm going to tell the landlord he's not going to get another nickel until she's thrown out." My God, he thought. Could she have done that? But on what grounds? What could she possibly invent as an excuse for getting Anne evicted from the building? The more he thought about it, the surer he became that it was Martha who had done it, but also the more confused he became as to why, and on what excuse. What could make a woman want to do a thing like that? What kind of hatred, or jealousy, would lead her to behave that way? She must be some kind of psychiatric case, he concluded. That's the only possible explanation, but it doesn't do much good right now.

He turned away from the parapet, wondering where he should go next. As he walked out of the park, he saw a figure sitting on a stone bench, huddled in a corner like a small bird. When he came into the park, he had been looking at the river and hadn't even noticed that the bench was there. He went closer, and saw that the figure was Anne. "Hi," he said quietly. "Can I sit down?"

She touched the bench with her hand, and he sat down beside her. He took her hand in both of his and held it in his lap, and they sat there in silence for a few moments. Her hand felt like a piece of old cheese. "Aren't you cold?" he asked.

She shook her head, and looked out at the river. A gust of chill wind blew off the water, and her body was convulsed with a long shiver. He took off his coat. "Here," he said. "Put this around you."

She let him put the coat over her shoulders, and then she leaned against him and rested her head on his shoulder. "I didn't have the nerve," she said.

"To do what?"

"To jump."

"Why should you, anyway?"

"You know what happened, don't you?"

"Yes, but there are other apartments. We could always help you find one."

"You've done too much already."

"Nobody's done anything."

"If you only knew."

"Evelyn said you mentioned you might go home. Would that be such a bad idea?"

She was quiet for a few seconds. "Just a little worse than jumping in the river," she said.

"All right, then, we can find you a new apartment."

"*We* can find you a new apartment—*we* can do this—*we* can do that—"

"O.K. Then *you* find yourself a new apartment. I don't see why moving out of the one you're in should look like the end of the world."

"How can I get an apartment in my condition? How can I take the time to do all I have to do? I don't have that much time—I don't have that much money—I can't *afford* to change."

"When do they want you out of this one?"

"When the lease expires. January."

"There's plenty of time, then. All the time in the world."

"No, there isn't. And it isn't only the apartment—it's everything. Everything's crowding in on me—everything's out of control—everything's gone wrong—oh, God, I'm so afraid!" She clutched at his shirt, and dug her fingernails into his chest.

"All right, then," he said gently. "All right. That's what we're here for."

"No, you're not! You shouldn't have to worry about me—it's none of your business what happens to me! Do you think I can keep on asking people to help me all the rest of my life?"

"Of course not. You won't have to. But everyone needs help at *some* time, so right now, when you need it, why not let us be the ones to do it?"

"Because it's not right! Because if I can't do it alone here in New York, then I'll have to go back home and live in misery all the rest of my life! But I'm not going to drag everybody else into it—is that clear?"

"Did it ever occur to you that we might *want* to do this?" he said. "Did it ever occur to you that this is something that none of us has ever had before?"

There was a long silence. "No," she said at last. "It didn't, and I don't believe it."

"It didn't occur to me until just now," he said. "But I do believe it."

"Mrs. Becker, too?"

"Mrs. Becker is not one of us. Mrs. Becker is off in her own little shell, barricading herself against I don't know what. Don't pay any attention to Mrs. Becker."

"She was the one who made the complaint, you know."

"Did they tell you that?"

"No, but it could only have been her. The agent said that the complaint listed—well, never mind."

"Don't worry about her. I really think she's crazy."

"A lot of good it does me to know that."

"Nothing is going to do you much good if you sit out here much longer—you'll freeze to death." He stood up, and held out his hands to her. "Come on. Let's go back and get something to eat, and then we can figure out what to do later."

She rose with the slowness of someone awakening from a long sleep, and when she was standing he put one arm around her, and together they walked out of the park. She shivered once again, and he held her tightly.

They had gone about a block when he saw a cigar store. "Let's duck in here for a minute," he said. "I want to tell Evelyn you're all right; otherwise she'll go out of her mind."

"I'm sorry I did that," she said. "I didn't mean to worry her."

They went into the cigar store, and he closed himself in the booth and dialed Evelyn's number. There was no answer, and then he realized that she was waiting in Anne's room, so he dialed that number. After four rings, Evelyn answered.

"She's all right," Montgomery said. "I found her."

"Thank God," Evelyn gasped.

"Are you O.K.?" Montgomery asked. "You sound winded."

"Well, I *am* winded! Did you just call my number?"

"Oh," he said. "Yes. I'm sorry."

"I heard it ringing, and I got all the way up the bloody stairs and into the room when it stopped, and then I heard this one ringing and had to lurch all the way down again. I'm a wreck."

"I'm sorry," he said again.

"How is she?"

"All right, I guess. We're on our way back now."

"I'll have something ready when you get here. And a medal for you, if you want one."

"It was nothing," he said. "Any member of Northwest Mounted Police would have done the same."

He hung up, and then called the city desk of the paper and told the desk man to relax. When he got out of the phone booth, he looked at Anne and knew that something was wrong. She was clutching the edge of the cigar counter, and her face was gray and shining.

"Take me to the hospital," she said. "Quick."

"Stay right where you are," Montgomery said, unnecessarily. "I'll get a cab." He ran outside, hoping that his voice had not betrayed the flash of panic that made him feel slightly sick.

The receptionist at the hospital was tired and disinterested. She took out a blank form and rolled it into her typewriter. "The name of your doctor?" she asked.

"Dr. Lipkin," Anne replied. "Dr. Edward Lipkin."

"Has he reserved a room for you?"

"I don't know. I don't think he—I mean, I think this is early."

"What did he say when you called him?"

"I haven't called him yet. I came here as soon as—I came right away."

The receptionist took the form out of the typewriter. "I think you'd better call him now," she said.

Anne went to the telephone booth, and Montgomery looked around the reception room. It was an old building, and the walls were an unpleasant shade of yellow which, combined with the dark woodwork, made the room look more like a museum than a hospital. There was a large potted plant in one corner, and a bench along the far wall, and between the two elevators was a bronze plaque in memory of some bearded doctor. The generally depressing atmosphere of the room was emphasized by the faint but recognizable smell of ether and disinfectants and creosote. A white-coated attendant padded through the room pushing a wheeled laundry hamper, and the smell became stronger as he passed. Then he was gone, and Montgomery wanted very much to be somewhere else.

Anne came out of the booth and went to the receptionist. "He's going to call you," she said. "He says it may be a little early, but that I might as well get a room now." Her face tightened, and then relaxed again. "He's coming over pretty soon," she said.

The receptionist put the form back in the typewriter. "All we have open are private rooms," she said, and typed something on the form. "Is that all right?"

"How much is a private room?" Anne asked.

"Twenty-five dollars a day." She typed something else. "What is your name?" she asked.

"Anne Waters. Look—I can't pay anything like that. Haven't you something cheaper?"

"Mrs. Anne Waters," the girl said, typing. "All the semiprivate rooms are taken. The only thing else is the ward. Do you have hospitalization or Blue Cross?"

"No," said Anne. "I guess I'll have to take the ward, then."

"Wait a minute," said Montgomery, surprised at the firmness of his own voice. "Give her a private room. I'll take the responsibility."

"Oh, no," Anne said to him. "I can't let you do that."

"Shut up," he said quickly, and then, to the receptionist, "Put Mrs. Waters down for a private room."

The receptionist looked at him. "Are you Mr. Waters?" she asked.

"No," said Montgomery. "My name is Arthur Montgomery. I'm—her uncle."

The girl typed some more. "Are you the next of kin?" she asked.

Montgomery took a deep breath, looked at Anne, and cleared his throat. "I suppose you could call it that," he said. "Yes. I am."

When the registration had been completed, the girl gave Anne a slip and told her the room number. Then she looked at Montgomery. "It will be a little while before you can go up," she said. "You can wait on that bench, over there."

Anne smiled at Montgomery. "You don't have to stay," she said.

"Don't be silly," he said. "I wouldn't think of leaving."

When she had gone up in the elevator, it occurred to Montgomery that he ought to call Evelyn. As he went to the phone booth, he glanced at the wooden bench and hoped that he wasn't going to have to wait too long.

Evelyn was just beginning to get worried again, when the phone rang. She picked it up quickly and said, "Hello?"

"Well, if it isn't one thing, it's another," Montgomery said, at the other end. "Now we've got her in the hospital. Things seem to be getting under way."

"You mean the baby?"

"That's the way it looks."

"Oh, for Heaven's sake! Do you want me to come over?"

"I don't think there'd be much point. There's not much going on at the moment."

"Are you going to stay there?"

"I might as well. I think somebody ought to be with her."

"By all means. Let me know if there's anything I can do."

"I will."

"Oh—and Arthur."

"What?"

"I think you're magnificent."

There was a silence at the other end of the line. "Thank you," he said finally, and hung up.

Evelyn put down the phone, and looked around the room. There's no use my staying around here any more, she thought. I might as well go back to my own room, where I can be a little more comfortable.

She had just got into her room when Duncan Lapham came clattering down the stairs, laughing. "He did it!" he said. "He got the bed! But do you know something? I meant for him to take it to my *store*, not to my room! He must have had an absolutely *murderous* time getting it up these stairs— I wish I'd been here to see it!"

"He had help," Evelyn said, and then she told Lapham of the day's developments. The laughter faded from his face, and his lips turned gray.

"It was that old bitch that did it!" he said. "She must have been the one that complained."

"I guess it was," Evelyn said.

"I think I'll go down there and give her a piece of my mind," said Lapham. "She ought to be hung up by the heels and flayed!"

"I don't think it would do much good."

"No, but *really!*" He was breathing deeply, and his nostrils dilated with each breath.

214

"I think there must be something wrong with her," Evelyn said. "I think she's probably a little unbalanced."

"Oh, unbalanced my foot. She's just an old biddy who can't keep her nose out of other people's business. She pretends to be outraged, and she's loving every minute of it. But to get the poor girl thrown out in the street—no, I'm going down there and have a few words with her." He turned and went out the door. Evelyn followed him.

"Duncan, I really don't think it will help," she said.

"It may not help," he replied, as he went down the stairs, "but at least it will make *me* feel better." He knocked on the Beckers' door, and Evelyn watched from the stair landing. After a moment, Ernest Becker opened the door.

"Excuse me, Mr. Becker," Lapham said. He could see into the room, and he saw Martha sitting in a chair, looking out the window. "I'd like a word with your wife." He went past Becker and addressed Martha, who did not look up. "Mrs. Becker," he said, "I want to say that I think what you did to Anne Waters was the most disgraceful, dishonest, disgusting thing I have ever heard of." Martha continued to stare out the window, and gave no sign that she was aware of him. "Do you understand me?" he said. "Do you hear what I'm saying?" Martha did not move. "Mrs. Becker!" he shouted. *"Listen to what I'm saying to you!"*

Behind him, Ernest Becker said, "I don't think she hears you."

Lapham turned and looked at him. "What's the matter?" he asked, his voice suddenly quiet.

"I don't know." Becker motioned him to the door, and they went out into the hall. "She's been like that for two days," he said. "She hasn't moved."

"My God," Lapham said. "Did you call a doctor?"

Becker shook his head. "No. For a long time now, she's been quiet, but it's only a couple of days she hasn't moved. I don't know if it's serious or not."

Lapham looked up the stairs, and saw Evelyn. "Come on,"

he said to Becker. "We'll see what Evelyn thinks, but I think we ought to call a doctor."

When Montgomery was allowed into Anne's room, he found her in bed, wearing a wrinkled white hospital gown that tied in the back. Her eyes were bright, and she smiled at him.

"Hello, Uncle Arthur," she said.

"Hi," he replied. "How goes it?"

"All right."

"Has the doctor been here?"

"No, not yet."

He shifted from one foot to the other. "How long is this supposed to take?" he asked.

"There's no set time," she said, and laughed. "I guess it kind of depends on me."

"Oh." He looked around, and saw a chair with green cushions and highly varnished flat wooden arms. "May I sit down?"

"Of course. I told you, you know. You don't have to stay here."

"I've got nothing else to do. Is there anything you'd like?"

"No, thank you." She winced, and bit her lip. "Ow," she said.

Montgomery got up quickly. "Should I get the nurse?"

"No," she said, smiling. "It's not that important yet."

He sat down. "How about something to read? Would you like it if I read something to you?"

"You get something if you want it. I don't really feel much like reading right now."

"I don't care one way or the other. I just thought you might like it."

"No, thanks."

"Oh, by the way," he said. "Is there anyone you'd like me to tell about this? I called Evelyn and told her, but I wondered if there's anyone else you'd like to have know."

There was a long silence. "No," she said at last. "Just you."

The door opened, and a nurse came briskly into the room. Her rubber-soled shoes made a squeaking noise on the polished floor. In one hand she had a shot glass, in which were two pills. She handed it to Anne, and poured a glass of water. "Here," she said. "Take this."

Anne raised her head, and put the pills in her mouth, then swallowed the water and lay back again. "What was that for?" she asked.

"None of your business," said the nurse, and she left the room.

"I must say, this is a friendly joint you've come to," said Montgomery. "Were they all booked up at the Tower of London?"

Anne laughed, and stopped in the middle of the laugh and closed her eyes. Then she opened them and said, "I'll tell you one thing you can do."

"What's that?"

"You can come over here and hold my hand whenever I get one of these things. I need something to hang onto."

"Done and done." He moved the chair alongside the bed, and put one hand near hers. "There it is," he said. "Do whatever you want to with it."

"Thank you." She held his hand gently, and her palm was warm and moist.

There was a sound outside the door, and then it opened and a doctor came in, wearing a long white coat. He was thin and cadaverous, and the curved earpieces of a stethoscope protruded from a side pocket of his coat.

"Oh, here he is!" Anne said. "Dr. Lipkin, this is Mr. Montgomery."

Montgomery rose, and the doctor shook hands with him. "How do you do," the doctor said. "Would you excuse us, please?"

"I beg your pardon?" said Montgomery.

"Would you mind waiting out in the hall for a few minutes?" The doctor looked at him coldly, as though he were an unpleasant specimen under a microscope.

"Oh—yes. Of course," Montgomery said. "I'm sorry." He went out into the corridor, and the door closed silently behind him. At one end of the corridor was an alcove, in which were a few random items of bamboo furniture, a potted plant, and a wicker table with magazines scattered on top of it. A weary, unshaven young man was sitting in one of the chairs. His head was back and his eyes were closed, and his hands hung limply over the arms of the chair. When Montgomery sat down, the young man opened his eyes and looked at him speculatively, then nodded. Montgomery nodded back.

"Just get here?" the young man asked.

"Yes," said Montgomery, and he reached out and took a magazine from the table.

"Good luck," said the young man. "I've been here since five this morning." Then he closed his eyes again.

Montgomery looked at his watch, and saw that it was half-past eight. My God, he thought. I didn't know it could take *that* long. He opened the magazine and tried to read, but the type was meaningless. He put the magazine back on the table, and got up and looked out the window. He could see the lighted buildings of the city, and above them drifted the winking red light of an airplane coming in for a landing. He watched the airplane until it disappeared, and then it occurred to him that he was hungry. I wonder what I do about eating, he thought. I wonder if there's some kind of restaurant nearby, or a hot-dog stand, even. He thought of asking the young man, since he must have had something to eat in all the time he had been there, but he looked so exhausted that Montgomery hated to disturb him. Then he saw the doctor coming out of Anne's room, and he walked down the corridor to meet him.

"How's she doing?" Montgomery asked.

At first, it didn't seem as though the doctor had heard him.

Then he said, "She's still got a long way to go. Labor hasn't really started yet."

"What?" said Montgomery. "What about those pains—what were they?"

The doctor shrugged. "It's too early to tell," he said, and looked at his watch. "I've got to go now, but I'll be back in another couple of hours."

"Oh," said Montgomery. The doctor started off, and Montgomery said, "By the way—is there someplace here where I can get a bite to eat?"

"There's a cafeteria in the basement," the doctor replied. "But if I were you I wouldn't try it. You've got plenty of time to go out and get a good dinner."

"Thanks," said Montgomery, and the doctor turned and left and Montgomery went into Anne's room. She waved two fingers at him, and smiled.

"Welcome back," she said.

"How do you feel?"

"I feel fine, except everything seems to have stopped."

He sat down in the chair. "Well, I guess that's not unusual," he said, thinking of the young man outside. "From what I gather, this kind of thing can take quite a little while."

"It makes me feel kind of stupid, though."

"I wouldn't worry about that."

"Listen to me, my dear sir," she said. "I've said this twice, and I'll say it again—there is no possible reason in the world for your staying around here. Why don't you go home, and laugh and play with the others?"

He looked at her. "Do you mean you'd prefer to be alone?" he said.

She hesitated. "No, of course not," she said. "But it's just that—"

"All right, then." He stood up. "I'm going downstairs and get something to eat, and I'll be back in about a half hour. If you want me for anything, you can have them page me in the cafeteria. O.K.?"

"O.K.," she said. "Paging Dr. Montgomery in the cafeteria."

The cafeteria was small, but it was not crowded when Montgomery got there. Three internes sat at a table in one corner, and two nurses sat at another, and the rest of the tables were empty. The lights were bright and glaring, and the room smelled of steam-table food and disinfectant. Montgomery had a cup of vegetable soup that was mostly water and tomato, and then a dish of rubbery pork chops with applesauce and wet succotash. As he mechanically ate the chops, he reflected that this was the first time in many years that he hadn't had at least three drinks before dinner. But for some reason he didn't miss the drinks, either because the dinner was so unlike what he was used to eating or because his mind was on other things. He felt a sense of unreality, of being a different person in a completely different world, and he noticed small details in things he would never have paid any attention to before. He noticed the crusted sugar on the rim of the chrome-lidded sugar bowl; he spent a long time staring at a hole in the linoleum where a radiator pipe went through the floor; and he could see the places on the window frame, high on the wall, where new putty had been applied and left unpainted. Time seemed suspended, and he moved in a brightly-lighted vacuum, seeing but not feeling, and aware only of a dim, gnawing worry in the back of his mind. Finally, when he could eat no more of the food, he lit a cigarette and walked out of the cafeteria and up to the reception room. There was a new girl at the desk, and she looked at him and smiled questioningly as he approached her. "Yes, sir?" she said.

"Is there a magazine stand around here anywhere?" he asked. "Or a place where I could buy a paper?"

"I'm sorry, the paper stand is closed," she replied. "But there's a place across the street."

He thanked her, and went outside. The night air was cold and clear, and he breathed deeply and gratefully as he went across the street to the stationery store. He bought all the evening papers, and on his way back to the hospital he noticed the saloon on the corner. I wonder, he said to himself. I wonder if one little shot might not be just what I need. This may be a long evening. Then he shook his head, and hurried across and into the hospital, back into the warmth and the smell of disinfectant.

When he got into Anne's room, her face looked somehow thinner, but she was smiling. "It's started again," she said.

"Good!" said Montgomery. "I guess all that was needed was for me to turn my back."

She laughed. "Sit down and tell me about your dinner," she said. "What did you have?"

He put the papers on the floor and sat in the chair by the bed. "It's kind of hard to tell you what I had, because all of it could so easily have been something else. To begin with, there was a soup—"

She dug her fingernails into his hand, and closed her eyes. "Just a minute," she said, and then she relaxed. "Now, about the soup."

"Well, it was about eight parts water," he began, and then the door burst open and a stocky, big-toothed nurse sailed into the room like a yacht before the wind. Her uniform made a sharp crackling noise as she came.

"Well!" she exclaimed. "So we're having a *baby!*" She put one hand under the covers, and turned the other hand so that she could see the watch on the underside of her wrist. "How often are we having the pains?" she asked.

"I don't know," Anne replied. "They're not regular."

"Well, now, we must keep track," the nurse said. "That's the only way we can tell." She straightened the covers, patted Anne on the top of the head, and then turned and blew out of the room.

"Now that I come to think of it," Montgomery said after she had gone, "I guess I prefer the surly ones, at that."

The next time Anne had a pain, Montgomery marked down

the time on a piece of newspaper, and the following pain came eight minutes later.

"That's not so good," she said. "I've got to do a lot better than that."

In the ensuing half hour, the interval narrowed from eight to seven to five minutes, and then the pains stopped. Anne closed her eyes, and her hand, which Montgomery was holding, went limp. In a sudden panic, he groped around and found the call bell, which was entangled in the head of the bed, and he jabbed the button several times. Then, more calmly, he leaned over and listened to her breathing, and was relieved to find that it was slow and even, like that of a person in normal sleep. Still and all, I shouldn't have to be doing this, he thought. There ought to be someone here who knows what's going on. The doctor ought to be here, just for one. How do *I* know if it's all right or if it isn't? He tried to remember all the news stories that he'd read or written about policemen delivering babies in patrol cars or taxis, and not one helpful detail came back to him. He was about to push the button again, when the door opened and the stocky nurse came in. "And how are we doing now?" she asked, brightly, and then saw that Anne was asleep.

"They've stopped again," Montgomery said. "Where's the doctor?"

The nurse said nothing, and reached out and took Anne's pulse.

"They were coming every five minutes, and then they stopped," Montgomery said, trying to keep his voice from sounding plaintive. "I think the doctor ought to know. Will you tell him?"

"I'll tell him as soon as he calls in," the nurse said, and she put Anne's arm back down on the bed.

"As soon as he *calls* in?" Montgomery said, incredulously. "Do you mean to tell me he's not in the hospital?"

The nurse looked at him without expression. "He has a lot

of other patients, too, you know," she said, and left the room.

Montgomery sat down, and was swept by a feeling of rage that abated only when he realized the impossibility of doing anything. Obviously, the doctor had other patients, and just as obviously, he had to be where the need was the most immediate. Still, there ought to be some way of—just supposing the pains *hadn't* stopped—supposing everything had gone quickly, then how would he.... Montgomery decided to let the doctor take care of his own schedule, and he settled back in the chair and tried to read a newspaper.

The pains started and stopped once more before the doctor arrived, and this time they were severe enough so that Anne cried out and arched backward with each one, like a fish fighting against the hook. She said nothing coherent during the intervals, and then she finally lapsed into a sleep that was much deeper than the one before. Montgomery, whose hands were torn and wet from her clawing, watched her and tried to make his mind a blank, tried to block out all feeling so as to be a more effective support for her, but he found that he was tense and trembling, and he could not make his thoughts take any rational form.

Then suddenly the doctor was in the room, and Montgomery rose and went toward him. "I'm glad you're here," he said.

"Yes," said the doctor, and he had his stethoscope in his ears and was bending over the bed, as Montgomery left the room.

Out in the corridor, Montgomery walked slowly and dazedly, like a man just out of an accident. He noticed, without thinking much about it, that the tired young man was no longer sitting in the alcove, and then, around the corner and down another corridor, he saw a telephone booth. He stared at it, trying to think what it reminded him of, until finally it came to him that he ought to call Evelyn. He looked at his watch, and saw that it was half-past eleven. I wonder where the time went, he thought, as he stepped into the booth. I had no idea it was that late.

Evelyn and Lapham and Ernest Becker stood on the front steps and watched until the ambulance carrying Martha Becker had disappeared. Then they turned and went back into the building.

"I was the one that did it," Becker said quietly. "I did it to her."

"No, you didn't," said Evelyn. "You heard what the doctor said."

"What was the word he used?" Becker asked.

"Catatonic. And there's nothing you could have done that would have caused it."

Becker shook his head, and Lapham said, "Anyway, she's going to get good care now. There are lots of things they know about schizophrenia that they never knew before."

Becker sighed, and said, "I suppose so."

"I tell you what," said Evelyn. "Let's go up to my room and have some tea, or coffee, or something like that. What do you say?"

"Good," said Lapham, and together they took Becker up the stairs.

Evelyn had just put the water on to boil, when the telephone rang. Quickly, she picked it up and said, "Yes?"

"Just checking in," came Montgomery's voice.

"How is she?"

"I don't know." He sounded tired and discouraged. "I may be here all night."

"Oh, no. Is she all right?"

"I guess so."

"Do you want any of us to come over?" She thought briefly of telling him about Martha Becker, then decided against it.

"No. There'd be no point in that."

"Is there anything you want?"

"No, thanks. I'll let you know if anything happens."

"All right." She paused. "We're all here, waiting."

"Good. I'll let you know."

She hung up, and relayed the news to Lapham and Becker.

"Oh, I didn't know," said Becker. "When did she go in?"

"This afternoon," Evelyn replied. "It was—ah—unexpected."

Becker looked at Lapham. "What was it you were trying to tell Martha?" he asked. "What did she do to Anne?"

"Well, actually, it's hard to say—" Lapham began, floundering in his embarrassment.

"It doesn't matter now," Evelyn cut in. "It's all over and done with. And about you, now," she went on, to Becker. "Isn't there something I could do to help you? I'd be very glad to cook, or help you clean up, or whatever."

He smiled. "No, thank you," he said. "I've been cooking for myself for quite a while now."

"If there's anything you need, or want done," said Lapham, "by all means call on us. I really mean that."

"Thank you," Becker said again. "I will."

"And I think that right now I ought to go help poor old Arthur," Lapham said. "What a perfectly dismal way for him to spend the night!"

"I don't think there's much anyone can do," Evelyn replied. "I asked him if he wanted anyone to come over, and he said no."

"I know, but still," said Lapham. "He ought at least to have someone to talk to, instead of pacing up and down those halls all alone."

"Well, I'm sure he'd be glad to see you," Evelyn said, as she poured the tea. "But from what I gathered, he may just go to sleep there. It seems to be simply a matter of waiting."

"I just hate to stand by and do *nothing*," Lapham said. "I mean, this has been a community project for so long that I feel now is the time for everybody to put his shoulder to the wheel—although that's possibly not quite the simile I'm groping for."

"I would go if I thought I could help," Becker said. "But

right now I don't know. Tonight I feel too tired to help much."

"One thing we could do is get at her room," Evelyn said. "There's a lot to be done there before she can bring a baby back to it. I don't think she's even bought any of the necessities yet."

"Sweet God," said Lapham. "Yes. And the bed, and all. I *would* like time to get it lacquered, but I guess that's just out of the question. Do you know how much he paid for it, by the way?"

"No," Evelyn replied. "There were—other things on my mind by the time he got back."

Lapham chuckled. "I wish I'd been there to see it," he said.

When they had finished their tea, Becker stood up. "I thank you for all you have done," he said. "I think now I had better go to bed."

"Wait a minute," said Evelyn. "Forgive my saying so, but I noticed your room hadn't been—attended to in the last couple of days. At least let me help you straighten it up before you go to bed."

Becker smiled. "All right," he said. "That would be very kind of you. It does make a difference to have a woman do it."

It was a long time before the doctor came out of Anne's room, and Montgomery hurried down the corridor toward him. "How is she?" he asked.

"She's having a hard time," the doctor replied, in an off-hand way. "It's twisted around, and may turn out to be a transverse arrest. I can't tell yet."

"Isn't there something you can do about it?" Montgomery asked.

"I'd rather she did it herself," said the doctor. "It's too soon to start interfering."

"Too *soon?*" said Montgomery. "When does it get late?"

"When she gets too weak," said the doctor, and started away.

From Anne's room came a muffled shriek *"Arthur!"* and Montgomery ran to the door.

"She's pretty heavily sedated," the doctor said. "I don't think she'll recognize you."

Montgomery flung open the door and went into the room. It was dark except for the light at the head of the bed, and the shadows looked tortured and grotesque. Anne writhed on the bed for a moment and then was still, and Montgomery went over and took her hand. "Here I am," he said. "I'm here." Her hand tightened slightly in his, but otherwise she gave no sign of having heard him. Still holding onto her hand, he sat down in the chair and settled back, prepared to wait it out.

How long he sat there he had no idea; the pains came and went and stopped again, and occasional nurses bustled in and out; and Montgomery sat in a kind of grinding trance, holding the small wet hand in his and saying things that he knew could not be heard or understood. Then an attendant came in with a wheeled stretcher, and Anne was bundled onto it and taken out, and Montgomery lay back in the chair and closed his eyes.

About five minutes later, the door opened quietly, and Duncan Lapham came in, carrying a round cardboard container. "How are things?" he asked, in a loud whisper.

Montgomery sat up, surprised. "Oh," he said. "Hi. They took her up a while ago. I don't know."

"I brought you some coffee," Lapham said. "I thought it might come in handy if this delivery bit was going to last all night."

"My God, how wonderful," said Montgomery. "Thank you."

Lapham took the cover off the container. "I didn't know whether you wanted cream or not," he said. "So I figured black would be best under the circumstances. I've got some sugar here, if you'd like it." From his pocket, he took a small envelope and put it and the coffee on the bed table beside Montgomery.

"This is very nice of you," Montgomery said, as he picked up the coffee. "Have you had some yourself?"

"Yes," Lapham replied, and then he laughed. "You should have seen the time I had with that bitch on the reception desk," he said. "She tried to tell me that visiting hours were over at nine, and that I couldn't come in. I certainly told *her* a thing or two." He laughed again, and said, "I didn't know I'd remembered so much from my medic days. When I got through, I'm sure she thought I was the son of Dr. Kildare, at least."

Montgomery sipped the hot coffee, and felt his strength return with the warmth in his stomach. "How are things back at the house?" he asked.

Lapham sat on the edge of the bed. "Oh, I almost forgot," he said, and told Montgomery about Martha Becker. When he finished, Montgomery took another sip of coffee, and then was quiet.

"Is she curable?" he asked, at last.

Lapham shrugged. "It's too early to tell," he said. "But at least she's getting treatment."

"Yes, I suppose that's something," said Montgomery, and then he paused, and drank the last of his coffee. He set the container down gently. "That poor little guy," he said.

"Evelyn's doing what she can to take care of him," said Lapham. "I don't think there's much, but she's damned well going to try. Things like all this bring out the mother in her."

"Yes," said Montgomery. "I guess they do in everybody."

A small, energetic nurse came bustling into the room. "If you gentlemen will excuse me," she said. "I'll get this room ready. Do you mind?" She stripped the crumpled sheets off the bed, and threw them in a corner.

Lapham and Montgomery started for the door, and as they went, Montgomery rubbed his hand across his chin and felt the stiff crackling of his beard. "Say, I could use a shave," he said, and then to the nurse, "You don't by any chance have a razor around here, do you?"

"Not one that *you'd* want to use," she said, and flung a clean sheet onto the bed.

"O.K.," Montgomery said. "I just wondered." They went out into the corridor, and he said to Lapham, "I guess I'll never understand nurses."

"Most of them are bitches," said Lapham, and they went into the alcove and sat down.

Montgomery felt completely revived by the coffee, and for some reason he also felt a little silly. Either it was the release from the tension of watching Anne, or it was the pleasure of having someone to talk to, or it was possibly something in his subconscious building up for the further ordeal that lay ahead; whatever it was, he felt like laughing. He looked at Lapham and said, "I don't suppose you know any good games, do you?" he said. "Games suitable for playing in hospital corridors?"

"We could have a paper chase," Lapham replied, after a moment's thought. "We could tear up little bits of bandage, and track each other in and out of all these dreadful little rooms."

Montgomery laughed. "That would be good," he said. "Only no fair hiding on the operating tables."

"God, no. We hide only in the beds of the wealthier patients."

"Just climb in with them and say, 'I'm terribly sorry, but I've got a dreadful cold and my doctor told me to go to bed right away.'"

"Or 'I hope you don't mind, but the bubonic ward is full up.'"

They both collapsed with laughter, and it was some little time before they could talk. Then Montgomery had another idea, although this one did not seem quite so funny, and after a while they ran out of ideas and simply sat, staring at the walls. Then Montgomery looked at his watch. It was quarter-past three.

"Say," he said quietly. "We should have heard something by now. She went upstairs hours ago."

"Did they say how long it would take?" Lapham asked.

Montgomery shook his head. "But they don't go up until they're pretty nearly ready," he said. "Something must have gone wrong."

"Well, they'd have told us if that had happened, wouldn't they?"

"I don't know. They could be too busy."

There was a long silence. "By the way," Lapham said. "Who's her next of kin?"

Montgomery hesitated. "On the records, I am," he said.

"*You* are?"

"It seemed like a good idea at the time."

"Who's really her next of kin?"

"I don't know."

"Does Evelyn know?"

"I don't think so."

"Oh."

There was another silence. "It never occurred to me that it would be important," Montgomery said.

"Oh, God," said Lapham. It was not profanity.

Then something began to close in on Montgomery; the absolute certainty that things had gone wrong filled the air like an evil fog, and everything he saw was tinged with ter-ror. He clasped his hands between his knees and closed his eyes to block out the sight, but he could not block out the feeling. Then a hand touched his arm, and he opened his eyes and saw Lapham sitting beside him.

"It's going to be all right," Lapham said gently. "I can promise you it's going to be all right." Montgomery shook his head, and Lapham went on.

"Look—I know just enough about this sort of thing to know. If anything goes wrong in any hospital—anywhere—"

He thought ahead quickly, trying to invent something that would sound convincing—"no matter where it is or what's happened, they let you know right away. The fact that we *haven't* heard is the best sign there is that everything's all right. I know what I'm talking about—I really do."

Montgomery took a deep breath and stood up. "I hope you're right," he said. "I just hope to God you're right." He walked to the end of the corridor, then came back and sat down. "They've got the room made up now," he said. "We can go back there if we want."

"Is that any better than here?"

Montgomery looked around the alcove. "I don't know," he said. "But I've got the feeling that I've been in this place here for the last five years."

"All right, then. Let's go."

Lapham reached out to pick up his cigarettes, and the doctor appeared around the corner. He had come so quietly that they hadn't heard him. He wore his white cap and gown, and his surgical mask was pulled down loosely under his chin. He looked first at Lapham, and then at Montgomery. "Well," he said. "She had a son."

Montgomery stood up. "How is she?" he asked.

"All right," the doctor said, in a voice filled with weariness. "She had a tough time, but she's all right." Then he looked at Lapham, who was standing beside him. "Are you the father?" he asked.

"No," said Lapham. "I'm just a friend. An old friend, from way back."

Montgomery laughed, and reached out and shook Lapham's hand, and then both he and Lapham shook hands with the doctor. "Will we be able to talk to her?" Montgomery asked.

"Not tonight," the doctor said. "We had to knock her pretty far under. Tomorrow morning, you can talk to her all you want." Then he turned and left, brushing against the wall as he went.

❧ 16 ❧

CHRISTMAS AT THE APARTMENT turned out to be quite a production. It was more or less a community project, with everyone doing something ostensibly for the baby, but by the time Christmas day arrived, there was an overflow that spread out into every room in the building. Lapham had bought a tree and some pine boughs from a cut-rate dealer on the West Side, and Becker had unearthed some old German tree ornaments from the storeroom in the basement. When the tree had been put up in Anne's room, and every available inch of it covered with ornaments, there was still enough left over to do a little decorating in the hall. And, once the hall was started, Lapham wasn't satisfied until it was festooned with sprigs of holly all the way up to the third floor. Montgomery came home with a massive holly wreath for Anne's door, but by the time he got there Lapham had the door covered with tinsel stars, so they hung the wreath on the front door of the building, agreeing that it was more appropriate there anyway.

In the matter of the presents, there was the simple problem of space. Anne's room was small, and with the tree and the cradle and the baby's equipment and the already-accrued presents such as Montgomery's panda, there was very little room left for the unopened Christmas presents. As many as possible were put around the tree, and the others were kept across the hall, in Becker's room. Not all the presents were for the baby; many were for Anne, and somehow in the confusion Montgomery's present for Evelyn got mixed in with the pile. He found it late Christmas afternoon, after a frantic search.

On Christmas Day, people wandered indiscriminately from room to room, leaving their doors open. Montgomery announced that he was holding open house all day, in honor of which he set a punch bowl in the middle of the room, with a ladle and glasses for those who wanted to sample it. He had gotten the recipe for the punch from the bartender at the saloon, and it involved eggs and Bourbon and cinnamon and was not very good. By the end of the day, however, there was only a small puddle of it left in the bottom of the bowl. Evelyn's problem was more complicated. She had said that she would serve a buffet dinner around three o'clock, and to that end she cooked a turkey and a ham, and bought a canned plum pudding, but she had also appointed herself official baby-sitter for the apartment, and she insisted on staying in Anne's room with the baby as much as possible, in order to let Anne visit with the others. In this, she had some competition from Becker, who got a tumbler of Montgomery's punch and then settled himself at the head of the cradle, where he rocked it gently and sang German Christmas songs in a reedy tenor. Lapham, in his apartment on the third floor, turned up the volume on his phonograph and played a program that alternated between Gregorian chants and "Swan Lake," and then he went down through the house, leaving in each room a small stocking with a present in it. For the baby, he left an antique cast-iron bank, in which the money was shot into the bank by a crossbowman.

Montgomery, after sampling his punch until he was sure

that it was as good as it was ever going to be, produced a piece of mistletoe that he had secreted in a dresser drawer and then, when Evelyn left her room to see that all was well with the baby, he put it up over her door. He never did anything more about it, because at that point he discovered that her present was missing, and it took him most of the rest of the afternoon to find it. At one point, Sam Ulm appeared with a present for Anne, and although everybody asked him to stay and celebrate with them, he was curiously ill-at-ease, and he left after about half an hour.

Finally, as it was getting dark, the party or celebration or whatever it had been began to lose momentum. Anne, who was listening to records with Lapham and Montgomery, looked at her watch and realized that it was time for the baby to be fed. She excused herself, and Montgomery followed her downstairs, where they found Evelyn giving the baby his bath, while Becker heated the formula on the stove. Anne tried to get them to leave, but they refused, so she turned to Montgomery and said, "Let's go outside for a minute. I'd like some air."

"Done and done," he replied, and he opened the door and they went out onto the front steps. The air was sharp, and from somewhere came the clanging, wailing noise of a fire engine. Then it faded, and there was quiet. Anne looked up at the sky, and breathed deeply.

"Oh, my, I'm going to miss this," she said.

"You don't have to go, you know," Montgomery replied. "I've told you that before."

"Yes, I do."

"You certainly do not. We can fix it with the landlord in no time. The whole thing was a mistake, to begin with."

"It wasn't a mistake."

"Well, a fluke, then."

"Maybe. But still, I've got to go."

"Why?"

"Lots of reasons."

"I can't see any."

"Maybe, but I can. Remember, I've always been talking about doing things on my own?"

"Yes."

"Well, it's about time I did. I can't let you all take care of me the rest of my life."

"We're not."

"You certainly are. Look at Evelyn—she's been with the baby more than I have. And Mr. Becker, and—well, all of you. It's just too much, that's all. It's no good for anyone."

"What are you going to do in your new place?"

"I'm going to take that job with Sam, so I'll have more money, and I'll have more room in the apartment, and everything will be more—well, more convenient. And I'll be on my own."

"What about Sam?"

"I don't know what about Sam. I guess that's up to him."

"I'm sorry. It's none of my business."

"I'd tell you if I knew. I just don't know."

"That won't be for long."

"He doesn't talk much, does he?"

"He will."

"You seem pretty sure."

"It's just a hunch."

She laughed. "You and your hunches. You know what you ought to do, don't you?"

"What?"

"You ought to come work for the magazine, too."

"Oh, no. We've been through all that."

"That's what I mean. You have a hunch you'd be no good, and I have a hunch you're wrong."

"Well, I don't."

"I'm not going to nag."

"Good."

"But I wish you'd think about it. I'd like to think I was still going to see you every day."

He took her arm. "Come on," he said.

"Where?"

"Back inside. I'm getting cold." It came to him that he might better have said old, but he let it pass.

The first Sunday in January was brisk and clear. A light snow had fallen during the night, but by noon most of it was gone, and when Sam Ulm brought his new station wagon around and parked it in front of the apartment, the sidewalk was clean. Evelyn took the baby up to her room and stayed with him there, talking and singing bits of old show tunes to him, while Lapham, Montgomery, Becker, Anne, and Ulm began to load Anne's possessions into the station wagon.

The loading didn't take very long, partly because of the number of people working and partly because Anne left a lot of her stuff behind. She took the brass bed and the cradle and the footstool and the marble-topped table, but she left the worn rug and the red overstuffed chair and a couple of the lamps. The biggest item in all the moving, in fact, was the baby's possessions. Aside from such necessities as bottles, diapers, food, bathinette, and the like, there were boxes of clothes, toys, and equipment that had poured in on him during the past three months.

When, finally, the wagon was packed, they all stood and looked at each other. Lapham turned to Anne. "Listen to me," he said. "I think you're insane not to let us come help you unload this. It'll take you a week if just the two of you do it."

"No, thank you," she said firmly. "I've made all the arrangements. There's a janitor and a handy man in the building, and they've agreed to help. Thank you just the same."

Lapham shrugged. "Very well, then," he said.

There was a short silence. "Well," said Anne, and then she hesitated. "I guess we're all ready. I'll go call Evelyn."

"I'll do it," said Lapham, and he darted into the house and called up the stairs.

Anne looked at Montgomery. "There's no point in saying good-by," she said. "Because, I mean—well, after all, I'll still be seeing—" Then her eyes filled with tears, and she ran to him and clasped him about the neck. He put his arms around her, and after a couple of moments she looked up at him and smiled wetly and said, "Damn. I wasn't going to do that." She snuffled and laughed and kissed him hard, then turned and kissed Becker, and then she kissed Lapham, who had just come out of the house. Laughing and snuffling, she got into the station wagon, and then Evelyn came out with the baby all bundled up in a blanket, and put him in Anne's lap. Anne kissed her, and Evelyn said something unintelligible to the baby, and then she closed the door. Ulm waved his hand in an embarrassed farewell, and got in the car and started the engine, and they drove off. Anne turned in her seat and waved back as long as the car remained in sight.

When it had turned the corner at the end of the block, Montgomery took a deep breath. "Well," he said. "It's cold out. Let's go back inside."

Evelyn blew her nose. "Come on up to my room," she said. "I'll make us something hot."

They went into the apartment, past the open door of Anne's empty room, and as they started up the stairs, Becker stopped and went to his door. "I'll be with you in a minute," he said, and disappeared into his room. The others continued quietly up to Evelyn's. She left the door open behind them, so that Becker could come in.

"What do you want?" Evelyn asked, as she went into the kitchen. "Coffee? Tea? A drink?"

Montgomery, who was sprawled on the couch with his head against the wall, said, "I don't particularly want a drink. I'll have whatever everybody else is having."

"Me, too," said Lapham, sitting crossways in an armchair.

"You don't by any chance have any cocoa, do you?" Montgomery asked.

"I'll see," said Evelyn. "I think so."

"That sounds wonderful," said Lapham. "I haven't had any cocoa in years."

"Neither have I," Montgomery said. "It just came to me, in a flash."

"Cocoa and marshmallows," said Lapham.

"And thin bread-and-butter sandwiches," Montgomery added.

From the kitchen, Evelyn said, "Yes, I've got some."

"Good!" said Montgomery. "Hurry it up—we're driving ourselves crazy thinking about it."

"I suppose it would be too much to ask if she has any marshmallows," Lapham said.

"Probably," Montgomery replied. "I can remember the day when I would have walked *out* of a house in which I found marshmallows."

"Oh, well," said Lapham. "We can get some tomorrow."

"Sure." There was a silence, and then Montgomery said, "You know, I've always held that once you've seen one baby you've seen them all, but I must say that that baby of Anne's was a remarkable child."

"He certainly was," said Lapham. "Of course, your judgment might be colored by the fact that he was named after you—I, on the other hand, can be completely impartial about the whole thing."

"Like hell you can." Montgomery grinned briefly, and then was quiet. Evelyn came in from the kitchen.

"My, but *this* is a merry crew," she said, looking at the two men. "What happened here?"

"Nothing," Montgomery replied. "We were just thinking."

"Oh."

"I wonder who'll be in that room next," Lapham said.

"Some slob, probably," said Montgomery.

"I've been thinking, too," said Evelyn, who had gone to the window and was staring out at the street. "I've been thinking I'm going to give up all this acting business, and go straight for a change."

"What?" said Montgomery. "What do you mean by that?"

She turned back and looked at him. "Just that. You asked me once if I really liked acting, and it has finally come over me that I don't—at least, not the kind of acting I've been doing. So I'm going to do something else."

"Like what, for instance?"

"I don't know like what. I might open a shop of some sort, or I might—I don't know. I'd like to do something with children, but I don't know who'd let me."

"I'll tell you one thing you can do," Lapham said. "You can come and work with me, if you'd like. You won't make a lot of money, but it'll be something."

She considered this, and then went slowly into the kitchen. She poured the rich-smelling cocoa into three cups, put them on a tray, and brought them back into the room. "That might be wonderful," she said at last.

"Think about it," said Lapham. "You don't have to decide within the hour."

"Just don't do anything that takes you away from here," Montgomery put in.

"Oh?" she said. "And why not?"

He shrugged, and took a sip of his cocoa. "You get used to having a person around. You break up a pattern too much, and things could go all to hell."

She looked at him, and then sat down beside him on the couch.

They drank their cocoa quietly, and then Lapham said, "You know, we ought to think of some Easter present for Anne and the baby. Something that would be so spectacular as to be unspeakable."

"Say, that's right," Montgomery said. "Easter is in just a couple of months. Or I guess three. The overall-mean date for Easter in the last hundred years is April 8.3."

"Good," said Evelyn. "That's nice to know."

There were footsteps on the stairs, and then Becker came into the room, carrying a carved wooden bowl, with two

239

handles on it. "What do you think of it?" he said. "It isn't finished yet, but when I get it lacquered it will shine like glass."

Evelyn took the bowl, and examined it. "It's just beautiful," she said.

"What's it for?" Montgomery asked.

"It's for the baby," Becker replied. He took it back from Evelyn, and rubbed his thumb along the rim. "It could still be a little smoother," he said.

"Sit down," Evelyn said. "Would you like some cocoa?"

Becker sat down. "No cocoa, thanks," he said. "I want to get back and work some more on this." He rubbed the bowl again, and then said, "Oh, yes—another thing. I think I'll take down the window box. I don't think anybody else ought to have her window box, do you?"

"Hell, no," said Montgomery.

"Certainly not," said Lapham.

"Not in a million years," said Evelyn.

"Good," Becker said. "I'll take it down today. I can fit it onto my window just as well—unless one of you would like it."

"No," said Evelyn. "You made it. You ought to have it."

Then she looked up, and saw that a tall, dark young man was standing in the door. He wore a gabardine topcoat and a brown Homburg hat. "Excuse me," he said. "Could any of you tell me where Anne Waters is living now? She used to have the apartment below."

They all turned and stared at him, and after a long pause Montgomery said, "May I ask who you are?"

"My name is Curtin," the man said. "Roy Curtin. I used to be a—friend of hers."

"Oh, yes," Montgomery said, although the name meant nothing to him. Then he took a long chance, and said, "You left town about a year ago, didn't you?"

"That's right," Curtin said, a little uneasily.

Montgomery continued to stare at him, and now he was

almost sure. "Well, I'm sorry you can't see her," he said. "Because she died about three months ago. In childbirth." He heard Evelyn catch her breath, and he saw Curtin grasp the edge of the door, and he knew he had been right.

"Oh," said Curtin. "I'm—I'm sorry." He turned and drifted out of sight, and they heard his footsteps slowly descending the stairs, and then the click of the front door as he went out.

Montgomery got up, and went and looked out the window. "Happy memories, you son of a bitch," he said, quietly.

ABOUT THE AUTHOR

ALTHOUGH NATHANIEL BENCHLEY was born and educated in New England, New York City has been his home for the greater part of his adult life. He worked for a time as a reporter for the *New York Herald Tribune,* and was on the editorial staff of the magazine *Newsweek.* He now devotes most of his time to free-lance writing for such magazines as *The New Yorker, McCall's, Ladies' Home Journal, Holiday,* and *Esquire.* He is also the author of a 1953 Broadway play, *The Frogs of Spring.* Mr. Benchley served as editor of a selection of his father's stories published in 1954 under the title *The Benchley Roundup.* His own original books are *Side Street* (1950) and *Robert Benchley* (McGraw-Hill, 1954).